ST. MARTIN'S

MINOTAUR
MYSTERIES

IF BLOOD COULD TALK . . .

The drying blood had blackened the brown carpet crusting the pile into spiky tufts. At the rear of the room, a sliding glass door led to a tiny balcony. The small closet stood open, empty except for a few bony hangers.

I didn't need to walk in. The atmosphere was as charged as a mid-western summer afternoon before a thunderstorm. With just one glance at the bloodstains on the floor by the bed, images began pushing into my consciousness like fresh memories from an unwelcome nightmare.

A darkened form emerging from the closet, raising a hammer over a man's head, bringing the blunt tool down with cruel force. The body crumpling into a heap. The one with the hammer striking three more furious blows. Bending down, peering at the fallen body. After a time, walking out the front door, hammer in hand.

None of this affected me emotionally. I was an impartial observer, an objective audience. That was good, that meant the channel was clear. I waited for more, but that was it . . .

PISCES RISING

MARTHA C. LAWRENCE

St. Martin's Paperbacks

PISCES RISING

Copyright © 2000 by Martha C. Lawrence.

Excerpt from *Ashes of Aries* copyright © 2001 by Martha C. Lawrence.

ISBN: 0-312-97447-7

Printed in the United States of America

St. Martin's Press hardcover edition / March 2000
St. Martin's Paperbacks edition / September 2001

St. Martin's Paperbacks are published by St. Martin's Press, 175 Fifth Avenue, New York, NY 10010.

10 9 8 7 6 5 4 3 2 1

Out of the wreck, I rise.

                         —Robert Browning, *Ixion*

ACKNOWLEDGMENTS

Grateful thanks to a host of generous experts who shared their knowledge: Detective Howard LaBore of the San Diego Police Department; Thomas A. Jones, M.D.; Elizabeth Porterfield and Bill Collins of the San Diego District Attorney's Office; Sal Lara at the Rincon Indian Reservation; and Rebecca Huston.

More than ever, thanks to my outstanding editor, Hope Dellon, and Matthew Shear, Kelley Ragland, Regan Graves, and Maureen Drum at St. Martin's Press. As always, thanks to my cherished agent, Gina Maccoby. Endless thanks to Carroll Driggs and Clark Lawrence, whose patience, understanding, and love sustain me.

AUTHOR'S NOTE

In November 1998 California voters passed Proposition 5, giving Native Americans the right to continue gambling activities on reservation lands. Believing that Indian gaming had broken the cycle of poverty on many reservations, eighty-eight tribes representing ninety-six percent of Native Americans on California reservations endorsed the measure. In August 1999 the California Supreme Court overturned Proposition 5. While this story takes place in the year prior to these events, it is a work of fiction. The Temecu Reservation, the Mystic Mesa Casino, and the 77th District are figments of the author's imagination. The denizens of these fictional places are likewise the author's creations. Any resemblance between the real world and the places and characters in this book is coincidental and unintentional.

PISCES RISING

PROLOGUE

It's been nearly ten years since I earned my Ph.D. in parapsychology from Stanford University. The certificate collects dust on the wall of my office, framed parchment from the archives of a more innocent era. I suppose the degree has a place in my life, but these days it doesn't serve me as well or as often as my 9-millimeter Glock, from which I can hit a bull's-eye at fifteen feet, four times out of five.

My name is Elizabeth Chase. I'm a licensed private investigator with a specialty: I am a psychic.

I know—I hate the word, too. So many charlatans and rip-off artists have hung out their shingles under the term psychic that it's hard to take the title seriously. I use it for lack of a better alternative. To call myself a *sensitive* makes me sound like a character in *Star Trek: The New Generation. Parapsychologist detective*? Too many syllables, wrong image. Makes me sound as though I hunt ghosts instead of people—people being the more dangerous of the two.

Ironically, the person who encouraged me to take pride in being a psychic detective was a lieutenant commander for the NYPD, hardly a touchy-feely organization. "Don't apologize," he told me when he caught my self-deprecating tone. "We've closed several cases on psychic tips. Under the right circumstances, using a psychic certainly merits consideration." So sayeth the NYPD.

Like any other professional, a psychic isn't infallible, even a good one. I'd like to think that my successes as a psychic—finding lost children, fingering rapists and murderers—have alleviated some suffering. The thought helps me deal with my black moments, when I'm face-to-face with my second-sight failures.

My second sight failed Tom McGowan.

I first met McGowan five years ago, when he was still a sergeant with the Escondido Police Department. His friend's recent death had been classified as a routine traffic fatality, but McGowan suspected murder. The quintessential doubting Thomas, he hired me as a last resort. I don't know who'd been more skeptical of whom: the hard-headed cop of the psychic, or the psychic of the hard-headed cop. In time our differences bonded us like the opposite ends of a magnet. I was attracted by his down-to-earth street smarts; he was drawn to my metaphysical skills. But those skills let me down at a critical moment during my last investigation, when McGowan had needed them most. By the time I realized my mistake, he was dead.

Anyone who's lost their beloved knows how cruel grief can be. The mind replays scenes from the past in heartbreaking detail, and not necessarily the ones you'd expect. I keep remembering McGowan's first kiss, a peck on the forehead. Over and over I hear the poem he recited that moment: "Take this kiss upon the brow/And in parting from you now/Thus much let me avow—/All that we see or seem/Is but a dream within a dream." How could I not have fallen in love with a cop who quoted Edgar Allan Poe? The most relentless memory is from last summer, the night he nearly pitched us out of a hammock under a star-filled sky. He'd been reaching into his pocket for a diamond ring. Three weeks later he was dead. I put the ring away in a cedar box, along with my PI license. I'd intended to let the license expire.

Then came a 4 A.M. phone call on a Sunday morning in September. It was Scott Chatfield, an investigator I'd met during that last terrible case. The sound of his voice jerked me right back to the horror of those final dark days in June.

"Scott," was all I could muster.

"Sorry to call at such an uncivilized hour, but this won't wait. Is there any way you can get down to the University Medical Center, like in the next hour or so?"

My heart jumped. An urgent call from a hospital at four in the morning has that effect.

"Has someone been hurt?"

"No," he said, clearing his throat. "I mean, yes, but—"

I heard a commotion in the background and then the

conch-shell sound of his palm covering the receiver. After a few seconds he was back.

"Shoot. I gotta go. I'll meet you out front." And the line went dead.

1

San Diego was still asleep, shrouded in the cool gray mist that settles along the coast when temperatures drop. I turned into the University Medical Center parking lot and claimed the kind of space you only find at 4:30 in the morning. The hospital wasn't fifty yards away, but the fog was thick enough to blur the edges of the main building. Fog this dense always made me think of my mother's Crawling Eye. When I was small, I used to wonder how Mom knew about the childish misdeeds I thought I'd concealed so well. How did she find out I'd snitched the candy, not brushed my teeth, read with a flashlight under the covers after lights out? "I have a crawling eye," she'd say. "It slithers through the crack under your door and watches you when you think I'm not looking." In my little-girl mind it became a monster, this Crawling Eye—a giant, bloodshot orb that lived on foggy hillsides and slinked through the darkness to peer in my window. I smiled as I got out of my truck. Perhaps my second sight was my own version of the Crawling Eye, inherited from my mother.

In the misty darkness overhead I could hear but not see power lines buzzing, set off by the heavy moisture in the air. It was a disturbing sound. I wrapped my jacket across my chest and hurried to the entrance. A man's figure, silhouetted in the mist by the bright lights behind him, stood at the top of the hospital's wide cement steps.

"You," Scott Chatfield said as I trotted up the stairs, "are an angel to come at this hour." His red hair was slightly disheveled, but a vibrant band of energy glowed around his head and shoulders, signaling to me that he was fully awake and aware, despite the early hour. I'd been well into grade school before I learned that these bands of light weren't visible to everyone. Sometimes I see colors in the bands, but not this morning.

"Is this business or personal?" I heard the urgency in my

own voice. All the way to the hospital I'd been combing my memory for acquaintances we had in common, hoping that tragedy hadn't struck. Again.

"Business," he said.

The muscles deep in my chest relaxed.

"Well, thank God for that."

He realized then that I'd taken his urgent call personally because his mouth dropped open and he slumped apologetically.

"Oh, jeez, I'm sorry. I didn't mean to scare you."

"It's okay." I was still drinking in the relief.

"I was so absorbed in our little drama here I completely forgot—"

"Don't worry about it," I assured him. I genuinely liked Chatfield. It wasn't his fault that the case that had brought us together had ended so badly. He'd sent me a thoughtful card after McGowan's death.

"You're really okay?" His voice was soft, concerned. "I mean, you're working again and everything?"

"Looks that way. So tell me about this little drama."

"This is sort of a lame excuse for my being such an abrupt jerk, but I was calling you from a cellular when the press got here. Didn't want details flying over the airwaves. David's going to have a tough enough time with damage control as is, without me throwing juicy tidbits to piranha newscasters."

"Tidbits about what? And who's David?"

"A lawyer friend of mine with a hell of a case on his hands here. I'd love to help him out, but I can't take this on now. I'm investigating a homicide up in Barstow. In fact, I've got a meeting there this morning."

"Hence the urgent call to me."

"Yeah. Also because you're perfect for this case, which is truly strange. David asked me jokingly if I could refer a psychic detective . . ." he paused to smile ". . . and I said that, as a matter of fact, I could. Come on, I'll introduce you."

The glass doors of the lobby slid open as soon as our feet touched the rubber doormat. In my haste to get to the hospital I'd thrown baggy chinos and a roomy tunic over skimpy silk pajamas. The smooth underthings against my skin felt out of place and slightly scandalous.

A news photographer with a Sony television camera perched on his shoulder stood just inside the hospital doors. Tape was rolling on a conversation between a reporter and a uniformed police officer.

"Looks like a feeding frenzy," I mumbled.

Chatfield didn't even glance their way as he led me with determined footsteps toward the far side of the lobby where a man in a rumpled trench coat leaned against the wall. The man stood straight as we approached and looked to me hopefully.

"David Skenazy," he said, extending his hand. "Thanks for coming down." Skenazy was hovering somewhere around forty but was going for a younger look, his dark brown hair cropped short on the sides, a shank of curls tumbling from the top. He exuded intensity, as if he had enough energy for two people.

"Elizabeth Chase," I said, returning his firm squeeze.

Chatfield looked at his watch.

"I hate to play matchmaker and run, but I've got to hit the road. It's a three-hour drive and—"

"Go on, get outta here," Skenazy teased in a Brooklyn accent.

We said our good-byes, and Skenazy and I watched Chatfield exit the lobby doors.

"Now there," Skenazy said, "goes a seasoned professional. I call him at 3 A.M. and ask if he knows a psychic detective. An hour later I'm standing here talking to one."

"What's going on here?" I asked.

Skenazy dropped the getting-acquainted mask and his smile disappeared.

"There was a murder last night at the Mystic Mesa gambling casino. My client was arrested at the scene. He was admitted to this hospital about two hours ago."

"Your client was injured?"

"Not exactly. At the time of the arrest he was overdosing on tranquilizers. He was completely unconscious when the body was found. The medics managed to revive him in the ambulance. He had the presence of mind to have me called when he got here."

"The Mystic Mesa Casino is on the Temecu Reservation, isn't it?"

Skenazy nodded and headed toward the elevator bay.

"That's got to be an hour away," I said as I followed behind him. "Why'd they bring him all the way down here?"

David pushed the up button.

"You ever wonder what happens to violent criminals who are too wounded from a day's work to be taken to jail? Stabbed drug dealers, burned arsonists, bullet-riddled bank robbers?"

"Never really thought about it," I admitted.

"They end up at hospitals with county contracts to accept custody patients. My client is upstairs being baby-sat by an armed guard."

"Why the heavy security?"

"The nature of the crime. It was . . . ugly."

There was a ding and we looked up, but the elevator was going down.

"Ugly how?" I asked.

Skenazy swiped upward at the hair tumbling onto his forehead.

"He was found unconscious in one of the beds at the Mystic Mesa Hotel. The casino manager was lying in a pool of blood at the foot of the bed. He'd been bludgeoned and scalped."

It took a moment for the word to sink in.

"Did you say *scalped*?"

Skenazy nodded.

"The victim died of skull fractures from a blunt instrument—not sure what yet—and the skin and hair on his head were peeled off. Scalped."

I hadn't heard the expression since school days. It conjured up dim memories of a history class on the French and Indian War. I vaguely remembered journal entries written by eighteenth-century Europeans, horrific accounts using the term *savages* instead of *Native Americans*. Long before I'd

ever heard about a thing called "revisionist history." I stared
into Skenazy's face, trying to imagine who'd do such a thing
today.

"You're going to get a nasty wrinkle between your eyebrows if you keep grimacing that way," he said.

"This happened at an *Indian* gambling casino?"

"Yeah. Mystic Mesa, on the Temecu Reservation."

"Is your client white?"

Skenazy nodded.

"Was the murder victim a Native American?"

He sighed. "Yes, he was."

I had a fleeting image of a crowd of angry protesters, placards waving.

"Who is this suspect?"

"Bill Hurston, an old client of mine. In spite of how it
looks, I really don't think Bill's capable of something like
this. He's a medical doctor—or was. I represented him several
years ago when he got into trouble selling prescription narcotics under the table. He lost his license, but I managed to
keep him out of jail."

I gave Skenazy a dubious look.

"He was arrested for dealing narcotics? Doesn't exactly
sound like a pristine client."

There was another elevator bell, and this time the up arrow
was lighted. We stepped inside, and Skenazy pushed the
eighth-floor button. I felt the ground give way as the elevator
swept us upward.

"You're right," he continued. "Bill's not spotless. But I was
able to talk with him tonight after they got him stabilized. He
says he could never murder anyone, and you know what? My
gut says he's telling the truth. Scott tells me you're good with
this intuition stuff. I'd like to know what you think."

"Your client was found OD'd in a room with a bloody
corpse. What do I think? I think you've got your work cut out
for you."

The door opened, and we stepped onto the eighth floor.
Skenazy led the way past the nurse's station and down the
gray-flecked linoleum hallway.

"I didn't mean I want your opinion. I want your, uh, you know—"

"My intuitive reading."

"Yeah. And if your gut tells you the same thing mine does, I'd like you to be my lead investigator."

The offer didn't appeal. This was the kind of murder that would inspire a blizzard of publicity and an endless stream of tasteless jokes. I pinched the bridge of my nose and applied steady pressure, a short-term fix for an ache that only caffeine would cure.

"Why don't you find someone who's hungry for a sensational gig? There've got to be a dozen PIs who'll jump at this."

"No doubt. But Scott's impressed as hell with your work." He slowed to a stop and turned to face me. "Honestly? This'll probably be the highest profile case of my career. I want to know what I'm dealing with, A, and I want the best investigator I can get, B. Of course, if it's too controversial for you—"

"It's not that it's too controversial. It's just that . . ." I hesitated, trying to think of a diplomatic way to put it.

"Yeah?" he prodded.

"I generally don't like working for defense attorneys. For the most part, all you guys do is help scum stay afloat. I prefer to *catch* criminals, not set them free."

He actually smiled.

"I'll say this for you, Elizabeth, you're a straight shooter. But I'm tellin' you, William Hurston isn't scum. He's a medical doctor—"

"An unlicensed medical doctor," I amended.

"—and a guest of the hotel who happened to be in the wrong place at the wrong time. All I want you to do is look at him. Just one look."

We resumed walking. At the end of the hall an armed guard sat in a cheap aluminum folding chair, a magazine open across his lap. He looked up as we approached.

"Still sleeping," he said to Skenazy.

"That's okay," he said. "We're just going to step inside for a minute."

The man lying on the bed had been handsome at one time, I could see that in his long, elegant nose and angled cheekbones. His fine blonde hair was receding now and streaked with gray, matching his closely trimmed beard. The halfdome of his forehead did not shine under the fluorescent light. His dull skin was just a shade or two deeper than the white pillowcase under his head. Looking at his face, I was overcome with a wearying sadness. My eyes traveled down the arms at his sides and stopped at his hands. His fingers were long and tapering. A healer's hands.

"Please don't judge by appearances because he looks like hell right now," Skenazy said.

I made a shushing sound.

"He can hear you," I whispered.

"You kidding?" he muttered. "He's out like a light."

"Doesn't matter. If he has a heartbeat, he can hear you."

Skenazy's wilting look accused me of being hopelessly New Age.

"You talking about his subconscious mind? Pardon me, but who the hell cares?"

I was about to answer when the patient's eyes opened.

"Hello," I said.

"Hello," Hurston answered, so quietly that I barely heard him.

Skenazy's mouth dropped open, but he recovered quickly, stepping to his client's bedside.

"Hey, Bill. Listen, I'd like you to meet Elizabeth Chase. She's an investigator and . . . Bill?"

Hurston's eyes had closed again. Skenazy shook his arm.

"Bill?"

It was no use. This time he *was* out like a light. Skenazy gave up and rejoined me near the doorway.

"So . . . any first impressions?"

I looked again at Hurston's hands. I couldn't connect them to the murder Skenazy had described. I wondered if physical evidence would back up my hunch. The police would have tested Hurston's hands for blood traces. If he'd scalped a man, those traces would show. Unless he'd worn gloves.

"I don't know," I answered. "I won't know until I talk to him. I'll have to come back later."

The guard looked up from the magazine draped across his thighs. He'd been reading an article about lawn care.

"Don't bother coming here," he said. "This guy's due to be transported, soon as he sleeps it off."

"Transported where?" I asked.

"Downtown Central Jail."

2

Deputy Capshaw carried a Ruger P85—I recognized the make from the distinctive ring at the corner of its grip. The gun bobbed slightly on her hip as she walked ahead of me to the visitor sign-in area of the San Diego Central Jail. I knew that jail policy did not permit officers to wear arms beyond this point, guns being invitations to trouble. I imagined how easy it would be to reach forward, slide Capshaw's Ruger from its holster, and press the barrel against her temple. The fantasy disturbed me, an example of my continuing preoccupation with violence. I chalked it up to another unwelcome symptom from that dreadful last case: seeing danger where none existed, anticipating escape routes when no escape was necessary.

Capshaw paused at the entrance, her hand on the door knob.

"You a family member?" She softened the inquiry with a quick smile.

I smiled back, grateful that she couldn't read my thoughts. "Investigator for the defense."

"I'll need to see some—"

But I was already flipping open my wallet. She inspected the California driver's and PI licenses that I held out to her.

"That'll do it."

She ushered me into a narrow room with a glass wall. A Formica countertop ran the length of the glass. Three telephones sat on the countertop, strategically placed in front of a half dozen or so plastic chairs.

"The guard will bring him out," Capshaw said. "Shouldn't be long."

I sat in the chair at the far end of the counter. I took a notebook and pen out of my purse and placed them in front of me. The room was chilly. I felt like a child at the zoo, waiting to see the bears come out of their artificial cave. I wrapped my arms around my chest for warmth and waited.

I *felt* Hurston coming before he appeared, his despair seeping into my consciousness like water dampening a sponge. Seconds later he came around the corner. He was a tall man, over six foot, and could have used more flesh on his large, bony frame. The guard stood back while Hurston dropped into the chair opposite mine and picked up the telephone.

"Hello again," he said. He had on a pair of small, wire-rimmed glasses that he hadn't been wearing in his hospital bed. His blonde-gray hair was combed straight back, and his beard was freshly trimmed.

"So you remember me."

"You, yes. But I'm afraid I don't remember your name." His delivery was smooth, his tone cultured and polite. The color rose faintly in his face.

"My name's Elizabeth. I'll be David Skenazy's investigator on your case."

In truth, I'd made no promises to David. Hurston's attorney fees were being picked up by his parents, a pair of elderly Philadelphia aristocrats who'd stepped in when their middle-aged son needed them. David had tempted me with a generous retainer, plus points on any proceeds he might collect from a civil suit. I'd told him I'd have to talk with Dr. Hurston before committing to the case, but I didn't want Hurston to know that. I figured he'd be more forthcoming if he felt I were already on his team.

Hurston's right hand worried the phone cord, working its way along each of the coils.

"I've never been in jail before," he said. "It's quite an experience. Humiliating—" he let out a pained laugh "—just when I thought I couldn't fall any lower."

I was at a rare loss for words.

"I'm sorry we couldn't have met under more pleasant circumstances, Elizabeth."

He projected a helpless sweetness; I could feel it tugging at my sympathies. I observed the cord in a detached, curious way.

"I have a lot of questions," I began. "I'll probably be covering much of the same territory Mr. Skenazy has already gone over with you. He's happy to share his notes with me, of course, but I prefer to get my information firsthand. Keeps me from repeating other people's mistakes."

"You're a hard worker, then."

He gave me a sad smile and continued to massage the phone cord, working the coils as if they were beads in a rosary. It was a nervous gesture, not the picture of an innocent man. When he reached the last coil, I spoke.

"First question."

"Yes?"

"How many coils in that phone cord?"

His hand froze, as if I'd caught him doing something naughty. He peered up at me through his glasses with an embarrassed grin.

"Hundred forty-seven."

I had a hunch the number was correct. During my brief career as a psychotherapist, I'd had a client who compulsively counted: birds on a wire, bricks on a path, Fruit Loops left in her daughter's cereal bowl. Anything had been fair game.

"Do you do that often," I asked, "count like that?"

"All the time. Cards, especially."

"Cards, yes. So tell me what happened at the casino Saturday night."

"If I had to sum it up, I'd say that I made the worst mistake of my life."

It almost sounded like a confession.

"What mistake is that, Dr. Hurston?"

"*Dr.* Hurston. No one's called me that for years. Ironic you're calling me that now, since my medical ineptitude is the very reason I'm sitting in jail."

It was a provocative statement. Surely he didn't mean that the scalped corpse in his hotel room had been a botched operation?

"What do you mean by that—medical ineptitude?"

He switched his phone to the other ear.

"You would think that having practiced medicine for nearly twenty-five years, I'd know how to end my own life. But I botched it."

"You mean you killed someone else instead?"

He lowered his eyes, trying to hide the emotions warring inside him. My body picked up his tension like a telegraph wire, and I felt a tightening in my throat. The silence stretched. In a court of law, the judge would ask him to state his answer out loud. But this wasn't a court of law, and I wasn't a judge. At last he looked up and cleared his throat.

"Have you ever gambled?" he asked.

"Not to speak of." I noticed that he hadn't answered my question. "Gambling makes me nervous."

He laughed a little, but there was pain in it.

"Then you're not going to understand what brought me to this point."

"Right now I just want to understand what happened in that hotel room. Did you kill Dan Aquillo?"

"No, I didn't kill anyone, which is precisely the problem. I failed to kill the person I'd intended to kill: Me." He stared at me with eyes so full of pain that I had to look down at my notepad. The tug on my heartstrings was stronger now, and I was determined to resist it. I wondered how many women in Hurston's life had succumbed to the urge to mother him.

"Why don't you just start from Saturday night and give me a rundown of the events up until your arrest."

"There's not that much to run down. I gambled my last hundred dollars at Trish's table—"

"Trish?" I scribbled the name on my notepad.

"One of the blackjack dealers. When my last hundred was gone, that was it. I'd already planned it. I went back to my hotel room, made one last phone call to Natalie—"

"Natalie?"

"My ex-wife. I didn't tell her I was killing myself, of course. Just offered a general apology for the years of hell I'd put her through. I prepared a solution of Versed—it's a powerful tranq—injected it, and laid down to die. The next thing I

knew police officers were shoving me into the back of an ambulance. It was barbaric, really. They wouldn't even let me
use the bathroom."

"Bathrooms have faucets, and faucets can wash away evidence."

It was a statement that could prompt him to defend himself, but he didn't. He just massaged the phone cord with his
long, slender fingers. After several seconds of silence, I asked
the obvious.

"How do you account for the corpse at the foot of your
bed?"

"Preposterous as this sounds, I don't know a thing about it."

"A scalpless corpse is lying in a pool of blood not six feet
from you, and you don't know a thing about it? How can that
be?"

He rested his face against his palm, looking weary.

"I was nearly in a coma when the police arrived. It was all
they could do to rouse me. I passed out again in the ambulance. Whatever happened after I dosed myself, I didn't hear a
thing."

His undramatic delivery was convincing, however dubious
his story. And the story did match the few facts I'd been able
to glean from David.

"A crime this messy leaves a tremendous amount of forensic evidence. I'm sure you're aware of that."

"Of course."

"I need to know how it is that you can be in the same room
as someone who's been violently murdered and not know a
thing about it."

"I told you. Versed is a very potent tranquilizer. With
twenty cc's coursing through my veins, I could have slept
through the Battle of Normandy."

"Did you know the victim, Dan Aquillo?" I asked.

His forehead tensed.

"Yes. I was a regular at his casino. It's awful what happened to him."

"How long had you known him?"

"Many years. Fifteen, at least." His mouth was pulling

down at the corners and for a minute it seemed like he might cry.

"Did you like Aquillo, hate him? . . . What was your relationship?"

"He was my friend." His voice quavered on the last word, and he pursed his lips, biting back tears. This time the tugging reached into my belly. He was either telling the truth, or he was an actor with uncanny talent. "Can you imagine trying to kill yourself and then waking up to find that your good friend is dead and you're still alive?"

"And arrested for murder to boot," I added.

He dismissed that with a flick of his hand.

"That doesn't matter. My life's the prison I can't escape from. The fact that I'm behind bars is so beautifully symbolic it would amuse me, if I could feel amusement."

I wondered if Hurston was being treated for depression and made a note of it on my pad.

"What are you writing there?"

"Just making a notation about your mental state."

"Have you ever wanted to die, Elizabeth?"

I hesitated. Why not be honest?

"Yes," I said.

"Tell me."

I stared through the glass with a level gaze and tried to keep my voice as dispassionate as possible.

"Three months ago, the man I loved was shot in the spleen with a .44 Magnum. He died in my arms. I had a couple of shaky days."

His face registered shocked compassion. He reached forward and touched the glass, the tips of his fingers flattening against the transparent barrier.

"I'm so sorry. What was his name?"

"Tom." As always when I said the name, my nose began to sting.

"I'd give anything to trade my life for Tom's, right here, right now."

Hurston's comment slipped past my defenses. I felt myself responding to his kindness, hoping he was innocent.

"You're familiar with the casino," I said. "Who'd be willing to talk to me about Dan Aquillo?"

"About his personal life? Probably your best bet would be Trish Brown."

"The blackjack dealer."

He nodded. "She's also Aquillo's girlfriend."

"Do you think Trish believes that you killed Dan?"

A door slammed off to the right, and I turned toward the sound. When I looked back, Hurston's eyes were filled with tears.

"Ask her. Ask my ex-wife. Ask anyone. I'm a failure, but I'm not a killer."

3

I rolled down the driver's side window and inhaled the dry, sage-scented evening air. For natural southern California scenery, few trips are more beautiful than the one to the Mystic Mesa Casino, which occupies a premium spot on the Temecu Reservation. At an elevation of nine hundred feet, the combination gambling hall/hotel is nestled about halfway up the boulder-studded foothills that peak at Palomar Mountain, home of the world-renowned observatory.

Driving east, I couldn't help but think about my last trip into the backcountry. After McGowan's death last summer, I'd taken his ashes and his favorite car deep into the Sonoran Desert and burned them together in a final, blazing farewell. A strange thing had happened as I'd watched the brilliant orange glow of the fire. As the bereaved often do, I'd wondered if his spirit really did live on and if so, did he know how much I loved him? He'd answered as clearly as if he'd been sitting at my side.

Always and ever.

That was the last time I'd heard his voice. I'd waited to hear it again, prayed to hear it again. The silence had stretched now for nearly three months. I was beginning to wonder if it hadn't been an auditory hallucination brought on by intense grief and desert heat.

A green road marker ahead snapped me into the present. The small white lettering read "TEMECU RESERVATION, NEXT RIGHT." Just past a ramshackle place called Ed's Country Cafe I made a right onto Mystic Mesa Road. The seat vibrated as my tires rolled over the cattle crossing that marked the western entrance to the reservation. I sped under clear skies along smooth black asphalt, hoping I wouldn't get lost. A half mile later I could see this wasn't going to be a problem. The casino complex was impossible to miss, distinguished as it was by a

gigantic fiberglass tepee rising into the sky like Disneyland's
Matterhorn.

I turned at the tepee and pulled into acres of parking spaces
filled with more cars than I'd been expecting on a Monday
evening. Instead of letters or numbers, the lot was divided into
sections marked by painted metal sculptures of desert
wildlife: jackrabbit, eagle, coyote, lizard. I parked under a
cranky-looking coyote, chuckling at the goofiness of the
neo–Native American motif.

Following the footpath to the casino, I reviewed what I'd
learned from David about the victim, Dan Aquillo. Thirty-
seven-year-old male. Luiseno Indian. Black hair, brown eyes,
five-eleven, one-eighty. Statistics only—I had no sense of the
inner man. I was hoping Aquillo's girlfriend would remedy
that for me tonight. The casino grounds were beautiful; I felt
more like I was going to summer camp than a house of gaming. A man-made stream gurgled over some granite boulders to
my right, and a high desert breeze rustled the pines overhead.

The tranquil mood vanished as I neared the casino entrance. About a half-dozen men and women stood on the sidewalk, carrying placards above their heads. Each sign was an
enlarged photograph of a dark-haired man under the boldface
headline: **JUSTICE NOW.** The photograph of Dan Aquillo
was a two-dimensional image, no more revealing than the po-
lice-report statistics. A couple of the protesters gave me the
evil eye as I approached the door. I gave them a sympathetic
thumbs-up, and they parted to let me in.

I don't know what hit me first—the flashing lights, the ri-
otous noise, or the adrenaline rush. Swept into the crowds
milling past the slot machines, I suddenly felt high, as if I'd
taken something illegal. The good-time sensation baffled me,
since ordinarily I loathe casinos. I hadn't been kidding when I
told Dr. Hurston that gambling made me nervous.

Hurston had said that he'd lost his last hundred dollars at
the blackjack table of Aquillo's girlfriend, Trish Brown. I
weaved through the milling bodies and scanned shirt fronts,
hoping that the dealers might wear nametags. No such luck.

I moved through the casino in a daze, my senses overloaded by lights, noise, and the discordant vibes of the gamblers. Their emotions—numbness, excitement, anxiety, ecstasy, love, loathing—clashed all around me. It was the psychic equivalent of a heavy-metal band, jazz quartet, and full symphony orchestra all tuning up at once. Shaking my head to clear the fuzz in my brain, I kept my focus straight ahead, on the blackjack tables.

I stopped at a game where one of the few female dealers presided. Standing behind the players, I watched her toss cards onto the table with motions as fluid and precise as a dancer's. I studied the action for a few rounds and when a seat opened up, I slid in.

That's when it started. I began to *know* things. It's an unpredictable gift, an ability I can't force to come about. Nor can I stop it, once it's begun.

I *knew* that the short-haired brunette at the end of the table would lose. In spite of her pretty white smile and positive attitude, I could see her defeat as clearly as if she were wearing it like a dead albatross around her neck. I picked up nothing about the oily-looking man to my left, whose nicotine-stained fingers fiddled with his chips. As for me, it was as if I'd already played my hands and seen their outcome.

Tonight I was destined to win.

The dealer flicked our cards across the green-felt tabletop. I pulled two tens. When it was time to take or decline a third card, the brunette on the end smiled brightly at the dealer, eagerness shining in her eyes.

"Hit me," she said confidently.

In the split second before her top card landed on the table, I foresaw her whole night. A series of losses, just like this one. On my inner movie screen I watched her taking a long car ride with friends, back to wherever home was. She was in the backseat looking out the rear window at the black highway retreating behind her. I could feel her disappointment.

The jack of hearts landed on her cards, wiping her out. She looked stunned. I was staring at her stricken face when I heard the dealer prompting me.

"How about it?"

I had twenty. Anything higher than an ace would wipe me out. The smart thing to do would be to hold, but now I had a perverse desire *not* to win.

"Go," I said.

She flicked her wrist, and the ace of spades flew onto my stack. Twenty-one. So much for altering destiny.

The oily man on my left drew a high card and folded. He got up and nodded to the dealer.

"See you tomorrow, Karen."

So the dealer's name was Karen, not Trish. I'd sensed this wasn't the one I'd wanted, but I had to start somewhere. An eager young man took over the vacated seat. As the new player settled in, I leaned over and spoke to Karen.

"Have you seen Trish?"

She shook her head and began tossing us our cards.

"Trish Brown? She's off tonight."

There went my primary contact. Now what? I stayed put, deciding to play until I lost a hand. My winning streak lasted for so many rounds that I lost count. By the time I drew a losing card, I'd amassed over six hundred dollars. Not bad, considering that I started with a twenty. I killed another hour trying to lose some of my winnings and pick up some gossip about the murder. Failing to do either, I scooped up my take and made my way toward the back of the casino.

I paused at one of the slot machines, which was being fed a steady diet of coins by a hump-backed woman in an orange cardigan sweater. I *knew* she was about to win. When the moment came and the machine burst into a spasm of flashing lights and ringing bells, I shook my head. I had to admit it was a little thrilling, *seeing* this way. It wouldn't go on forever, but I was enjoying it while it lasted.

Using two hands, the woman scooped her coins into a wicker-weave satchel and walked away with a smile on her face. Almost as an afterthought, I stepped up, slipped a coin into the slot, and pulled the handle. Again the machine erupted, this time with sirens on top of the flashing lights and ringing bells. A small mountain of coins piled up in the trough. Twice in a row, the machine had relinquished a jackpot. What were the chances? People gathered around as I scooped up the coins. Added to my blackjack winnings, my take came to nearly two thousand dollars.

I found the cashier's window and read a notice mounted on the wall: ANY WINNINGS OVER $1199 MUST BE RECORDED ON A W2G FORM. I approached the clerk behind the bars.

"Guess I'll need a W2G," I said.

He was smooth and dark and adorable, with eyelashes like Bambi's. He looked too young to be betting, let alone working in a gambling joint.

"Those white forms? Um, I just ran out, and I'm not sure where to find more. I gotta call my manager. Can you wait a minute?"

I nodded and listened as he picked up a phone and made his call.

"Yeah, this is Mark in the cash cage. There's a lady here who needs a W2G form, and I'm all out." He studied my face. "Uh-huh. I'd say so. Okay."

He hung up.

"Go upstairs," he said as he pointed past my shoulder, "to the second door on your right. Peter Waleta's office. You can get the form there."

I walked up the carpeted spiral staircase and looked out over the casino. Mystic Mesa was funky. It had the homespun feel of a bingo hall but reached for glamour with a few glitzy Vegas trappings, like the mirrored balls hanging from the ceiling. Eyes in the sky, each containing a video camera, I was sure.

I reached the hallway at the top of the stairs. The second door on the right stood ajar, and I could hear the sounds of a televised ball game floating into the hall. I tapped gently the first time. When I got no response, I gave the door a knuckle pounding.

"Come in."

The first thing I saw were the soles of two large shoes. They belonged to a man, heavy-set but not fat, sitting behind a plain steel desk with his feet propped up. He seemed mesmerized by the football game coming through the small Sony Trinitron on the corner of his desk. His thick black hair was pulled back into a neat ponytail, his Dockers were pressed, and his sage-green polo shirt looked new. The game cut to a commercial, and he turned to me without smiling.

"Mr. Waleta?" I said.

"Yeah. You're the one who needs the W2G?"

I nodded and he swung his feet off the desk. He opened the top drawer, took out a stack of forms, and slid the bundle across the desk to me.

"Would you mind taking the rest of those down to that dip-shit in the cash cage?" He caught the swearword too late and added, "Sorry, no offense."

"It's okay. I'm not that delicate."

That cracked a smile.

"So how lucky did you get tonight?"

I shrugged.

"Eighteen, nineteen hundred. Something like that."

He lifted his dark brows.

"You got photo ID and a Social Security number? We'll need to see both before you can collect."

I stepped forward and put my open wallet on Waleta's desk. He flipped through my ID cards, nodding slightly. When he got to my PI license, he looked up.

"No shit?"

"No shit. Come to think of it, mind if I ask you a few questions?"

4

Peter Waleta took a hard look at my PI license, folded my wallet shut, and handed it back to me. I could see in the casino manager's dark eyes that he'd shut something else, as well. An open mind, perhaps.

"Questions about what?" he asked.

"William Hurston. The man who was arrested here night before last." I put my wallet back in my purse and spotted a pack of sugarless gum at the bottom. I fished it out and held it up to Waleta. "Want some?"

He shook his head. He had the air of a man who did not trust easily. I unwrapped a piece and popped it into my mouth, aiming for a casual, nonthreatening impression.

"Who you working for?" he asked.

"I'm not working for anybody just yet. That's why I'm asking questions. I want to get your take on the guy."

"I already made a formal statement to the police. Once is enough." He turned back to his football game.

"Informally, can you just tell me if Hurston was a trouble-maker or a problem of any kind? His attorney wants me to in-vestigate the case, but if Hurston has a reputation around here, I won't do it. Simple as that."

It appeared that the Vikings had plundered the Packers. The Minnesota team was up by six in the fourth quarter, and from the looks of things on the four-yard line, they were about to score again. When a time-out was called, Waleta returned his attention to me.

"So the defense attorney sent you."

"Nobody sent me. I came on my own. To see what I could find out about Hurston before I agree to join the defense team."

The amped-up volume of a beer commercial filled the room. Waleta grabbed the remote and muted the sound.

"Like I said, I've already talked to the police. I'd like to help you out, but without an attorney here I don't think it's such a wise idea. I'm sorry." He was gentle but firm, handling me the way you might turn down a Girl Scout hawking Thin Mints.

"Can you just tell me if Hurston's one of those guys who's rotten inside but charming on the outside? Because when I spoke with him this morning, he seemed like a genuinely nice guy. Pathetic, but nice."

"I'll go with the pathetic part," Waleta said.

"You know him, then."

He watched the TV, ignoring my comment.

"I wonder," I said, "could a pathetic man do the kind of damage that was inflicted on Dan Aquillo?"

Waleta pointed the remote in my direction, his dark eyes flashing.

"Don't go there, okay?"

I held up my hands in mock surrender.

"Sorry. Please don't mute me."

A smile tugged at the corner of his mouth.

"Can you just tell me if Dan Aquillo knew Bill Hurston?"

He crossed his arms over his chest and glared at me.

"This is beginning to sound like official-type questions."

"No, not at all. I'm just trying to get a sense about Hurston. Because if Dan ever mentioned that Hurston was an asshole or a problem or something like that, then I'm off the job, period. Let someone else take up the cause of the sleazeballs, that's what I say."

My eyes were drawn to the muted television set. The game was back on. In a precognitive flash I *saw* the final score. I was definitely having one of those nights.

"Packers have got this one," I said, "twenty-one to twenty."

"Yeah, right. Dream on. So you're one of them emotional Packers fans, huh?"

"A branch of my family lives in Wisconsin, so I follow the team. But I'm not particularly invested."

"Well, that's good, because they've got fifty-three seconds to pull off a miracle." Waleta leaned his bulky body back. His chair squeaked in complaint. The Vikings tried a sweep to the right but the running back's feet slipped on the pulverized turf. Loss of three yards. Waleta shifted uncomfortably. "You know, I would like some of that gum, if you don't mind."

I fished the pack out of my purse and tossed it onto his desk. "Keep it," I said.

"Thanks." He unwrapped a piece and chewed thoughtfully for a minute or so.

"You promise this is just between you and me?" he asked.

"Yeah, I promise."

"Okay. I didn't know Hurston personally, but he ran up some debt awhile back and was about to be cut off here. Dan and I were partners in the casino, so we discussed it. Like I said, I didn't know Hurston personally, but I knew he was trouble. I was you, I'd turn the job down."

"Thanks for the advice. And—" I held up the stack of W2Gs "—for the tax forms."

"No problem. So how much was it you won tonight?"

"Eighteen hundred something," I said again.

He dug in his back pocket and came up with a slim black wallet. He fished out a hundred-dollar bill and held it out to me.

"Sounds like you're hot. Go win some more."

I stepped forward and took the Ben Franklin from his fingers.

"Why, thank you," I said with feeling.

"Don't mention it."

It looked like an expansive gesture, but I knew that Waleta was counting on his hundred dollars to shut me up and lure me back to the game tables, where he hoped I'd play until the house recouped some of my winnings. I walked to the door and when I reached it, turned back.

"One last thing. Hurston said he made a phone call to his ex-wife from his hotel room the night of the murder. I'll trade you this hundred for a look at the phone record."

"Your attorney can subpoena those records, you know."

"I know. But time is money, Mr. Waleta."

He smiled. "Yes, time is money, and the Packers have less than a minute to live. All right, you got a deal. This game's over, anyway."

I handed the hundred back to Waleta as he walked past and followed him down the stairs. The game room was more crowded as the night wore on; the cacophony of vibes raised to an even higher pitch. Waleta and I dodged customers drunk on alcohol and anticipation. Beneath the din of the ringing slot machines and conversational noise, I heard the PA system piping out a steady stream of moldy oldies. *"If you want to know if he loves you so, it's in his kiss."*

"What kind of lousy relationship advice is that?" I shouted into Waleta's ear.

"What's that?"

"That song. Telling girls that they can know how much a guy loves them by his kiss."

He shrugged. "Sold a lot of records, didn't it?"

True, I thought. No wonder baby boomers were so confused.

At the rear exit, Waleta held the door and I stepped outside. The night air had the kind of chill that let me know summer was on its way out. We stood facing a single-story building with a row of gold-numbered doors. The Mystic Mesa Hotel.

"So this is where it happened." I glanced over at Waleta as we walked toward the main office. His profile was as stony as a Mt. Rushmore carving, and he was about as talkative. "I feel sorry for whoever found Aquillo's body," I went on. "Jesus, that must have been awful."

He turned and fixed me with a heavy look. He'd seen the body, I knew by his haunted eyes. When we reached the hotel office, he held the door for me.

I heard a familiar sound as we walked in. A television set was mounted in the corner of the room near the ceiling, tuned to the Packers-Viking game. A frowning gray-haired woman sat behind the registration desk, arms crossed over her chest. She was wearing a shapeless floral-print dress that could have fit a woman twice her size.

"Hey, Rosemary," Waleta said.

"Shhh!" She glared at him, her deeply lined face full of menace. "This is an important play."

I glanced at the set. In the time it had taken Waleta and me to walk to the office, Wisconsin had intercepted the ball and tied the score. With seventeen seconds left, the Packers were kicking for the game-winning extra point.

Waleta didn't notice. He walked to the counter and spoke quietly but firmly.

"This lady needs to see some records."

"Hold your horses," she said, without taking her eyes off the TV.

The play went through and the crowd roared. Waleta looked up at the TV. As the final score—Packers twenty-one, Vikings, twenty—flashed on the screen, he did a double take on me.

"Son of a gun. You psychic or something?"

"Sometimes," I said.

Rosemary turned away from the television and gave us her attention, a satisfied look on her face.

"Okay. What is it you need?" She peered at me with eyes that looked like they'd seen it all at least twice. I wasn't fooled by the grandmotherly flowered dress. It would be difficult, if not impossible, to get anything by this woman.

"She's an investigator," Waleta said before I could introduce myself. He looked at Rosemary with an expression that left something unspoken, I wasn't sure what. "She needs the September thirteen phone record for Room 109."

Rosemary rolled her chair to a computer and tapped the keyboard with her bony fingers. She'd put her gray hair up in a bun, but some of the hairpins had fallen out and the left side was drooping in back.

"You want a copy of this?" she asked.

"If you don't mind," Waleta said.

A dot-matrix printer churned out the invoice. She tore it off and handed the track-fed sheet to Waleta. He placed it on the countertop, and we scanned the listings.

"This just gives the date and cost of the call," I said to Rosemary. "Do you have something that shows the actual phone number that was called?"

She looked to Waleta, a question in her ancient eyes.

"Go ahead," he said. "The attorneys are gonna get these anyway."

She made a few more keystrokes, printed out another sheet, and handed it over. Again Waleta and I scanned the page. Hurston had made two calls that night. I pointed to the number with the coastal prefix.

"This must be the ex-wife's number. But he also called extension 303. Is that a room number at the hotel?"

"No," Waleta said slowly, "that's Dan Aquillo's extension at the casino."

"So Hurston called Aquillo from his room at 11:30 the night of the murder. That doesn't look so great, does it?"

Waleta raised an eyebrow. "I told you I'd decline his case if I were you."

The facts were falling into a straight line that pointed directly to Hurston's guilt, but I wasn't getting a straight feeling. I folded the phone record and put it in my purse.

"Maybe you're right," I said. "Is there any chance I could take a look at the room where it happened?"

"That area's out of bounds," Waleta said firmly.

"I just want a sense of where it happened, is all."

Rosemary was surfing through the channels now, pretending not to listen.

"Tell you what," I said. "I'll give you half of the money I won at the casino tonight if you let me take a look at that room."

"Fifty percent of eighteen hundred is nine hundred bucks." Waleta's voice had climbed half an octave. "Are you crazy?"

"Sometimes," I said with a shrug.

He shook his head.

"Sorry, but the cops have got that all roped off."

"They've already taken prints and fibers," I said. "Besides, I won't touch a thing. I just want a look."

"For crying out loud, Peter," Rosemary mumbled without moving her eyes from the TV. "Take the money and let her look at the damn room."

5

I followed Peter Waleta's linebacker-sized body past the Mystic Mesa Hotel guest rooms, their curtains shut tight. An occasional wall sconce lit the passageway, leaving dark patches of shadow in between.

"We grew a lot faster than we ever expected to, so we're adding a second story to the hotel," he said. "That's why the area up ahead is roped off."

The passageway ended sharply in an L. Sawhorses strung with yellow "CAUTION" tape blocked off the wing that continued to the right. A cardboard sign on the middle sawhorse apologized for the construction mess beyond:

PARDON OUR DUST!

I chuckled under my breath.

"What's so funny?" Waleta asked.

"Oh, nothing. Just that phrase, 'pardon our dust.' Always reminds me of what Dorothy Parker wanted put on her tombstone."

"What's that?"

" 'Excuse my dust.' "

In the dim light of the hallway, Waleta's face scrunched in puzzlement.

"This Dorothy sounds weird. She a friend of yours?"

"No," I said with a smile. "She was a writer. She's dead now."

I stood behind the sawhorse and looked at the wing under construction. The half-finished framing of the second-story add-on was silhouetted in pitch black against the night sky.

Waleta moved the sawhorse a few inches and slipped behind it.

"Watch out for nails," he said. "They're all over the place."

I followed him down the dark hallway, weak light from the

parking lot the only source of illumination. I studied Waleta from behind, trying to get a sense of him. He swayed slightly from side to side with the lumbering gait of a large man. His aura was calm, almost placid. If he had any troubles, they were buried deep inside. He stopped at the last door at the end of the wing. Room 109.

"Why was Hurston staying in this room, if this part of the hotel was off limits?" I asked.

"Looks like Dan comped him a room last weekend. I noticed there was no charge on that invoice Rosemary gave you. Dan let him bunk for free, I guess, since we're not making any profit off these rooms anyway."

"Why would he do that?"

"I dunno. Maybe he didn't want him to drive drunk. Maybe he was giving him a break." Waleta pulled a plastic key from his shirt pocket and slid it into the door lock. The tiny light on the lock flashed green.

"Was there any sign of forced entry?" I asked.

"Not that I'm aware."

"How many of those card keys do you issue for each room?"

"Two, usually."

Waleta covered the knob with his shirt tail.

"The cops finished taking their prints and pictures yesterday, but you can't be too careful," he said as he pushed the door open.

The room was pitch dark. Waleta reached for the wall switch but nothing happened.

"Shit. Just a second. Wait here."

He walked in, and a few seconds later light from the bathroom cast an oblong shaft across the floor.

"Has this wall switch been dead like that for a while?" I asked.

"Don't think so. It usually turns on the wall lamp. Must be burned out or something."

Waleta walked over to a sconce on the far side of the room. He put his hand behind the frosted glass, and the light came on.

"Bulb was loose, is all."

I made a mental note of it. Had someone loosened the bulb intentionally?

Light from the sconce made plain a wide bloodstain at the foot of the unmade bed. The drying blood had blackened the brown carpet, crusting the pile into spiky tufts. At the rear of the room, a sliding glass door led to a tiny balcony. The small closet stood open, empty save for a few bony hangers.

I didn't need to walk in. The atmosphere was as charged as a midwestern summer afternoon before a thunderstorm. With just one glance at the bloodstains on the floor by the bed, images began pushing into my consciousness like fresh memories from an unwelcome nightmare.

A darkened form emerging from the closet, raising a hammer over a man's head, bringing the blunt tool down with cruel force. The body crumpling into a heap. The one with the hammer striking three more furious blows. Bending down, peering at the fallen body. After a time, walking out the front door, hammer in hand.

None of this affected me emotionally. I was an impartial observer, an objective audience. That was good, that meant the channel was clear. I waited for more, but that was it.

"Thank you, Peter," I said. "That's all I need for now."

He switched off the lights, came back out, and pulled the door shut with a click.

"For nine hundred dollars? The pleasure's mine."

6

I parked across the street from a sand-colored condominium along Sea Lane Drive. I couldn't see the breaking waves as I climbed out of my Chevy pickup, but the squawking gulls and salty air left no doubt that an ocean was on the other side of the building. This was the address I'd tracked down from the reverse directory when I'd looked up the number Bill Hurston had dialed from his hotel room—or the murder scene, depending on how you wanted to look at it. It was the same address listed beside "Hurston, N." in the phone book. I'd called the number several times with no answer.

I was heading up the walk when a woman wearing navy blue running shorts and a white tank top came out of the middle condo and locked the deadbolt behind her. Her dark auburn hair was pulled back under a white visor, and she was carrying a pair of wraparound shades. She was petite, with deeply tanned skin and very little flesh, as if years of sun had shrunken her. Her sinewy limbs moved quickly, like an insect's.

"Ms. Hurston?"

She tucked her key into a zippered pouch around her waist and eyed me warily.

"If you're here from the press, you're out of luck. I've got to run. Literally."

She put on her shades and brushed by me, moving swiftly down a stairway to the beach. In the split second she passed me I picked up her vibe: Fear.

"I'm not from the press," I said, hurrying down the stairs to catch up. "I'm working with your ex-husband's attorney. Can I ask you just a few questions?"

She hit the sand and headed south at a jog.

"You want to run with me, fine. Otherwise, it'll have to wait. I have a one o'clock meeting, and I do *not* miss my daily run."

She didn't strike me as a particularly shy person, which

made me wonder what she was afraid of. Grateful that I'd worn shorts and Adidas, I ran after her.

"Don't mind if I do," I called. "A run sounds good."

I sprinted through the thick, dry sand and caught up with her where the water met the shore in a wide, glassy slick. The air was calm—just the merest hint of offshore breeze—and the tide was out. Our footsteps made slapping sounds, the earth giving just slightly under our feet.

"So you work with David Skenazy," she said, glancing at my khaki shorts. "You don't look like an attorney."

"I'm a private detective."

She nodded and turned her eyes straight ahead. Natalie Hurston was well into her forties but had the body of a life-long runner—one of that determined species with rock-hard leg muscles and just enough torso to hold a gigantic set of lungs. The pace she set was daunting.

"I guess the most important thing I need to know," I began, "is whether or not you think your ex-husband is capable of the crime he's been charged with."

She trotted on, shaking her head.

"Who knows? If I could figure him out, I might still be married to him."

She didn't elaborate. Just continued to run, breathing steadily.

Her response gave me hope. I've discovered that if you're looking for an unsanitized character assessment of someone, former spouses are good sources. Sometimes they'll volunteer the ugly stuff without you even asking. Natalie, however, was being noncommittal, making me pull the ugly stuff out of her. Putting me through my paces, literally.

"Did you know he was suicidal?" I asked.

"He'd been down before, but I never thought he'd actually try it. I don't know what happened to him. He used to be my hero. You wouldn't know it looking at him today, but there was a time when he was a decent husband and one hell of a good doctor." I thought I heard a little anger now, mixed in with her fear.

"Did you know the casino manager he's been accused of killing, this Dan Aquillo guy?"

"Not personally, no," she said.

"But your ex did mention him?" Already I was beginning to get winded.

She veered left around a pile of rubbery orange kelp that had washed up on the sand. I veered to the right. When we jogged back together, she answered.

"I'd heard Aquillo's name before. I don't even remember the context. Bill and I have been divorced several years, you know."

"So do you hate Bill's guts, or are you still friends?" I panted.

"I don't hate his guts, but I wouldn't call him a friend. He let me down too much for that."

We were jogging toward a covey of sandpipers that pecked at the tiny crabs just beneath the surface of the sand. When we were nearly upon them, the birds scattered in a fan-shaped cloud.

"What happened to the marriage?" I asked.

"In a word? Gambling. It started out slow. I even went along with it at first. Weekends at our time-share in Las Vegas. Off-track wagering. Then we started hanging around the track. We used to be big names at Del Mar. I'd plan months for what to wear opening day. We even had part ownership of a thoroughbred at one point. Those were the good old days."

"What were the bad old days?"

She took off her visor for a moment to swipe at the perspiration that was beading on her forehead. Her pace slowed.

"It's so damn typical. He was away from home more and more. He withdrew. I started getting calls from the bank. I'm sure there were other women. I kept hoping it would turn around and go back to the way we used to be, but it kept getting worse. With each shitty new development I'd tell him that was the last straw." She laughed joylessly, arcing around some kids making a sand castle. "There were a lot of last straws."

"What *was* the final straw?"

"When the Medical Board of California shut down Bill's practice and suspended his license. That came as a total shock. Seems he was selling prescription narcotics—Percodan, mostly—to fund his gambling hobby. The attorney you're working with—Skenazy—kept him out of jail, but that was the end of our marriage."

"You think Aquillo's murder could have something to do with your ex-husband selling narcotics again?"

"I have no idea."

I looked out to sea. A pod of Pacific dolphins—I counted at least eight of them—was swimming just beyond the breakers, their sleek black bodies weaving in and out of the water. A few surfers sat languidly on their boards, waiting for the next set to roll in. Sometimes the dolphins will hang out and surf with the locals, but not today. The friendly mammals were heading north at a steady clip, swimming right through the gathering of surfers.

"Look at that," I said, pointing.

Natalie turned to look, breaking out of her jog.

"Let's walk," she said.

I took a deep, relieved breath and slowed to a walk.

The exercise seemed to have put Natalie more at ease. The fear I'd picked up earlier had toned down several notches. But I could still sense it, so I tried to make my next question sound as casual as possible.

"When was the last time you spoke with Bill?"

"The night of the murder. He called me from the hotel and said he was sorry for all the pain he'd put me through. I didn't like the tone of his voice. It worried me."

"What do you mean?"

"It's not like this was the first time he'd called me drunk and morbid, believe me. But there was something different this time. A real resignation."

I searched Natalie Hurston's face. She seemed to be talking frankly, but I couldn't read her eyes behind the wraparound sunglasses.

"Maybe he'd killed Aquillo," I said, "and felt that suicide was the only way out."

"No. If he'd been involved in a murder, he wouldn't have sounded so calm. It was like he was just . . . tired. This is where I turn back."

She pointed to a high bluff lit the color of saffron by the bright midday sun. Sedimentary rock layers created an elegant pattern of horizontal stripes along the sandstone face. We rounded a large outcropping of algae-covered rock and began jogging north again. The way of the dolphins.

The conversation lapsed as we fell into a steady pace back up the beach. By the time we reached the steps to Natalie's condo, my leg muscles were complaining and my mouth was dry.

"Thanks for your time," I said.

"Let me at least give you a drink of water for the road," she said. "Come on up."

The offer surprised me.

"That's very kind of you," I said, following her up the stairs.

The inside of Natalie's condominium was lovely but crowded, as if she'd condensed a houseful of treasures into a smaller space and hadn't been able to part with too many favorite pieces. She went to get my water, leaving me standing in the entry. I examined the bric-a-brac on a table nearby. Hand-carved wooden candleholders, an exquisite urn of polished pewter, a Montblanc pen. To my disappointment, she displayed no framed photographs. I can read a lot from photographs.

"Here you are." She returned holding out a goblet of ice water. As I took the drink, I noticed that her nails were painted a warm poppy-red that complimented her tanned fingers. I work my hands too hard to go in for fancy manicures myself, but I appreciate women who can pull it off. Natalie's poppy-colored nails suited her nicely.

"Thanks." I swallowed half the water in one draw, then held the cut crystal to catch the light. "You have such gorgeous things."

"Thank you. Now if only I had a suitable house to put them

in. Bill still owes me six figures from our marital settlement agreement, but I gave up collecting on that long ago."

"Do you ever see him anymore?"

"Not in ages. It's too painful."

I didn't have to see behind her sunglasses to know that she was telling the truth about the painful part.

"Do you have children that see him?"

"No."

Her terse reply let me know that the subject of children was painful as well.

"When did you last see him, do you remember?"

"Oh, Jesus. I don't even know. Months ago. Our lives went separate ways after the divorce." She looked at her wristwatch. "I'd better get into the shower. I have a meeting with a client within the hour."

"Of course." I finished up my water and handed her the empty glass. "What kind of work do you do?"

"I'm a sales rep for Calloway golf clubs."

Natalie probably sold a lot of golf clubs to people who wrongly assumed that a few holes of golf would give them her deeply tanned, razor-ripped body.

I reached in my pocket for a business card and handed it to her as I stepped toward the door.

"If you think of anything that might throw some light on this casino mess, could you give me a call?"

She nodded as she took the card. She lifted up her sunglasses, glanced at my title, and looked at me with wary green eyes.

"*Psychic* Investigator?"

"Niche marketing. Comes in handy."

Her fearful vibe was back.

"No offense, but you people give me the creeps. The last psychic I went to scared the daylights out of me. Said he saw negative energy around me, bad fortune coming to a loved one, danger, all this crap. No, thanks. No more psychics for me."

I took my card back from her, picked up the Montblanc from the hall table, and drew a line through the offending adjective.

"There," I said, handing the card back. "Consider me just an investigator. Thanks for your time. *And* the run. I needed it."

I left her with a smile, biting my tongue about the fact that her psychic had been right about bad fortune coming to a loved one.

7

I was wondering what Natalie Hurston might have been afraid of as I stepped onto the elevator with a man and a dog. The man was a complete stranger, a twenty-something hipster sporting a trendy microfiber jacket and short spikes of two-toned hair. The dog was my best buddy, a hefty Rhodesian ridgeback that I'd inherited from McGowan after his death. When the doors closed, Nero sat back on his haunches and stared straight ahead. The dog had impeccable elevator etiquette, which was more than I could say for the hipster, who shamelessly eyed us both.

"Nice dog," he said, keeping his hands stuffed in his microfiber pockets.

"Thanks," I replied civilly.

He looked as if he wanted to pat Nero's gigantic head but wasn't quite sure if it was a good idea.

"Does the dog . . . *live* in this building?"

"No," I said, "we're just visiting."

Nero and I stepped off on the third floor, leaving the hipster to ascend alone. We stepped along the outside hallway, and I took in the view: The lights of downtown San Diego to the north and the San Diego Harbor to the south. Ninety years ago this building housed a mattress factory. Today it was home to a small colony of young urban professionals.

I pressed the buzzer at Suite 3A. When the door opened, I was looking into the face of my other best buddy, Thomasina Wilson. Her coarse jet hair was pulled back into a tight chignon, making her strong ebony features look fierce.

"Prepare for your doom," she said, "because I'm feeling deadly tonight."

"Ooo, I'm scared." I stepped inside, and Nero padded in after me, tail wagging.

Thomasina closed the door with a bang.

"Go ahead with that nonchalant attitude. I know you're scared. I see it in the whites of your eyes. This is gonna be Black Tuesday for you, girl."

Tuesday was "Girls' Night In," a tradition Thomasina had started when she noticed me turning into a recluse after McGowan's funeral. Rain or shine, good mood or bad, we gathered every Tuesday night, alternating between her place and mine. The tradition included eating exotic food, drinking exotic beverages, and reveling in the main event: no-holds-barred Scrabble.

"Dream on," I said with a confidence I didn't entirely feel. "No way I'm losing tonight."

She leaned over and patted her thigh.

"Come here, Nero, and say hello to your Aunt Thomasina."

The dog stepped forward and licked her hand. Her face softened but didn't lose its edgy, intelligent quality. The first day I'd seen that face it seemed I'd known Thomasina for lifetimes. Later she told me she'd felt the same about me.

Nero quickly lost his inhibitions and began drenching Thomasina's lovely sunflower-yellow sweater in slobber. She didn't seem to care.

"How's my favorite mutt?" she cooed. "How's my big boy?"

"Your big boy is mad at me. I've been out a lot this week. He liked it better when I was a grief-stricken shut-in."

"That makes one of you, Nero," she said. She straightened and gave me a hug.

I hugged back, reveling in the energy of the strongest human being I knew. The victim in a serial rape case I'd investigated, Thomasina had been stabbed twenty-one times by her would-be murderer. Instead of setting her back, the experience had strengthened her, the way two thousand degrees Fahrenheit forges steel.

"Good to see you," I said.

"You, too."

She led me into the living room, an expansive space with exposed brick interior walls and an atypical view of the city. The high pine ceilings were crisscrossed with a colorful network of pipes for water and ventilation. A Nepalese rug warmed the slate-colored floor. The furniture was sparse and sleek, suiting both the space and the occupant.

"So what's lured you out of doors this week?" she asked as she dropped onto the sofa. The Scrabble board was ready to go on the chrome-and-glass coffee table before us.

"I took a case," I said.

"Anything interesting?"

"A murder case. Maybe you heard about it. That situation on the Temecu Reservation."

Her dark eyes flashed.

"You're involved in that nasty thing?"

"Working for the defense, if you can believe it. The man they arrested was a client of a friend of a friend, sort of. Scott Chatfield. You don't know him." I rambled into silence, and Thomasina looked at me dubiously.

"Is the guy guilty?"

"If I thought he were guilty, I wouldn't have taken the case. I talked to his ex-wife today. She dinged him for being a gambler, but she didn't cast aspersions on his innocence. Which is saying something, if you know ex-wives."

"Unless she's in cahoots with him. What do you think's going on?"

"I don't know. Hard to tell. I need to spend more time out at the reservation. I got some information out of the manager and the hotel clerk—a wise old bird, that one—but it's a tight-knit vibe out there. I definitely feel like an outsider."

"Yeah, they can be like that."

I leaned toward her and gave her the eye.

"*They?* You're not going racist on me, are you?"

"Just tellin' it like it is. When I was a kid, I used to go to the spring powwows in Temecu to visit my dad's relatives."

Her statement struck me dumb. Thomasina and all her family members I'd met were African American.

"You have relatives on an Indian reservation? How—"

"I'll tell you how. My great-grandfather on my dad's side was a full-blooded Luiseno Indian. He married a black woman—my great-grandmother Shoshena. Both of them died before I was born, but some of their progeny still live up in Temecu."

I stared, wondering if my leg was being pulled.

"You don't believe me," she said. "Wait here. I'll prove it."

She hopped off the sofa and went into the next room, returning with a framed photograph. It was a picture of a group of at least thirty people gathered outside a church, dressed in their Sunday finest. From the clothes I guessed the picture had been taken sometime around the first World War.

"That's my grandfather," she said, pointing to a small dark-skinned boy, "and that's my great-grandfather." Her finger slid over to a young man who wore baggy pants and a starched white shirt that contrasted dramatically with his long, straight hair. "He took an Americanized name, Clay Wilson, but the family always called him Night Cloud."

"And this is his wife?" I asked, pointing to the black woman at his side.

"Um-hm, that's Shoshena."

"Where was this photograph taken?"

"At the Temecu Mission, on the reservation." A buzzer went off in the kitchen. "Come on," she said, hopping off the sofa, "let's eat. I'm starved."

Nero lay curled on the Nepalese rug, eyes closed. Thomasina sat cross-legged on the floor in front of the coffee table, facing me. I sat on the sofa staring at the six letters she'd just placed across a triple word-score square: *WHYDAH*.

"Yeah, right," I said.

"African bird with long, drooping tail feathers," she replied calmly.

"Hey, we already discussed the ground rules. No Swahili."

"It's English. You challenging me?"

A formal challenge according to the rules of Girls' Night In meant that the winner selected any item she pleased from the Victoria's Secret catalog, and the loser picked up the tab, exorbitant shipping fees included. I was tempted to challenge her but wasn't entirely sure that her word didn't exist in English.

"No," I said, "if you're desperate enough to try to get *why-*

dah by me, I can hardly be so cruel as to humiliate you with exposure."

"Listen to you. So full of shit, Elizabeth Chase, Ph.D. That stands for Piled Horrifically Deep, right?"

"Sticks and stones," I said, laying down *VEX,* the eight-point *X* snuggling nicely into a double word-score square. I picked up my new tiles with a smug grin. "Do you still keep in touch with those relatives on the Temecu Reservation?"

Thomasina promptly used my *X* to spell *SEXY,* virtually cutting off yet another triple word score. I tried to stay philosophical about it.

"We stay in Christmas-card touch," she answered, "if you know what I mean." She picked up three more tiles from the box, looking confident in her lead. If I was going to catch her, I needed a miracle here.

"You think any of your Luiseno Indian relatives would talk to me?" I asked.

She slid the tiles around on her wooden letter tray.

"I don't see why not. I could ask, if you like."

"I'd like that," I said absently, beginning to see possibilities in all seven of my letters. "I need someone on the inside to talk to."

I looked up suddenly, then picked up a tile and placed it on the board.

"What?" she said, wrinkling her brow. "I don't like that smile on your face."

"This can't be a coincidence," I said. "It's a sign."

"What's a sign?"

Using the *Y* on the board, I laid down all seven of my letters and spelled *ROSEMARY.*

"Shit," she said with a respectful smile. "That's a fifty-point play, damn you. It's a sign, all right—a sign that I'm losing this game."

"It's more than that. Remember the wise old bird I was telling you about in the casino hotel office?"

"Yeah, so?"

"Her name is Rosemary."

8

I called the Mystic Mesa Hotel first thing the next morning and asked for Rosemary. Some people might think me silly, attaching significance to the coincidence that the letters of Rosemary's name came up in a Scrabble game. But I stopped believing in coincidences long ago. Too many times I've ignored so-called chance happenings, only to regret not having paid attention to the message my subconscious was trying to send me. The day-shift clerk in the hotel office told me that Rosemary Andreas wouldn't be in until 5:30 that evening, so I spent most of Wednesday finding out what I could from police reports and public records.

The public records were scanty. The Temecu Reservation belonged to a sovereign nation, a tribal government that generated a lot less paperwork than the State of California. *Inconvenient for me but a positive reflection on the Temecu tribe,* I thought.

Even though the crime had been committed on reservation lands, the case was being handled by San Diego Deputy District Attorney Milton Coben. Murder cases are the domain of the State of California, and the paperwork was already piling up in abundance. I obtained the police reports from the SDPD. They made for sobering reading.

According to the report, Peter Waleta had called 911 at 1:32 A.M., stating that two people were hurt, possibly dead, at the Mystic Mesa Hotel. Deputy Valquez of the Temecu Tribal Police, the first officer to arrive at the scene, recorded Waleta's statements. Valquez described the body:

THE HAIR AND SKIN ON THE VICTIM'S HEAD WERE PEELED OFF, RESULTING IN EXCESSIVE BLOOD LOSS AND RENDERING THE VICTIM UNRECOGNIZABLE. WALETA STATED THAT HE RECOGNIZED THE CLOTHING OF THE VICTIM AS BELONGING TO HIS BUSINESS PARTNER, DAN AQUILLO.

It was an image that stayed with me as I drove out to the reservation. The late afternoon sunshine painted the landscape in warm hues, but I couldn't shake the coldness that came over me.

I bypassed the coyotes, eagles, jackrabbits, and mountain lions of the big lot and parked my Chevy on the asphalt in front of the Mystic Mesa Hotel. When I walked into the registration office, Rosemary was sitting with her arms crossed over her chest, looking up at a *Dallas* rerun.

"Hello again. Rosemary, wasn't it?"

She was wearing a shapeless blue dress this evening, with big white buttons down the front. She either didn't hear me or was pretending not to.

I came forward and leaned on the counter. A melodramatic bar of music underscored a close-up of JR's devious face, and after several torturous seconds, the show mercifully cut to a commercial. She turned to me and frowned.

"You think it was worth nine hundred dollars to look at that room the other night?"

"I guess only time will tell," I said.

Her wide mouth turned down like a fish's, and she nodded almost imperceptibly.

"What'd you do with the other nine hundred?"

"I'm saving it for a worthy cause. How late do you work nights?"

"Shift ends at 2:30 A.M."

I gave her a good, hard look. She couldn't be a day under seventy.

"Those are long hours."

She shrugged.

"Always been a night owl. I'd just be sitting home watching TV anyway. Might as well do it here and get paid for it."

"What do you like to watch?"

"*Judge Judy*'s my favorite show. Ever seen it?"

"Oh, sure. Judy's awesome."

Her lips pulled into something close to a smile, and her eyes turned crafty.

"I'm a worthy cause," she said.

I started to open my mouth, but she held up a wrinkled hand to stop me.

"You're gonna ask me if I was here that night and if I noticed anything strange. You'll probably follow it up with questions about Dan: Did I know him? How long? Did he have any enemies, yadda, yadda, yadda. You'll probably want to know if I knew this Hurston fellow."

"Very good."

"I watch a lot of *Law & Order*," she explained.

"*Did* you notice anything strange that night?"

"That depends. If you consider me a worthy cause, maybe I did."

"Very worthy. I have two hundred dollars in my wallet that say so."

"Peter got nine."

"Peter took me to the crime scene."

She made the frowning fish face again.

"That's all I've got on me," I said. "Besides, I already read your statement to the police. So unless you've got something new, it's probably not worth my time and mon—"

"I didn't tell them everything," she said.

"Why not? Are you protecting someone?"

"You betcha I am." She poked a gnarled finger into her chest. "Me. The reason people don't talk to the police is because sometimes people who talk pay a price for not keeping quiet. All's I'm going to say is there's a bad element around here sometimes. 'Course, the cops know that already."

"Who?"

She shook her head.

"You're not paying me enough to name names. That ain't worth two *thousand* dollars."

"But you saw someone here that night—someone who shall remain nameless—who may have had something to do with Aquillo's murder?"

"You better start with a different question."

"All right. You said in your interview with the police that Dan Aquillo was your boss."

"That's right."

"What was he like? Not just as a boss, but as a person?"

"Nice enough fellow. Respected by his people. Most of 'em."

"Who didn't respect him?"

She hesitated.

"So far I'm not hearing anything new, Rosemary."

"I didn't think his girlfriend treated him with the respect he deserved."

"Trish Brown?"

"Um-hm."

"Is she working tonight?"

"She's off until Saturday night. Seein' a shrink, I heard. This whole thing shook her up pretty bad."

"Does she live on the reservation?"

"Nope. Lives in Escondido."

My town. I should be able to track her down there without much help.

"Thank you. Okay, tell me something the police don't know."

The phone rang, and she picked it up.

"Mystic Mesa Hotel. Yeah. Eight-five dollars. Uh-huh. That's right."

She hung up.

"You answer the phones that come into the hotel on your shift?"

"Kind of looks that way, doesn't it?"

"Did anyone call Hurston's room that night?"

She reached for a box of Kleenex on the desk.

"My memory's not bad for an old woman, but I sure don't remember which calls go to what room on any given night." She pulled out a tissue and honked her nose without a trace of self-consciousness. "There was a woman who came by, though," she said, wiping at her nostrils. "She asked for Hurston."

If Hurston's mystery visitor had been mentioned in the police report, I'd missed it.

"Did you tell this to the police?"

"No. Didn't remember it till just now."

"What did this woman look like?"

Rosemary scrunched her face and stared into the lobby, as if she were seeing the woman again.

"Looked like she needed to eat. Skinny little thing."

Natalie Hurston's sinewy limbs instantly came to mind.

"Woman with a dark tan, reddish-brown hair, mid-forties, about five-foot-five?"

"That sounds about right."

"Did you see her go to Hurston's room?"

"It's against hotel rules to give out room numbers, but she looked pretty harmless, so I told her she might find him in the room at the end of the breezeway. Last I saw she was headed that direction."

"What time did she come by, do you remember?"

She shook her head. "After midnight, but before one o'clock. I was watching *Xena.* No wait, or was it after one, while I was watching *Hercules?* I honestly don't recall."

"But you're sure it was after midnight?"

"Yeah, I'm pretty sure of that."

I figured I'd gotten my two-hundred-dollars' worth and pulled the bills from my wallet, along with one of my cards.

"Thank you, Rosemary. I would appreciate any other information, day or night, if you happen to remember anything else."

She took the bills and slipped them between the buttons of her dress, tucking them away in her bosom.

I went back into the casino and played four games of blackjack, which won me just about enough cash to cover a cup of coffee and my gas mileage to and from the reservation. On the drive home I felt both tired and jumpy, an irritating combination.

The moon would come up later, but for now the mountain road was black. Most of the headlights I encountered were heading uphill, toward the casino. A few miles into my journey headlights appeared behind me, coming fast. I slowed and pulled over to let the speeder by. As the car pulled around me, I heard a popping noise. An old engine backfiring, I assumed as I watched the taillights racing away.

Suddenly my steering wheel pulled hard and uncontrollably to the left. I took my foot off the gas and, for one desperate moment, thought that I might be headed into oncoming traffic. I regained control and was able to coax my truck to a stop on the shoulder.

Blow out.

I sighed, thinking it might have been worse. A blown tire I could deal with. I got out and retrieved the jack from the supply box in the truck bed. My Chevy was practically new, and the parts were so shiny and clean they were almost fun to work with. The lug nuts were tight but came off with a little muscle. I threw the damaged tire into the truck, popped on the spare, and was just tightening the nuts when a pair of headlights slowed and pulled up behind me.

I glanced back over my shoulder and caught the full glare of somebody's brights. Whoever it was turned off their motor but left their lights on. I couldn't see the make of the car, only the driver's side door swinging open. Heavy footsteps crunched toward me along the gravelly shoulder.

"It's okay," I called out. "I got it handled. Thanks anyway."

The footsteps kept coming. I began to get the feeling this wasn't a good Samaritan.

"Really," I said hurrying to my feet and dusting off my knees, "I'm outta here."

I opened the door and was hopping into the cab when a rough hand jerked me back by my hair.

"Not yet, you're not."

9

My scalp burned with a searing pain as the bad Samaritan dragged me by my hair away from the road. Still blinded by the headlights, I stumbled backward, unable to get a foothold. I finally managed to dig a heel into the loose dirt and spin left, where a fist glanced my cheekbone. It wasn't enough to knock me out, but I dropped like a stone anyway, employing the old play-dead ruse.

"Get the fuck up, or I'm gonna pull all your hair out."

The voice was demon deep. I didn't recognize it. I kept my eyes closed and didn't move.

He grabbed another fistful of hair and pulled, inching my dead weight away from the road. I felt sharp pebbles under my back, and the pain in my scalp was all but unbearable. Just when it felt like the skin would rip right off my skull, he stopped.

I heard an impatient sigh and felt his grip loosen. I waited three beats and rolled sideways. He lost his hold on me. I'd just made it to my feet when I felt him catch me by the tail of my shirt. He grabbed my hair again and jerked me around hard.

"If you don't knock it off, you ain't gonna have any fuckin' hair left."

"I can't do a thing with it anyway."

This time the fist came from the right side, connecting solidly with my nose. I cried out in pain and started to tumble backward, but he clamped his ham-hand around my arm and held me upright. With my vision impaired by instant tears and a black, moonless night, I couldn't make out his finer points, but I got the basics. Five-eleven, maybe six foot. Huge—two-sixty, easy. Knit ski cap on a block head. No heart.

"You oughta watch your big mouth, bitch."

I was too stunned to duck the final blow, which caught me on the right temple and put me out before I hit the ground.

* * *

Someone was bending over me, holding me. In spite of the dark I could *see* the look of tenderness and encouragement on his Native American features. Even though I'd never seen him before, somehow I knew him. He didn't speak, but he didn't have to. I was sure he was here to help me. And somehow he knew everything that had happened, without me telling him.

I tried to sit up to see him better. My head felt three sizes too big for my body. My ears were ringing like a bell tower. I had the mother of all headaches. The inside of my mouth was gritty and sour with dirt and blood, but I couldn't muster the energy to spit. I couldn't muster the energy to do anything but fall back and stare into the sky, where the Milky Way cut a dazzling swath across clear black space and disappeared behind Palomar Mountain. I realized I was slipping away again. There was nothing I could do about it. It crossed my mind that it wouldn't be so bad to die, now that McGowan had passed on.

The cold brought me around the second time. It was still dark. My headache was worse, which I wouldn't have thought possible. But I felt a little stronger. I rolled onto my side. I was alone, about thirty feet from the side of the road. The Chevy was parked where I'd left it.

Getting up was slow going. I tried sitting, a dizzying experience. My first attempt to stand left me bending, hands on knees, close to vomiting. The severity of my injuries made me wonder if the bad Samaritan had kicked my head in a bit after I'd passed out. Crawling seemed a better idea than walking.

It was a slow, laborious journey back to the truck, with lots of rest intervals. When I finally reached the passenger's side, I was able to stand. Leaning against the truck, I fished in my pocket and was grateful to find the keys still there.

I was in no shape to drive. I opened the door and searched the front seat for my cell phone. No phone. When I leaned down to check the floor, a tidal wave of blood pressure made my head feel like it was going to explode. Trying to keep my head upright, I searched the floor with my fingers three times before admitting that the fucker had stolen my phone. Not to mention my purse.

I climbed in, locked the doors, and bundled my jacket into a makeshift pillow. I rested my sorry head and lost consciousness again.

I was awakened by what felt like an earthquake. The sun had risen over the mountains and was casting a blinding glare on a shiny steel-and-aluminum semi roaring past me down Highway 76. It was early—not yet nine by the dashboard clock. I still hurt but was past the worst part. I started the engine and headed back to Escondido, poking along like a tourist.

As soon as I walked through the door of my house, my animals let me know they'd been worried sick. Nero went into a sniffing frenzy, making a series of low growls and yelps I'd never heard from him before. Whitman, my Himalayan, jumped defiantly onto the sofa—something he rarely does—meowing loudly for an explanation. I gave him a reassuring pet and headed immediately for the aspirin bottle in the bathroom cabinet. I was wholly unprepared for what met me in the mirror.

My nose had been pummeled to the point that it listed to the left. Both of my eyes were swollen, with blackening lids and blood-red blotches in the whites. There was a neat circular shiner like a bright crimson blossom on my left cheekbone. That part wasn't so bad. It was the right side of my face that made me look like something out of an *Alien* movie. My temple had swollen grotesquely, as if about to give birth to some hideous facial offspring. Blood had run from a cut on my brow bone and dried in streaky rivulets along my cheek and jaw line.

The phone was ringing. I walked back to the kitchen and answered with a meek hello.

"Hey, girl. What's up?"

My spirits lifted.

"Thomasina, God love you for calling."

"How you doin'?" she asked. "I had the weirdest dream about you last night."

The fear and agony of the last few hours hit me full force. I felt tears welling in my swollen eyes. I tried to think of some-

thing light-hearted and witty to say, but all that came out was
a wordless stammer.

"Hey," she said. "You sound funny. Are you okay?"

My voice was so small that I hardly recognized it.

"No, I'm not."

10

I was coming up from unconsciousness again. This time I was lying on a wheeled bed behind gauzy green privacy curtains. I heard emergency-room sounds: a game show outside in the waiting room; a nurse calling for Dr. Pomidor. I smelled emergency-room smells: rubbing alcohol, cheaply scented antibacterial soap, the sour aroma of unfamiliar bodies. I rolled my head sideways and saw that I had company.

"Now this is a switch," Thomasina said with a smile.

I was fuzzy from sedatives but knew right away what she was talking about. Years ago it had been me sitting by her bed as she recovered from the rapist's knife attack.

"Yeah," I said, "but your injuries were a lot more serious than these."

She nodded thoughtfully.

"True. You look worse, though."

I flinched as she placed a bag of ice against my face.

"Thanks for calling the ambulance. The EMTs got there so fast I barely had time to pack my bag. Hey, that ice kinda hurts."

"Sorry. I know it's uncomfortable, but this really does reduce the swelling." She smiled at me sweetly, her liquid brown eyes shining. "The doctor said your forehead stitched up just fine. Unfortunately, he wasn't able to save your nose."

Thomasina and her nose jokes.

"No loss there," I said and had to chuckle. The pain in my sinuses stopped me short. "No more comedy—hurts when I laugh."

Her face was dead serious.

"Who in the hell did this to you?"

I closed my eyes, which were nearly swollen shut anyway.

"I don't even know."

"Come on, psychic detective, surely you have a clue."

I shifted on the bed, trying to get comfortable. A futile effort.

"Maybe somebody doesn't want me hanging out at the Mystic Mesa Casino. I went out there to question the woman in the hotel office—Rosemary, remember?"

"The woman who inspired a fifty-point Scrabble play. How could I forget?"

"I was going to talk to Trish Brown at the casino, but Rosemary told me she was on bereavement leave until Saturday. So I played a couple of hands of blackjack and left. On the way home I had a blowout, and when I pulled over to change the tire, somebody pulled up behind me and did this."

She took the ice pack off my face and stared at me.

"You had a blowout, huh?"

I thought back to the car that had passed me and backfired.

"Either that or the car that passed me shot out my front tire."

With gentle hands, she replaced the ice against my swollen face. Her jaw was clenched tight.

"I talked to one of my relatives out at the reservation. He said he'd be happy to talk to you, but I'm thinking maybe you should drop this case. This is the last thing you need now."

"Need shmeed," I said.

"What's that supposed to mean?"

"If there's anything I learned from you, Thomasina, it's how to be a fighter, not a quitter. No way I'm dropping it. Especially now."

She didn't smile, but I could see by the fire in her eyes that she knew where I was coming from. She repositioned the ice pack, which didn't feel quite so uncomfortable now that it was beginning to thaw.

"You need some protection? 'Cause I know some pretty badass bodyguards. You just say the word."

"I can take care of myself."

She let out a sound that was something between a cough and a laugh. She put down the ice pack and pulled a mirrored compact from her purse. As she held it up to my face, I got a good look at myself. The bandages mercifully covered some of the damage, but the parts that were visible looked ghastly. Thomasina's eyebrows arched high into her forehead.

"Say that again while you look at your face. Go ahead, now. Tell me how well you can take care of yourself."

"Forewarned is forearmed. If it happens again, I'll be prepared."

"You damn well better be. Otherwise your ass will be hanging out of a hospital gown. If you're lucky."

I met her scolding stare with a request.

"Hand me my backpack, would you?"

She leaned down to pull the backpack off the floor and placed it on my lap. I unzipped the main compartment and, one by one, displayed the contents: My 9-millimeter Glock and lightweight polyurethane shoulder holster. My snub-nosed 22 and a DeSantis ankle holster.

"See? Not to worry. From here on out, my ass is covered."

11

"Hello?"

I stepped into the offices of David Skenazy, Esq., where my greeting met with nothing but the desperate first movement of Beethoven's Fifth Symphony. I walked across a threadbare Persian rug to the reception desk, a piece with a personality all its own. I glanced at the stately mahogany monster, piled high with legal briefs and court documents. The desk was unmanned, so I opened the door to the back office and peeked down the hall.

"David?"

From his office twenty feet down the hall, I could hear him arguing into the telephone. Some sorry soul was getting an earful about the indiscriminate release of information to the media. The aging decorum of the reception area completely disintegrated back here. I walked past plaster walls chipped and blighted by water stains, dodging the overstuffed files that spilled from the bankers boxes lining the hallway. The overall effect was like that moment, comic but disappointing, when you saw the disheveled Wizard of Oz behind the curtain. I poked my head into the wizard's office.

David took one look at my face, mumbled "gotta go" to his caller, and slammed down the phone.

"My God, you look awful. Who do you want me to sue?"

I think he was serious.

"Pretty hard to sue when you don't know who clobbered you," I said.

"You weren't in a car accident?"

"This was no accident."

His mouth dropped open.

"Have you filed charges?"

"Charges against whom? The guy who beat me up didn't exactly introduce himself."

"You've at least filed a police report, then."

"You don't have to play lawyer with me, David."

"What do you mean, play? We're talking egregious assault here. You can't simply ignore—"

I put a hand up to stop him.

"It's okay. The doctor who repaired my face contacted the PD. An officer dropped by the ER and took a report. I called American Express about my stolen card—fortunately I still have a Visa card in my office. I'm going to stop by the DMV for a replacement driver's license on my way home. With any luck, I'll have a new cell phone by tomorrow and my replacement PI license in a week or two." I realized I was rambling. Sedative hangover.

David got up and walked around his desk, pulling out a chair for me.

"You were robbed, too? Was this some sort of random attack, or what?"

I sat down and endured his curious eyes peering intently at my bandaged face, as if he were inspecting bruised tomatoes at the market.

"Satisfied?" I asked.

He backed off and returned to his chair behind the desk.

"No, I'm not satisfied! What the hell happened?" Genuine concern was coming through the explosive outburst. I found it rather endearing.

"As you know, I've been spending some time out at Mystic Mesa." Given the pressing nature of the case, I'd been faxing David nightly progress reports. "On the drive home last night, a car passed me and I heard a popping sound. Next thing I knew my tire had blown out. I pulled over and had almost finished putting on the spare when a guy pulled up and beat the crap out of me. Told me 'you oughta watch your big mouth, bitch.' That's a direct quote, I believe. As far as whether it was random or not, your guess is as good as mine."

"Who was this guy?"

"No idea. I could barely see him in the dark. He had a deep voice. Five-eleven or six foot. Big. That's all I can remember."

While the wheels turned in David's mind, I looked over his desk, reading letterheads and whatever else was in plain sight.

Before I was an investigator, this used to be a rude habit. Now it was a job skill.

"How's Dr. Hurston?" I asked.

"Still in jail and likely to be there awhile. He's flat broke. His family will pay for the defense but not the bail. Don't blame them. Half a million is a lot of lucre."

"That's an excessive bail amount."

"It's an excessive crime."

"How's the case going?"

He rolled his eyes and swiped the air, as if fending off a world of woes.

"Fuggedaboudit. The man is all but indefensible. The client from hell. Apparently he made a negative statement about the victim when he was on his way to the hospital. I'm pretty sure I can get it thrown out—Miranda or no Miranda, he was practically overdosed on tranquilizers. Definitely a diminished-capacity defense there."

"What kind of negative statement?"

"One of the medics claims Hurston was mumbling that it was his fault. But that's not my biggest problem. My biggest problem is that he's giving me all the wrong answers about the night of the murder. Stuff like, 'I can't remember.' A jury hears that and it's rest in peace, Bill."

"Rest in peace?"

"The DA's filing special circumstances. They've deemed the murder heinous, atrocious, cruel, manifesting exceptional depravity, blah, blah, blah."

"Exceptional depravity? Don't tell me Aquillo was scalped alive."

"That's what the DA's suggesting. Still haven't seen the medical examiner's report."

He slumped in his chair and dejectedly tapped a pen on the papers in front of him, staring at my face.

"Ah, hell. It's probably a good thing you're out of commission. I worked a death-penalty case nine years ago. Nearly sucked the life right out of me. Chatfield and I shouldn't have dragged you into this in the first place."

"I'm not out of commission. My face is a little banged up.

Besides, you said yourself the worst-case scenario is a diminished-capacity defense."

"But—"

"Just give me copies of everything you have on the case so far."

He chewed the end of his pen with a gleam in his eye.

"I'm too selfish to stop you—you need to know that."

"I'm a big girl."

He pushed the intercom button on his phone.

"Kathy, can you bring me everything on the Hurston case, please?

Silence. I remembered the abandoned receptionist's desk. David raised his voice.

"Kathy!"

He mumbled something I couldn't hear, jumped from his chair, and stormed past me out the door. In two minutes he was back, fuming, his complexion bright red.

"Everything all right?" I asked.

He tossed me a sheet of paper, which read:

Dear Mr. Skenazy,
    I can't take it anymore. I'm out of here.
        Sorry,
        Kathy Kobler
    P.S. Do you realize your name rhymes with "crazy"?
Think about it.

I put my hand to my mouth, trying to cover my smile.

"That's the third damn secretary who's walked out on me." He twisted his face into a sneer. "*Mr.* Skenazy. She never once called me that when she worked here. Disrespectful little—"

"The files?" I reminded him.

"They're out there somewhere. Come on."

I followed him back down the hallway, dodging boxes. When we got to the secretary's desk, David looked at the piles of abandoned paperwork, and made a mournful sound. A half dozen more file-filled boxes cluttered the floor. I started sorting through the chaos on the desk.

"You don't need a secretary, you need a toxic-waste management firm," I said, stacking the files into a neat pile. "Hey—I found it."

The Hurston file had been near the top of the heap, and my hand had gone right to it. I held the folder out to David.

"Make copies of everything in here for me."

He didn't argue, just walked straight across the room and began Xeroxing. I continued sifting through the paperwork on the desk. In a mound of unopened mail I found an envelope from the San Diego Medical Examiner's Office. I held it up to show David.

"Is this the autopsy report?"

He rushed over and snatched the envelope out of my hand.

"Hey, I've been waiting for this."

He tore open the envelope and shook the contents onto the desk. A sheaf of typewritten pages slid out first, followed by a series of photographs. David grabbed the written report; I nabbed the photos.

The graphic images caught me off guard. Instantly queasy, I averted my eyes and took a deep breath. I'd seen crime-scene photos before, but nothing like this. The skin and hair had been ripped violently from Dan Aquillo's head, taking part of the left side of his face with them.

I took another deep breath. David was busy reading.

I moved on to the next photo, a close-up of the ravaged head. The exposed cranium rose up like a slick white rock where the scalp had been peeled away. A series of dents made a semicircular pattern where the skull had been caved in. Blunt force cerebral trauma, and how.

David peered over my shoulder.

"That's where the hammer came down," I said.

He squinted at the photo.

"You're sure it was a hammer?"

I'd faxed David a synopsis of my experience at Room 109, where I'd picked up a psychic image of someone striking Aquillo with a hammer and then leaving through the front door with the weapon.

"Yes, I'm sure. I saw the claw end. There's some construction being done on the wing of the hotel where the body was found. Wouldn't be surprised if some union worker's pounding nails with the murder weapon right now."

I flipped to the next picture, another view of what remained of Dan Aquillo's head and face. David was standing right next to me, and I could hear him take in a sharp breath.

"What do you think?" he asked.

I was examining the ragged way that the scalp had been ripped from the skull.

"Hurston was trained in surgery, right?"

"Yes. An ear, nose, and throat specialist."

I pointed to the ragged tearing of Aquillo's skin.

"I don't think this looks like the work of an experienced surgeon."

I flipped to the next photo, a close-up of the victim's open mouth. Something wasn't right, but the cavity was too dark to make out just what. The next photo made it perfectly clear. With the help of a pair of tongs, the tongue had been extended against a white background. It had been sliced in two down the middle.

"What the—?" David began flipping through the pages of the written report. He jumped in mid-paragraph, reading rapidly out loud. "Examination revealed dissected tongue and punctured epiglottis. . ." He peered again at the photograph. "This is weird. What's up with this?"

"Not sure, but I can venture a guess. Somebody thought Dan Aquillo spoke with a forked tongue."

Suddenly I felt light-headed. I'd stopped at David's on the way home from the hospital, promising myself I'd keep the visit brief. I'd already stayed too long.

"I gotta go, David."

"What about your injuries? You've got a robbery-assault case here."

"We'll worry about that later."

"You going to be all right?"

"I'll be fine." I opened my jacket and gave him a peek of the gun I had holstered under my armpit.

Frown lines appeared between his eyebrows as he lightly touched my arm and led me to the door.

"You call me day or night if you need anything, hear me?"

"I hear ya. Thanks. Let me get through this—" I nodded toward the bulging file tucked under my arm "—and maybe we can discuss it over lunch tomorrow."

"I've got a meeting with the tribal police in the morning."

"There's a restaurant, Ed's, just outside the entrance to the reservation. Why don't we meet there around one or so?"

"Ed's, one o'clock. You got it."

All the way home I couldn't shake the images of Dan Aquillo's mutilated head. Heinous and depraved indeed described this murder. Who'd do such a thing? And why?

By the time I walked through my front door, my temples were throbbing. The pressure was so great that I couldn't even bend down to greet the faithful dog and cat who met me in the front hall. My pets tagged along as I headed straight up the stairs for bed rest and a pillow. I'd just reached the first landing when the doorbell rang.

Nero bounded back down the stairs, barking the whole way. I continued up, hurrying to the bedroom window. From there I had a perfect view of the front porch. Fifteen feet directly below me, a large, dark-skinned man stood on my doorstep. His long black hair was pulled into a ponytail that streamed down his back. He wore a short-sleeved T-shirt, exposing heavily tattooed, muscular forearms. I couldn't see his face.

I took my gun out of its holster and went back downstairs. Nero continued to bark, his throaty woofs echoing loudly in the hallway. If this guy was here to hurt me, would he really ring the doorbell? I was staring at the front door pondering the question when a small piece of paper wormed its way through the crack.

12

Heart pounding like a bass drum, I froze in the hallway with the sights of my gun lined up on my front door. The paper made a faint scratching noise as it inched through the crack and onto the runner. Nero pounced on it and sniffed frantically. His tail began to wag.

Call me paranoid, but I wasn't about to step in front of that door. Maybe I've seen too many *Goodfella*-type movies, but who wasn't to say that a torrent of bullets wouldn't come flying through that hundred-year-old oak?

As Nero continued to sniff and wag, I went into the kitchen and got a broom. Staying off to the side, I approached the front door and swept the paper toward me. I unfolded it and read:

> Elizabeth,
>   Tom sent me.
>   S—

Other than the *S*, I couldn't read the scrawled signature. For a brief, illogical moment I thought that "Tom" referred to my deceased lover, Tom McGowan, and that somehow he'd contacted the land of the living and sent a messenger.

Impossible.

Scouring my mind for the other Toms I knew, I hurried back upstairs to look out the window. Now the man was bending over my cement planter, taking in the fragrance of my La Reine roses. I removed the Glock from my holster and held it in my right hand, opening the sash with my left.

"Tom who?" I yelled down.

He looked up and smiled. Damn, he looked familiar.

"Thomasina Wilson."

Oh, that Tom. It was true that Thomasina's close friends and family called her Tom. The original nickname had been

Tomboy, but somewhere along the way the second syllable had dropped off.

I put my gun into its holster and went back downstairs. I opened the door and with one glance took in more of his distinguishing features: a deep brown face as large and immobile as a statue's, an embossed copper earring, forearms tattooed with snakes, quads the size of Texas.

"Hi, I'm Sequoia."

Had Thomasina taken the initiative to send me a bodyguard? He was imposing enough to be one, yet so soft-spoken that I barely heard him. Nero was sniffing the man's legs, his tail wagging nonstop. The man patted him with a large, dark hand.

"Sequoia, like the tree?"

He was massaging Nero's ears now, making the dog a friend for life.

"Yeah. Sequoia Wilson."

"Wilson. You must be one of Thomasina's relatives from the Temecu Reservation."

"You got it."

I stepped back and he came into the hall, moving lightly for a man of his size. For a man of any size, in fact.

"I'm her second cousin," he said.

"I always forget what that means, exactly."

"We had the same great-grandfather."

"I'll forget that in a day and a half, but thanks for explaining it anyway."

His eyes met mine. They were dark as obsidian, deepened by black brows that nearly joined above the bridge of his nose.

"Does it hurt?" he asked.

Suddenly I remembered the wretched state of my face. All the excitement had taken my mind off the pain.

"Only when I think. Come on back and have a seat."

He didn't inquire further about my bruises and I didn't particularly want to tell the whole story. I led him down the hallway to the family room at the rear of the house.

"This is a great house," he said. "Looks old."

"A vim-and-vigor hundred and nine years."

"You keep it in excellent shape."

"Thanks."

We'd reached the family room. Sequoia stepped up to the back window, and looked out onto the garden.

"Tom tells me you had trouble on the res," he said.

"Just outside Temecu, actually, on Highway 76. I really appreciate your taking the time to come see me. Can I get you a drink?"

"No drink for me, thanks."

Late afternoon light was filtering through the trees and reflecting a golden shimmer off the large, glossy leaves of my giant bird of paradise. He stood as still as the glass he was peering through, taking it all in.

"Mind if I walk out there?"

"Be my guest."

I opened the back door, and Nero rushed out ahead of us. I escorted Sequoia into the yard, where he began inspecting the plants. With a delicate touch, he ran his fingers down the frond of a massive Boston fern hanging from the arbor.

"You love this fern."

It was an odd thing for him to say, but it couldn't have been more true.

"Yes, I do."

"You have the gift."

"What gift would that be?"

"You can talk with the earth and hear it talk back."

I laughed, feeling a little embarrassed.

"I don't know about that. People give me their sick plants, and I nurse them back to health. Like that fern you're admiring. It was all yellow and dry when the owner gave up and bequeathed it to me. After a year, I had to divide the thing, it got so big. That's actually the baby of the original plant."

"Who taught you how to heal plants?"

"Nobody actually taught me."

"Then how do you know what they need?"

I shrugged and bent down to snap a few deadheads from a stand of salvia blooms.

"I have a general idea of which plants like shade and moisture, which ones like sun. . . I don't know, I just kind of sense what they need."

I thought that would be the end of it, but he didn't let the subject drop.

"In other words, the plants talk to you, and you listen. That's good. I'm a plant lover myself. Small wonder, right, with a name like Sequoia?"

"True enough." I found myself admiring him. He was different, but not the least bit self-conscious about it. Both qualities appealed to me.

He pointed to some weeds growing along the fence. "You mind if I pull those?"

A lot of gardening chores had gone undone in the months since McGowan's death.

"Heck, no. Pull all the weeds you want."

He walked to the fence and carefully pinched the tops off the weeds, bringing them to his nose. He looked around the yard, as if searching for something, and went to a clay pot brimming with an overgrown aloe plant.

"How about this?" he called, pointing to the aloe.

"Help yourself."

Squatting on his haunches, he inspected the spiky plant and broke off one of its juicy leaves. He straightened and walked back to me, holding the assorted flora in his hands.

"You got a bowl?"

"Sure."

I opened the back door and motioned him inside, leaving Nero to his sniffing in the garden. I followed him into the house and directed him to the kitchen. Perplexed, I reached into a cupboard, handed him a bowl, and watched as he dropped the greens inside.

"You want some dressing for those? Bleu cheese, oil and vinegar?"

"Just a wooden spoon, if you've got one."

I opened the utensil drawer and handed him a wooden ladle. Leaning against the kitchen counter, I watched as he peeled the aloe spike and broke it into pieces in the bowl, then mashed the weeds into its juicy pulp.

"Are you going to *eat* that?"

He laughed and shook his head.

"You've been healing your plants, now it's time for them to heal you. You should probably lie down while I put this on."

Ordinarily I wouldn't kowtow to someone I'd met five minutes ago, but Sequoia had three things heavily in his favor. One, he was related to my best friend, Thomasina. Two, he had a gentle, reassuring vibration. Three, I had the unmistakable sense that I was about to learn something valuable here. I walked into the family room and lay back on the sofa. When I'd settled onto the cushions, he kneeled down beside me.

"I'm going to take off the bandage, okay?"

I nodded.

He carefully peeled the gauze and tape off my nose and cheeks and began smearing the salve onto my skin. The mixture smelled pungent and alive; its cool wetness was soothing.

"Your plants have a lot of life force. They'll heal you much faster than the junk in that little orange bottle."

The little orange bottle was an antibiotic sitting in my bathroom cabinet. Odd that he should mention it. On the other hand, it was reasonable for him to assume that I was taking something for my injuries, and most prescription bottles looked pretty much the same. Didn't they?

Through squinted eyelids, I watched his face. His expression was as tender as his touch, and somehow familiar. I flashed back to my last trip to Mystic Mesa, after I'd been beaten up by the side of the road. Déjà vu: A large man with Native American features, bending over me. Comforting me.

"I've seen you before," I said.

"I know."

"You do?"

He nodded.

I got the feeling he knew exactly what I was talking about, but I wanted a reality check.

"Okay, where?" I asked. "Where have I seen you?"

"You saw me in the spirit state a couple nights ago."

"How do you know that?"

Ignoring my question, he put down the aloe mixture and

rubbed his hands together, the friction making a shushing sound. He held them out, palms down, six inches over my heart, and closed his eyes.

Though his hands didn't touch me at all, a warmth began to emanate, either from his palms or my chest—hard to tell which. Perhaps both. Subtle at first, the warmth increased in intensity. Initially, the sensation was purely physical. Gradually—with a subtle, magnetic force—his hovering hands began to pull emotions from deep within me. At first I fought the sadness, but it was a losing battle. The unresolved grief from McGowan's death swelled up and there was no stopping it. Within minutes tears were rolling down my face, quite beyond my control. I shut my eyes, trying to staunch their flow. Above me I heard Sequoia's soft-spoken voice.

"Your face I'm not worried about. It'll heal okay. But your heart's been wounded pretty bad."

13

"What I'm doing is more or less an Indian version of Reiki healing," Sequoia said as his hands zeroed in on my wounded heart. I turned my face into the pillows and stared at the stitching in the upholstery, fighting to keep my emotions under control. When I was able to speak, my words came out sounding as defensive as a hurt child's.

"I don't want to do this now."

"Okay," he said lightly. "Come here, let me put your bandages back on."

His voice was so casual and devoid of judgment that I felt safe enough to open up a little. I swallowed and managed to sound almost normal.

"It's just that somebody really close to me died recently."

He nodded, his face completely neutral, and waited for me to continue. I got the feeling he already knew quite a bit about me. His quiet, unassuming manner made me very curious about him.

"Tell me about yourself. Apart from the fact that you're a distant relative of Thomasina's, I don't know a thing about you."

He arranged the gauze bandage over the bridge of my nose and pressed the surgical tape onto my temples.

"What do you want to know?"

"That thing you just did with your hands. What, exactly, was that?"

"Something I learned when I lived with my Aunt Christina in Mexico. She's a *curandera*."

"A healer?"

He smiled enigmatically.

"A healer, a seer, a powerful dreamer. Kind of like you."

"Why do you say that?"

"Tom told me about you."

"Thomasina, you mean."

He didn't answer but got to his feet instead.

"Would you mind if I have some water?"

"Filtered drinking water in the fridge. Help yourself."

As he walked into the kitchen, I studied the ponytail that reached to the middle of his back. His razor-straight hair was as black and shiny as a river at midnight. Were it not for his tattooed forearms and the swoosh logo on his Nikes, he could have walked into my life from another century.

Although the kitchen was in full view of the family room, it was several yards away. I cleared my throat and raised my voice so he could hear me.

"So this Aunt Christina of yours—is she related to Thomasina also? I didn't realize you guys had family in Mexico."

Sequoia found the correct cupboard on the first try, pulled out a tall glass, and filled it from the pitcher in the refrigerator.

"Aunt Christina isn't related by blood. It's kind of a long story."

"I like long stories. I'd love to hear it."

He came back into the family room and took a seat in the chair across from me. He drank his water in one long draw, put his glass down, and sat back.

"Maybe some other time. Thomasina tells me you're an investigator."

"That's right." The file from David's office was sitting before me on the coffee table. I pulled the folder onto my lap. "I'm looking into the Aquillo murder." I opened the file and began leafing through the papers. "Did you know him?"

"Not real well, but I knew who he was, sure. Seems like everybody knows everybody on the res. Although I stay on the mountain and keep to myself most of the time."

"On the mountain?"

"After my mom died, she left me her property up there. I built a house on it a few years ago."

"What do you do for a living, if you don't mind my asking?"

"Don't mind at all. I teach shamanic studies."

I'd heard of shamans, of course, but had never actually met one.

"Is that also something you learned from your Aunt Christina?" I asked.

He made a patient smile.

"More like something I put into practice after I got my degree in cultural anthropology."

"Really? Where'd you go to school?"

"The University of California at Santa Cruz."

The Santa Cruz campus, perhaps the most beautiful in the UC system, was nestled in a redwood grove on California's Monterey Peninsula.

"That's certainly appropriate for a man called Sequoia," I said. "Did you choose the name yourself?"

"No, I've had the name since birth. I was conceived in a Sequoia grove when my folks were visiting northern California." He pointed his chin toward the file in my lap. "You got any leads on the Aquillo murder?"

"Nothing concrete yet. Would you happen to have any theories about it?"

He shook his head.

"Not really. I steer clear of the casino. There's a bad element that hangs out around Mystic Mesa."

"I kinda got that impression," I said, gently touching my bandage.

He smiled at my little joke.

"The woman in the Mystic Mesa hotel office hinted about the bad element," I said.

"You must be talking about Granny Rose."

"Yeah, Rosemary Andreas. She was reluctant to name names or even go into details. What's the deal?"

"It's a gang thing. The Department of Housing and Urban Development moved some of the teenagers from the inner city back to the res. I guess the idea was to bring the housing-project kids back to their roots. Some of them have grown up into thugs. They've got Indian blood but no respect for reservation life. They're trying to get their inner-city thing going in Temecu. Could be one of them that messed you up."

"Maybe. I did get robbed. Then again, maybe someone doesn't appreciate my inquisitive nature."

"Did you see who beat you up?"

"Not much more than the basics. He was about six feet tall, and huge. Built like a linebacker."

"That could be about forty guys I know."

I noticed that my cordless phone was sitting on the coffee table. I was about to return it to the kitchen for recharging when it began to ring.

"Excuse me." I picked up the receiver and said hello.

"Late-breaking development." The voice on the other end spoke with an urgent rush.

I put my hand over the mouthpiece and whispered to Sequoia.

"Speaking of my case, excuse me a minute."

He nodded patiently.

"What's up, David?" I said into the phone.

"Do you have a cold? You sound stuffy."

I fingered the bandages on my nose.

"This is what I sound like with my face banged in."

"Jesus, I'm sorry—I forgot. Listen, I'm looking over the report you sent about Natalie Hurston. You saw her Wednesday, is that right?"

"Yes. We went for a run on the beach."

"And she stated that she did *not* know Dan Aquillo?"

"I think she said something like she'd heard his name but didn't know him personally. Why?"

"A white Volvo with a dented fender was seen in the hotel parking lot the night of Aquillo's murder. Natalie Hurston drives a white Volvo—"

"With a dented fender."

"You got it."

"Oh, man, I forgot." I was remembering an important detail I'd neglected to tell David this afternoon.

"Forgot what?"

"I talked to the woman in the hotel office last night. She said the night of the murder a woman fitting Natalie's description came to the hotel and asked which room Bill Hurston was staying in. With all the commotion on my ride home and my trip to the emergency room, I forgot to mention it."

"A woman fitting Natalie Hurston's description was at Mystic Mesa Hotel the night of the murder?"

"That's what Rosemary Andreas in the hotel office told me, yes. She works the night shift out there. It's a piece I don't think the police have yet."

"Thank you, Elizabeth." And he was gone.

I turned off the phone and opened the file, making a note about the conversation I'd just had with David. The police report sat on top, and the victim's address caught my eye.

"Aquillo lived at 546 Pala Verde Highway," I said to Sequoia. "You know where that is?"

"Sure. That's down the mountain from my place."

"On the reservation?"

"Um-hm."

"Damn." I said it to myself more than to him. "I really would like to case Aquillo's house, see what I can pick up out there."

"We can do that."

"I'm not so sure I'm ready to challenge anyone's authority on the reservation just yet."

Sequoia nodded and rose from his chair. He carried his water glass into the kitchen, where I watched him wash it out, dry it carefully with a towel, and return it to the cabinet. He came back into the family room and stood in front of me.

"I have to go now. Thanks for the drink."

I started to rise, but he stopped me with a raised hand.

"Don't get up. I'll lock the door on my way out. Get some rest." He got a wallet out of his back pocket, pulled out a business card, and handed it to me. "I'll pick you up at nine tomorrow morning, and we'll go out to Aquillo's. You'll be okay with me. Anything comes up in the meantime, call that number."

I glanced at the card, which was printed only with a line drawing of a snake, a post-office-box address, and a phone number. I tucked the card into the case file. By the time I looked up, Sequoia was halfway down the front hall. Just before he slipped out, he reached into his front pocket and slid something onto the credenza near the door.

"That's for you. Found it in the garden. I think it's lucky."

I jumped up as the door shut behind him. I reached the front window as a dusty green Jeep was pulling away. The old-model Jeep, with a tan canvas top. I looked on the credenza and spotted something under the rim of the antique porcelain bowl. I slid my fingers along the wood, leaving a trail through the dust. My fingers found the object, a coin. I studied it and chuckled. Yeah, right, he just happened to find an Indian-head nickel in my garden. Very funny.

I flipped the coin into the air and trapped it between my hands.

"Tails," I guessed out loud, and lifted my hand. The embossed buffalo on the tail side of the coin was encrusted with an old layer of dried mud.

14

"This is Aquillo's, coming up ahead."

Sequoia eased his foot onto the brake as we passed an un-fenced burial ground, small but lovingly tended. Mounds of earth rose in a haphazard pattern, the graves marked by rough-hewn stones and hand-carved wooden crosses, many with flo-ral wreaths looped over the top. Sequoia kept his eyes on the road, so he missed the long-suffering look I gave him.

"Graveyard. Very funny," I said. "Don't you know it's not nice to make fun of the dead?"

A faint smile crossed his face.

"Aquillo's isn't *in* the cemetery. It's *past* the cemetery."

Today Sequoia was wearing a black T-shirt with a small blue-green planet Earth printed above the left breast, where a designer logo might be. I liked it, and told him so. About a hundred yards beyond the last row of gravestones, he turned into a hard-packed dirt driveway. As we pulled to a stop I stared, somewhat shocked, at the scene before us.

"This is his house?"

He nodded.

It wasn't the crib I'd been expecting for a high-flying casino manager. The victim's residence was modest, more of a cottage than anything else. The white paint and tile roof were new, but the structure had an old, settled-in look. A weathered tool shed sat near a sagging fence along the side of the house. Bordered by leggy geraniums, the small yard was dwarfed by an ancient pepper tree with a two-pronged trunk as wide as a doorway.

Sequoia cut the engine, and the motor coughed before dy-ing. His Jeep had been around long before the phrase *sport-utility vehicle* had entered the general lexicon. He pointed at the pepper tree.

"That old tree marks the northern border of the reservation.

The limbs were bent apart like that when it was just a sapling. See how one points east and one points west?"

"That's pretty cool."

He smiled slyly.

"It's an Indian thing."

Untouched chaparral surrounded us on all sides, framed by deep-blue foothills. Aquillo had been a lucky man to live here. The natural setting was more spectacular than any developed landscape. I wouldn't have been particularly enthusiastic about living next to a graveyard, but I could get used to gazing at unspoiled wilderness like this every day.

Before getting out, I pulled down the sun visor, finding the mirror I'd hoped would be there. Morning sun streamed through the windshield, illuminating my face with plenty of natural light. I couldn't believe the difference a day had made in my healing process. Or had Sequoia worked some kind of magic? My misshapen forehead had returned to almost normal. My nose had been bent but not broken; the swelling above the bandage was almost completely gone. Even the bruises around my eyes were fading—into an ugly shade of green-tinged yellow, but fading nonetheless.

"You're so vain," Sequoia chided from the driver's seat.

"Amazed, is the word. Whatever you did, thanks."

"Welcome. Come on, let's have a look."

I stepped down out of the Jeep and into the brilliant morning sunshine. The air was completely still. In that soundless moment I could almost imagine what it must be like to be deaf. I cupped my hand over my eyes to reduce the glare and studied Aquillo's house. All the sunshine in the world couldn't light the darkness surrounding it. I often pick up an abandoned, forlorn feeling from houses where the owners have died. Aquillo's went beyond forlorn. There was something actively creepy here.

At the end of the driveway, an aluminum mailbox leaned at an angle, as if it were falling over backward in imperceptibly slow motion. I pulled open the latch and took a peek inside. I'd expected the police to have confiscated Aquillo's mail and was surprised to see a thick stack of circulars and envelopes lying in the box. As I shuffled through the pieces, I noticed a preponderance of two-day-old postmarks. This mail must have arrived yesterday, after the police had been by. I felt Sequoia staring at me.

"What?" I said without looking up.

"Isn't that a federal crime or something?"

"I think so."

A phone bill would have been helpful. I found nothing of obvious value. Real-estate flyers, credit-card offers, the local classified-ad booklet. I flipped to the next envelope, felt a vibe, and read the return address: Intertribal Gaming Regulatory Consortium. Whatever the hell that was.

A sound penetrated the silence—a faint but steady hum just coming into earshot. Sequoia and I turned toward the noise. A quarter mile away, a car was heading in our direction, kicking up a cloud of dust that grew larger as it approached. The teal Geo Metro pulled to a stop alongside the cemetery. I could see two passengers in front but couldn't make out their faces. After a minute or so, a woman emerged from the car. She wore jeans, a sloppy purple sweater, and Ugg boots. Her long, dark hair hung nearly to her waist.

"Hey," Sequoia said, "That's Lucy Aquillo."

I was just glad it wasn't the bad Samaritan, coming back to remind me that I was persona non grata on the res. The woman opened the back of the car and retrieved a large bouquet of flowers. From their improbable turquoise shade, I guessed they were silk.

"The victim's wife?" I asked.

"Sister," Sequoia answered. "Poor Lucy. So much tragedy in her family. She lost a father and a husband in the space of a few years. Now her brother Dan's been killed."

Lucy walked into the cemetery and knelt at a tombstone near the east corner. She arranged the flowers, pausing every now and then to survey her handiwork. After a while she got to her feet and fired up a cigarette. When she exhaled, the gray-blue smoke hung above her like a cloud in the still morning air.

Sequoia pointed to her with his thumb.

"I'm going to go say hi, okay?"

"Okay. I'll join you in a few."

As Sequoia walked over to the cemetery, I returned the bulk of Aquillo's mail to the box but slid the envelope from the Intertribal Gaming Consortium into my purse.

I was glad the woman had shown up—I could scope out the house more effectively without anyone to distract me. I sensed something here; just what, I wasn't sure yet. I tested the front door and wasn't surprised to find it locked. I rounded the house and gave each window a tug with the same negative results. The window coverings—a hodgepodge of venetian blinds and mismatched drapes—were all drawn closed. After circling the house, I walked out to the two-pronged pepper tree at the edge of the yard and leaned my back against one of its wide, sloping trunks. I took a deep breath, inhaling the fragrance of its spicy leaves.

A hundred yards away I could see Sequoia talking with Lucy Aquillo in the cemetery. The morning was dead calm, with no wind to carry their voices. I was mildly curious what they were talking about but, for the most part, was simply enjoying the beauty and uncommon hush at the edge of the reservation.

The screech of a hawk pierced the silence, and I turned north toward the sound. High above the rolling hills a red-tail circled against the rich blue sky. The magnificent bird banked to the left, its pale underside catching the sunlight. It seemed weightless as it floated above the earth, rising higher with each revolution. As I watched the hawk's spiraling motion, I could feel myself traveling inward, going into trance.

I felt the rough bark of the pepper tree beneath my back. I became keenly aware of how solidly the soles of my feet connected with the ground. I felt the pull of gravity, so much so that the sensation became exaggerated, as if I were standing on Jupiter. My attention was drawn to the crust of the earth beneath me. In my mind's eye I could see the roots of the old pepper tree stretching outward like gnarled arms. Then in a shadowy flash, I saw that I was not alone here. There was something else—some*one* else—under the ground.

With a chirp and rustle of leaves, a bird flew out of the branch above me. I sensed yet another presence—this time behind me.

"Hello," I said.

I turned around to see a scowling face—too young to be a man's, too old to be a kid's. His brown hair was parted in the middle and hung shoulder length around his face. The blue-green color of his eyes was as startling and improbable as the flowers Lucy Aquillo had placed on the grave next door. I gave him a friendly smile, but my charms failed to win him over. His scowl darkened.

"This is private property, lady."

His cheek was tattooed with a cryptic graphic that looked like a lightning bolt, or perhaps a lopsided *W*. He wore baggy pants and a loose coat of fringed leather. Something about him looked familiar, but I couldn't place it.

"I'm here with Sequoia," I said, pointing toward the cemetery. "I'm his friend, Elizabeth. And you're—?"

He didn't drop the scowl.

"What happened to your face, man?"

"Oh—" I put my fingers to my nose "—that. Had a little work done. You think this is bad, you should have seen it a couple days ago."

His hand dove into the pocket of his coat. When he pulled out a pack of cigarettes, I exhaled with relief. He tamped the pack against his palm and stepped forward, holding out the jutting smokes for me.

I took one, in spite of the fact that I don't smoke cigarettes as a habit. For some reason I felt a need to connect, and a ritual smoke seemed fitting. He flicked a lighter and offered me the flame. As I lit up, I did my best to keep the carcinogens out of my lungs.

"Thanks," I said.

He lit a cigarette for himself and looked at me through squinted eyes.

"What's Sequoia doing here?" he asked.

"You know him?"

"Everybody knows Sequoia, man."

"He was just giving me a little tour of the reservation."

"Why?"

"He's my teacher," I replied without hesitation. "He wanted to show me some things."

The explanation seemed to satisfy the boy-man. I wanted to know what *he* was doing here but refrained from asking outright.

"I didn't get your name," I reminded him.

"Wolf."

"That short for Wolfgang?"

"What?"

"Never mind."

If Wolf was his nickname, it was the most Native American thing about him. His skin was a beautiful creamy brown, but with his thin face and long nose, he looked more like a European import than a native.

Now that I had some assurance this guy wasn't going to undo all the healing Sequoia had achieved on my face, I became aware again of the ground under my feet. Once more my inner movie screen showed me the roots of the pepper tree spreading beneath the earth. And something else, something human—

"What's the matter, man?"

I'd been reentering the vision, and it must have shown on my face. I shook my head.

"Nothing. So you're here with Lucy Aquillo?"

"Yeah. We're putting some stuff on Dan's grave."

"Dan was your—?"

"My uncle."

"So Lucy Aquillo's your mom."

He sucked some smoke and held it in as he answered.

"Yeah."

"Sorry about your Uncle Dan. It's terrible to have a loved one murdered." I stared at the cigarette in my hand. "I know that firsthand."

The comment brought a cynical smile to Wolf's face, and

he shook his head, as if he didn't believe me. The smile revealed teeth that weren't perfectly straight, but they were perfectly white. He hadn't had the smoking habit for long.

"Yeah? Well Dan's death wasn't murder, man." His smile disappeared. "It was a casualty of war."

15

The scalping murder of Dan Aquillo, a casualty of war? I wasn't sure what Wolf had meant by that. Judging from the smug look on his face, my confusion pleased him.

"What war is that?" I asked.

He took a long draw on his cigarette and stared northward, his blue-green eyes scanning the horizon.

"Same war it's always been. Destruction of our people. Destruction of our land."

"Your uncle's murder was a hate crime?"

"No, man, I told you. He was killed in the war." He glared at me now, his voice rising. "This kind of violent shit didn't happen on this res before the capitalists came in, building their fuckin' casinos, raping the little earth we got left."

I was puzzled by his outburst.

"I thought that the Temecu tribe built the Mystic Mesa Casino."

"You think it was native money that built that casino? The white man put up the money for that place. It's a Trojan horse, man. Seeds of our destruction."

I arched my brows.

"Really? I thought the casino was a good thing. Jobs, prosperity, all that. Didn't I read somewhere that the estimated annual income for each member of the tribe has increased like three hundred percent since the casino went in? Doesn't sound like destruction to me."

He made a horrible noise in his throat and hawked a wad of phlegm into the dirt.

"Some of the tribe's become just like you people. Greedy and materialistic. Deaf to Mother Earth." With a stabbing motion, he threw the remains of his cigarette at my feet.

I couldn't help noticing that he had no problem littering Mother Earth with cigarette butts. The kid made me nervous.

He gave me the feeling you might get when you're rewiring a light fixture and not quite sure the power's been shut off.

"Hey, we've got company," I said.

Lucy and Sequoia were walking toward us up the driveway. When Lucy got within reaching distance, she grabbed the fringe on the bottom of Wolf's leather coat and gave it a playful yank.

"You boring this lady with all your radical Native American crap?" She smiled and held her hand out to me. "Hi, I'm Lucy." She looked at my nose bandage but didn't comment. Her deep brown eyes were steady and knowing. Old-soul eyes.

"Elizabeth," I said, shaking her hand. Her skin felt soft and warm. "Sequoia told me about your brother. I'm so sorry for your loss."

"Thank you." She wrapped her arms around her torso in a self-comforting gesture. "He's the last person in the world who should've been killed. Dan was a peaceful man. Unlike like this one, here." She nodded toward Wolf with a just-kidding smile, but her eyes were worried.

"Don't start," Wolf snapped.

For a moment, tension crackled in the air, like electricity was traveling down those wires after all. I looked over at Sequoia, who was looking back at me. His expression communicated complete understanding. *Yes, the kid's a time bomb.*

"I don't know about you guys," Sequoia said, "but I'm thirsty. Norm's got a Coke machine outside the old mine now. I'm buying, if anyone wants to come." He turned to me. "You got time?"

"I have a lunch date at one, but I'm free till then." I looked over at Lucy.

"A drink sounds good," she said.

I followed Sequoia back to his Jeep as Lucy and Wolf headed to the Geo. With all these people around, there was no point trying to investigate Aquillo's now anyway. I hated to leave, but since Sequoia was driving, I really had no choice. I'd have to come back later. I stared at the bumper of Lucy's Geo as we followed her back to Mystic Mesa Road. No bumper stickers, just a Christian fish symbol, which seemed odd. Perhaps it had come with the car.

"She's an interesting woman," I said.

"I know. I think every guy on the res has been in love with her at one time or another."

"She taken?"

He shook his head.

"Her heart's taken by something, that's for sure. Many have tried, but no one's been able to get anywhere with her."

"Wonder why."

"Lucy's husband passed away before her son was even born, back when she was living in Las Vegas. I think that hurt her so much that she closed her heart."

I caught a cautionary undertone in his voice.

"How old is her kid?"

"Sixteen or seventeen, something like that."

"He seems older."

"That's because he takes life so seriously. Always been that way. I think when he saw what having a soft spot did to his mom, he decided to harden his heart. You're not going to do that now, are you?"

He was talking about the effect my recent loss might have on me, and his question caught me off-guard.

"What—harden my heart? Not on purpose, I guess."

"I know what my Aunt Christina would say."

"The *curandera*?"

He nodded.

"She'd say that suffering is a natural part of life, and it can make us either brittle or wise. It's up to us to choose."

"You think people really have a choice what life does to them?"

His black eyes looked straight at me.

"Yeah, I do."

"Even people who suffer tremendous bad fortune?"

"Especially those people. Suffering is good medicine. But you have to know how to use it. If you use it wrong, you shut life out. If you use it right, you open up and become softer, wiser. Takes courage, though."

I contemplated the chaparral going by outside the car window.

"That's the Pisces lesson," I said.

"Say what?"

"There's an astrological parallel to what you're talking about. The Pisces experience is one of suffering, but it's also an opportunity for enlightenment. Is that what your tribe teaches?"

He nodded.

"Many cultures teach that. From the beginning of time, suffering has been a doorway to spiritual advancement. All you gotta do is walk through." We rounded a sharp curve and Sequoia pointed ahead. "Here we are."

The Pony Express Mine and Rock Shop was nestled at the foot of a sagebrush-covered hill that rose at a steep angle to the sky. We parked alongside Lucy's Geo and got out. The shop was fronted by an uncovered wooden porch, and our footsteps made creaking noises as the four of us climbed the old wood steps. Sunshine poured through the front windows, lighting the treasures on display: chunks of purple amethyst, fingers of pink and green tourmaline, geodes split open to reveal sparkling crystalline cores.

Sequoia held the door open, and I followed Lucy and Wolf into the shop.

"Hey, Norm," Sequoia said as he brought up the rear. "Scared up some customers for you."

A man standing behind the glass display counters looked up over a pair of half-glasses sitting on his nose.

"Sequoia, my man! Long time! Hey, Lucy, Wolf . . . and—?"

"Elizabeth," I said.

"Norm Clapp." He nodded his head in greeting. "What'd you do there, wrestle with a windshield?"

I put my fingers to my nose bandage.

"Something like that."

He respected my don't-ask tone and turned to Lucy.

"How you doin'? You okay?" Although Norm's gentle

voice didn't mention Dan Aquillo's murder, we all understood what he was talking about.

"We're okay," Lucy said.

There was a long, heavy silence. Feeling very much like an outsider, I walked to the glass cases and occupied myself with examining the goods inside. Several garnets, their color ranging from burgundy to rose, dominated the display. Norm had a good supply of topaz—including a gorgeous emerald-cut smoky the size of a thimble. I saw several gem stones I didn't recognize and even a few gold nuggets.

"These are all from your mine?" I asked.

Norm brightened, eager to move on to a happier subject.

"Got a few imports in there. The fire opal's from Arizona. But most of that stuff is ours, yeah."

"Where is the mine, exactly?"

Norm walked a few steps to the right and opened a heavy oak door. Beyond it, a hallway stretched into blackness.

"That's the entrance to the mine?" I asked.

"Yep. Didn't put in this steel-reinforced door for nothing."

I peered through the doorway. The black passageway was frightening but at the same time, compelling. I found myself wanting to go inside.

"Gold was discovered here in 1851," Norm said. "The mine's been open off and on for nearly a century and a half."

"Who owns this place?" I asked.

"You're looking at him. I bought the property with retirement money in '89."

I noticed video cameras mounted strategically around the ceiling of the shop.

"Looks like you've got a decent security system going here."

"Norm used to be a special agent with the FBI," Sequoia said.

I did a double-take on Norm.

"Really?"

He nodded and went back to inspecting the stone in his hand.

"Yeah. Owning a mine is not without risks. But hey, it's not as dangerous as police work."

Don't remind me, I thought bitterly. I wondered briefly if Norm had known McGowan, then thought about it and realized he'd probably retired from the bureau before Tom had even joined the FBI.

When I looked up, I saw that Sequoia was watching me. He blinked but didn't turn away. I could swear he read my thoughts. Lucy was looking into the display case. Wolf was across the room, inspecting one of the video cameras overhead.

"You ever have any shit go down here?" Wolf asked.

Norm looked up.

"Didn't used to, but things are changing since the casino went in."

Wolf shot me an "I told you so" look as Norm continued.

"A couple of those kids they brought in from the city tried to jump me in the mine a few months ago. Shot one of 'em—scared him more than anything else—and the other one ran. Cops caught him the next day."

"Exciting retirement," I said.

Norm's expression told me that he hadn't found the incident the least bit amusing.

"You've got to be prepared when you own a place like this. Some people consider these rocks more valuable than paper money."

"Yeah," I said dryly, "especially these gold ones, I'll bet."

I glanced around the place, tuned in to the energy. I sensed that Norm had enough artillery in this little rock shop to keep a small army at bay. You'd never know it from the latter-day miner's relaxed, friendly demeanor.

"You still at Temecu High, Wolf?" he asked.

Wolf shook his head but said nothing.

Norm looked over his glasses at the kid.

"You joining the Army or something?"

"Fuck off, Norm."

The former FBI agent furrowed his brows.

"Just a question, buddy."

I was standing right between the two. To get out of the line of fire, I wandered over to a display along the wall filled with Native Americana: silver and turquoise jewelry, kachina dolls, books, greeting cards, high-desert odds and ends. I picked up a small cardboard box with an illustration of a black bear on the front. The label read "Medicine Cards: The Healing Power of the Animals."

"My concession to the tourists," Norm called over to me.

"Hey, you even got a Coke machine outside now," Lucy chimed in. "How about some quarters?" She started to open her purse, but Sequoia stepped up and handed Norm a few dollar bills. Norm took the ones and opened the cash register.

"Yeah, I'm getting real high tech. Maybe one of these years I'll have a machine that makes change. Meantime, you're in luck—got plenty of quarters today."

The four of us walked outside and raided the soda machine. Without a cloud in the sky or the hint of a breeze, the morning was dry and hot. The conversation turned safely to the weather as we sat in the green resin chairs on the porch. When our drinks were empty, Lucy stood to go.

"Good seeing you, Sequoia."

Sequoia rose from his chair.

"You too, Luce."

There was such warmth between them that I expected to see a good-bye hug next. Instead, Lucy turned and walked down the stairs, her son following sullenly behind her. They got into the Geo and, without so much as a backward glance, disappeared around the curve of Mystic Mesa Road.

I looked back through the window of the shop. Norm was behind the counter, talking to someone on the telephone.

"Norm's white, right?" I asked.

"Part Cherokee, I think. Why do you ask?"

"Did he buy this mine from a full blood here on the res?"

"I don't know. What if he did?"

"Wolf told me that his uncle's murder was a casualty of war. I was just wondering if the robbery attempt here was an act of war as well."

Sequoia crumpled his can and tossed it in a green bin beside the Coke machine.

"Wolf said that, huh? He's taking himself more seriously than ever," he said darkly.

16

Ed's Country Cafe was outside the western edge of the reservation, just beyond the cattle crossing at the corner of Mystic Mesa Road and Highway 76. Whatever the building's original color, the paint had faded to a shade that matched the sun-bleached acres surrounding it. A worn wood shingle here and there had been replaced on the roof, giving the whole a blotchy complexion. A Suburban, a motorcycle, and a Toyota 4Runner were parked in front. I guessed that none of these was David's as I pulled into the gravel parking lot. On my way in, I put a coin into the newspaper machine near the door and grabbed the local *North County Times*.

The hinges squeaked to announce my arrival. A wood-planked floor filled with battle scars set the tone of the cafe. A man was handing foam-topped mugs to a couple of guys hugging the bar. Reigning over the beer taps were a camouflage battle helmet and a pair of rifles, crossed like a coat of arms. The place was a tad too testosterone-laden for my taste and made me uncomfortable.

Booths topped with red-and-white checked oilcloth lined the walls. I took a seat at one of them and opened my paper. An article about the casino murder appeared on the front page. It mostly rehashed events that had already been published, but there was one fresh angle:

> *Witnesses have stated that a woman and car matching descriptions of the defendant's wife and automobile were seen at the hotel shortly before the murder.*

I was so engrossed in my reading that I didn't notice the bartender until I heard his voice behind my shoulder.

"You need a menu, young lady?" His face was pouched and lined, his eyes blank.

It had been awhile since anyone had accused me of being a

young lady. I considered the source: a graying, grizzle-bearded man, not particularly fat, whose plaid shirt was tight across a protruding belly. Youth was relative, I supposed.

"Two menus, please. I'm expecting someone." I tried to cheer him with a smile. "Looks like your neighborhood's on the front page this week."

He wasn't cheered. "Last thing we need around here."

"Maybe it'll be good for business," I offered.

"Damn media. Half of it's lies, most the time." He walked off, leaving me with that thought.

David arrived five minutes later. I looked up from my newspaper as he slid into the opposite side of the booth, keys still jangling in one hand and an overstuffed briefcase in the other.

"Sorry I'm late," he said. The curls tumbling onto his forehead had grown a little longer. He pushed them out of his eyes with an upward sweep of his hand. "You look a helluva lot better than you did yesterday," he said. "No offense."

"None taken. I feel better, too. Did you leak this to the newspaper about Natalie Hurston being seen at the crime scene?"

David put on his best poker face.

"Witnesses stated that, not me. Although it does rather support reasonable doubt."

I gave him a disapproving look, which he ignored.

"Speaking of Natalie," he said, "when you talked to her on Wednesday, did she happen to mention going out of town?"

I thought back to Natalie, handing me a crystal goblet of ice water after our run.

"No. She said she had a meeting with a client within the hour. That's all I remember. Why?"

The bartender approached our table, menus in hand.

"No one can find her," David replied. "She didn't show up for work the next day. Or the next two days after that. Her condo's locked up, but no one's home. It's heading into missing persons territory."

I took the menu the bartender handed me.

"Hm," I said. "Woman spotted at murder scene leaves town. That would seem to support reasonable doubt, too."

The bartender gave the other menu to David.

"You two want drinks?" he asked.

Somewhere inside his briefcase, David's cellular started to ring. He dug through his papers in search of the phone, which continued to let out a high-pitched ring. I glanced at the menu. A brick-red banner printed above the food selections read: "Ed's . . . A Temecu Tradition."

"Coffee for me," I said. "Regular. And I'll have the BLT with onions instead of bacon."

David finally unearthed his phone and barked into the mouthpiece.

"David Skenazy. Just a minute." He covered the phone with his hand and turned to the bartender. "I'll have whatever she's having." The man walked away, and David said hello into the phone, twice, before he snapped it shut. "Crap. After all that, they hung up."

I was thinking about the fear I'd sensed from Natalie when she first brushed by me on the stairs of her condo. There'd been an almost desperate determination in the stride of her hard brown legs pounding the sand. Perhaps she'd run for good this time.

"Do the police know about Natalie being gone?"

"They do now. I spoke with the tribal cop who's working the case, Rubio Valquez. I got a chance to get out to the crime scene today. Talked to that guy you interviewed, Peter Waleta."

"What'd you think?"

"He wasn't telling me any more than he had to, although I did find out that Waleta was the victim's partner in the casino."

"Who gets Aquillo's interest in the business, now that he's dead?"

"I'm looking into that," he said.

I could hear the crack of billiard balls in the back room. There was only one man hugging the bar now. He loosened his embrace and headed to the game room. As he passed our table, his hard eyes lingered too long on me for comfort. David caught the exchange.

"You're brave to come back here after what happened Thursday night."

"I don't cotton to intimidation. Besides, I'm better prepared now. If I believe everything I hear, this reservation is something of a war zone."

"What's that supposed to mean?"

"There's a cemetery about a hundred yards from Aquillo's house," I said, "at the far end of the reservation. I met Aquillo's sister and nephew out there this morning. The nephew talks like a political radical. Said his uncle's murder was an act of war."

David's face lit up, as if a war were news to celebrate.

"Tension, tribal politics. That's all good for us. Look into it."

"I intend to," I said. "Have they set Hurston's preliminary yet?"

David smiled, still riding a wave of good news.

"No. The physical evidence isn't stacking up so well for the DA."

"In what way?"

The bartender arrived with our coffees.

"Thank you," I said as he slid the mugs onto the table.

David slurped a sip and continued:

"None of Aquillo's blood showed up on Hurston at all. Not in the sink or shower drains in his room, either." He put the mug down too hastily, and some of the coffee sloshed over the brim.

"And they still haven't found the murder weapon yet, have they?"

"No, they haven't." He mopped the spill with his napkin.

I watched the bartender walk away and thought about the vision I'd had at the Mystic Mesa Hotel, the man walking out the door. David was right there with me.

"I need you to tell me everything you saw or envisioned or whatever it is you did at the hotel," he said. "Start from the beginning and go slow. I want to hear every detail. You said something about someone hammering Aquillo, right?"

"Yes. The murderer left out the front door, and he had the hammer with him."

"You're sure he left through the front door?"

"Yes," I said, sensing doubt in his voice.

"The crime techs found footprints on the balcony and out back."

"Your point?" I asked.

"My point is, there's a strong possibility that the real killer may have exited via the balcony."

"That's not what I picked up."

"Tell me again what you saw. Can you give any kind of physical description of the person with the hammer?"

I thought about it and shook my head.

"No," I said. "Just a human form. I'm not even sure of the sex, to be honest."

"How can you know the weapon was a hammer and not even know the sex of the murderer?" He sounded exasperated.

I sipped my brew and shrugged.

"The murderer was shadowy. The hammer came through clearly. I know that's not how it works on television, but that's how it works for me. Sorry."

He let out an impatient sigh.

"Yeah, yeah. Chatfield explained to me how your psychic thing works. Told me you can't dial it up, that it just comes in flashes—"

I was having a flash at that very moment.

"Whoever killed Aquillo was more than angry. Almost zealous." I sensed the vicious hammer blows and shuddered.

David looked into my eyes, waiting. After several moments of silence, he prodded me for more.

"After you saw this person hitting Aquillo with the hammer, then what?"

"He bends over and peers at the body."

David was watching me so intently that I could see his black pupils shrinking to pinpoints inside his brown irises.

"You see anything else?"

I closed my eyes to view again what I'd seen that evening, standing outside the hotel room.

"I see a shadowy form coming out of the closet, raising a hammer over Aquillo's head, coming down on it several times. Then the murderer leaves out the front door . . . still carrying the hammer. I'm clear on that." I opened my eyes again.

"That's it?"

"That's it."

Across the restaurant, a man emerged from the billiard room. He was nearly as wide as he was high, wearing an over-sized T-shirt that hung almost to his knees. His head was shaved, and a smoky-colored tattoo adorned his scalp. It got me thinking.

"I don't remember reading anything in the police report about the scalp," I said. "Did they recover it from the crime scene?"

"They did not."

"Do they even know where Aquillo's scalp is?"

"They do not. Nor do they know the whereabouts of the knife or tomahawk or whatever was used to do that part of the job. From the bloodstains, the ME's saying now that Aquillo was probably dead when his scalp was removed."

"And they found none of Aquillo's blood on Hurston?"

"No."

The news brought a smile to my face.

"That's great for us, David."

"But lots of blood on Hurston's clothes, which were piled in a heap on the floor."

My smile faded.

"That's not so great for us."

"Doesn't necessarily do irreparable damage to our case," David said firmly. "He says that after he took the Versed, he removed his clothes before he climbed into bed and passed out. With all due respect to your, uh, vision, I'm building a case on those footprints on the back balcony."

He sat back and relaxed, looking around as if seeing the place for the first time. With his curly hair, round brown eyes, full bow lips, and curls, David was almost angelic looking when he wasn't stressed.

"Look at this place," he said. "What a time warp—Ed's Country Cafe." His eyes went to the military montage over the bar, where the grizzle-bearded man was serving up another round of beer. "He's a crusty old fart, isn't he? That must be Ed himself."

I was only half listening because my mind was fixed on a question. Who'd taken Aquillo's scalp, and why?

17

Dan Aquillo's girlfriend, Trish Brown, lived in an Escondido residential complex called Palm Vista Apartments. I'd picked up the name Palm Vista from the police report; tracking down the address hadn't required rocket-science sleuthing. The building was pleasant enough, although the absence of palm trees and proximity to Washington Avenue would have made Asphalt Vista a more appropriate name. I parked on the street and walked up a cement path that parted a struggling lawn with several bald spots. A rectangular swimming pool occupied most of the central courtyard, shaded by an overgrown shefflera that reached the second-floor balcony. I climbed a flight of outside stairs to Apartment 207 and rang the bell. As I waited, one of the shefflera's yellowing leaves dropped onto the pool's green-tinged surface with a soft plop. I heard the door unlocking behind me and turned back around. The door opened a few inches, and a woman's guarded face peeked out.

"Yes?" Her voice was as wary as what little I could see of her face.

"Hi. I'm investigating the murder of Dan Aquillo and wondered if I could I ask you some questions."

"You from the DA's office?"

"No," I said, handing a card through the crack in the door. "Private."

She took the card and inspected it. Her thin blonde eyebrows came together, and she looked at me more carefully this time.

"Is this for real, a psychic detective?"

"Yes." I was still waiting for my PI license to be replaced and hoped she'd take my word for it. "For real."

The door opened a few inches wider. She was a tall blonde, well fed but pleasingly proportioned in a casual knit pants and top set.

"I could use a psychic about now," she said. "If I answer your questions, will you give me a reading?"

"I'm not exactly the 900-number kind of psychic," I said.

"Come on in anyway," she said as she swung the door wide. "No sense you standing out there."

Trish Brown had eaten something Italian for lunch; the thick odor of tomato and garlic still hung in the air. I walked into the combination living/dining area and noticed an unfinished plate of pasta on the small table. The rest of the room was uncluttered. She closed the door behind me.

"So what kind of psychic are you?"

"I have occasional visions, for lack of a better term, that sometimes help me solve cases."

"Oh, like on that TV show," she said as she walked into the living room and lowered herself into a nearby recliner. "Please, have a seat."

I sat on a blue plaid sofa that made up for its lack of style with sturdiness and comfort.

"Those TV psychics tend to have very convenient visions," I answered. "Mine aren't always so straightforward or timely." I paused, then said, "I understand you were close to Dan Aquillo."

She nodded silently.

"I've read the statement you made to the police. You said that Dan was your boyfriend."

"I don't think that's what I said, exactly."

"How would you put it?"

"We dated for many years, off and on."

"And you last saw him that night at the casino."

"Yes. I was dealing blackjack that night. Dan was there all evening. I saw him when I took my ten o'clock break. That was the last time."

She had the shell-shocked look I'd seen in my own face after McGowan's death. Neither sad nor happy, just blank. Or was I projecting? This was the number-one reason my intuitive gift broke down: when I was too close to a situation emotionally. I reminded myself that, although we'd experienced a similar loss, Trish and I were two different people.

"The man they arrested," I continued, "said he gambled his last hundred dollars at your table that night. Did you know Bill Hurston at all?"

"Bill was a regular customer. A lot of us knew him pretty well."

"Dan knew him well, also?"

"Bill Hurston was a friend of Dan's. We'd both known Bill since back in our Las Vegas days."

"Where did you meet?"

"Me and Dan, or me and Bill Hurston?" She waved a hand. "Doesn't matter, actually. We all met at Caesar's Palace, ages ago. Back when I was still skinny." She smiled self-consciously. "Dan and I worked there; Bill was a customer. A good customer." She shook her head. "I just don't think he'd do something like that, even if Dan was sort of on his case sometimes."

"On his case about what?"

"Getting his shit together, being more responsible and stuff. Bill had a gambling problem, you know. A drinking problem, too, of late. He'd been passing out in that room by eleven every night. He was getting to be a joke around Temecu."

"Maybe Dan got on his case a little too hard, and Bill just snapped."

"Yeah, maybe. I don't think so, though. Dan had been pretty compassionate toward him. He'd been comping that room for Bill to let him sleep off his drunk."

"So in essence Room 109 was Hurston's regular home away from home?"

"It had been lately. It was in the part of the hotel that was being remodeled, so it wasn't like Dan was losing money on it."

I paused to think about it. If Hurston had a regular room and was passing out in it at the same time every night, someone who knew his habits could have framed him.

"I don't recall you commenting on this to the police," I said.

"I answered all their questions. I just didn't elaborate, is all. You've got to be careful what you say to the police, 'cause everything you say, you know . . ." She got halfway through the sentence and paused, probably realizing that I would use the information in very much the same manner the police would.

"When did you find out about Dan's murder?"

"I got a phone call at three in the morning." Again, her face got that blank, faraway look. "I didn't even get to say good-bye to Dan that night. I went home right after my shift ended. I was a little pissed, in fact, because I couldn't find him. I was beat, so I didn't wait around."

"Tell me about Dan. What was he like?"

"People really respected him. If you didn't know him real well, you might think he was a god. He did so many amazing things for the tribe."

"And if you did know him well?"

"You'd know he was human. He had his flaws. His family and I knew that."

"What kind of flaws?"

"Like everybody has. You know, he could be a jerk some-times, forget things, lose his temper. You know, typical stuff."

"Did he have a temper?"

"Not a bad one, no."

"You mentioned his family. Who are they?"

"Dan's parents passed away, but his sister and her son live in Temecu. He was real close to his sister."

"You're talking about Lucy and Wolf?"

"Yes."

"What was Dan's relationship with Wolf like?"

She straightened a pair of candlesticks on the coffee table between us. When she answered, she spoke slowly, as if choosing her words carefully.

"It was . . . Dan was a good influence on Wolf. He can be a difficult kid sometimes."

"I can see that. I talked to him this morning. He seems to feel that his uncle was a traitor to his tribe. He called his un-cle's murder an act of war. Do you have any idea what he was talking about?"

She shook her head.

"That kid says a lot of crazy things. As far as what he meant by that, I couldn't tell you."

"Perhaps the police already asked you this, but did anyone directly benefit from Dan's death?"

"What do you mean?"

"The new manager, Peter Waleta, said that he and Dan were partners. Did he mean that literally? I mean, who owns the casino?"

She inspected her manicure.

"Yes, Peter and Dan were partners. There are some other investors, too, though."

"Like you?"

She looked at me with candid blue eyes and laughed.

"Like I know anything about investing!"

Not a straight answer. I felt as if I were chasing a cat around the room, one who'd almost let me get close, then dart away when I was within touching distance.

"Is it possible that after Dan's death, his shares in the casino went to Peter Waleta?"

"I suppose it's possible."

"What was Peter's relationship with Dan like?" I asked.

"They worked real well together," she said. "Anyone will tell you that." She was moving away again, her tone becoming the slightest bit defensive.

"You like Peter pretty well, don't you?"

She averted her eyes, and again rearranged the candlesticks.

"Yeah, I do. He's a nice guy."

I tired of the game and decided to try something else.

"Do you have a picture of Dan?" To her puzzled look I said, "I'd just like to get a sense of who he was."

"I think I have a photo that'll help you do that. Just a minute."

She got up and went into the back of the apartment. I heard a door close, a toilet flushing, water running. When she came out a few minutes later, her lipstick was fresh and she carried a glass-framed picture.

"This was taken at a fundraising event for the library Dan got going out on the res."

It was a fine photograph. Dan Aquillo stood at a podium, his profile etched against a clear blue sky. His long black hair was blowing in the breeze, and his mouth was slightly open, as if the camera had caught him in midsentence. It was such an entirely different man from the one I'd seen in the crime-scene photos that I never would have recognized him.

"What was he talking about?" I asked.

"Dan was really into preserving the Luiseno culture. The old ones who speak the native tongue are dying off. Dan was talking to the reservation kids about a native-language program at the library. Encouraging them to take lessons with the elders, so that the language could be passed on to a new generation."

She looked at her watch.

"Look, I don't mean to rush you, but I've got things to do today."

"Of course," I said. "Thanks for your time."

As I passed back the photograph, I put my fingertips on Dan Aquillo's face, hoping to sense his essence. Instead, an image flashed to mind. It was the view from his home, looking past the two-pronged pepper tree to the chaparral beyond.

18

It was a macabre search, this hunt for Dan Aquillo's scalp, and it led me once more to the pepper tree. I leaned against its east-facing trunk and felt the rough bark under my back, the solid earth beneath my feet. This day was not so pleasant. Under a gunmetal-gray sky, the foothills looked like the backs of angry black bears. I heard a screech overhead and looked up to see a vulture, the tips of its wings drooping like arthritic fingers. My arms and legs were cold—I was wearing just my running clothes, shorts and a tank. I looked around to see if Natalie had caught up with me yet, but she was nowhere in sight. I hoped she'd hurry because it was going to rain any minute now. No sooner had the thought crossed my mind than the sky opened up. Dark red blotches appeared on my legs and arms where the heavy drops landed on bare skin. I dabbed at the wetness and brought my fingers to my nose, wincing at the pungent smell. The sky was raining blood.

I opened my eyes and lay motionless, shaken from the nightmare. Outside my bedroom window, the sky *was* gunmetal gray. It was early, but with cloud cover this heavy, there'd be no sunrise. I pulled a spiral-bound notebook and pen from my bedside table and recorded the dream just as I'd seen it. Dreams this lucid usually contain messages, and this one was no exception. By the time I was done writing, I knew that I had to take that return trip to Aquillo's right away.

I went downstairs, found Sequoia's card in the case file, and dialed his number. By the sixth ring, I figured out that he didn't have an answering machine. By the tenth ring, I was formulating Plan B. After fifteen rings, I hung up. I would have preferred to go out to Aquillo's with Sequoia as my guide, but I couldn't expect him to be at my beck and call every minute of every day.

I showered and dressed, putting on jeans, a plaid flannel shirt, my shoulder holster, my nine, and a rain-proof parka that did a decent job of concealing the gun. I stood before the mirror and gingerly brushed my hair, careful not to tug a scalp that was still tender from being dragged along the roadside three nights ago. I looked almost normal this morning, except for a disturbing blotch near my right eye. I could have covered it with makeup, but my features are ordinarily so pleasant and nonthreatening that I actually enjoyed looking a little scary.

Nero watched my entire getting-ready process. As I donned my gun, he sat up, fixing me with an expression at once serious and eager. I suppose in some way he connected this ritual with his late master. I kneeled down and scratched his ears, to comfort myself as much as the dog. He'd been hanging out with law-enforcement types since puppyhood. I smiled, remembering Nero's disastrous career with the Escondido PD, back when McGowan was still a cop there. They'd hoped to use the Rhodesian ridgeback in an experimental K-9 program and had trained him as a tracker. He'd been excellent at the tracking but miserable on discipline. "Too damn friendly," Tom had told me, proudly scratching the dog's ears. When it was clear Nero would never make the grade, Tom had adopted him.

Then it hit me: A tracker might be just what I needed today.

"Want to go for a ride today, buddy?"

Nero's vocabulary was limited, but he knew what *ride* meant. He jumped to all fours, ears forward, and bolted down the stairs as soon as I was on my feet.

Forty-five minutes later my truck was rumbling over the cattle crossing that marked the Temecu Reservation. Maybe it was the early hour, maybe it was the weather, but for whatever reason the roads of the res were all but deserted this morning. The parka had been a good idea. It started to sprinkle just about the time I was passing the cemetery.

I pulled into Aquillo's driveway and stopped the truck. As soon as I cut the engine, I was pervaded by the same unsettling feeling I'd had here yesterday morning. Outside the sky was close, weeping softly. No vultures.

I felt exposed, parked in full view of hundreds of unspoiled acres. Aquillo's dirt driveway continued down a small incline and led to a landing behind the house. I restarted the engine and parked the truck out of view of the road.

As soon as I opened the door, Nero jumped out and loped back up the driveway. He honed in on the pepper tree, where he sniffed first one side of the two-pronged trunk, then the other. Talk about the horns of a dilemma. He finally relieved himself on the west-facing trunk. I had no scent for him to follow, no piece of clothing or pillow or shoe to put under his nose. But he got down to business anyway, muzzle to the ground. He trotted north for about ten feet and stopped near a stand of tall pampas grass. He let out a little yelp, the muscles quivering under his shiny coat. He looked to me, as if asking for permission.

"What is it, boy?"

He put his nose to the earth again and began digging. His paws made a hissing sound as the damp dirt flew up behind him. When he'd made an indentation about four inches deep, he let out a bark.

"Whatcha got, Nero?"

He skittered back, unable to stand still, and made worried noises. I came forward and kneeled down to brush the loose clay and granite soil out of the depression, but I didn't see anything.

"What is it?" I goaded.

Nero went back to his digging, more purposefully now. I kept my eye on the earth beneath his fast-moving paws.

"Nero, stop!"

Something white—it looked like a grub—had begun to protrude from the side of the hole. I picked up a sharp rock and carefully chipped away at the surrounding earth, feeling like some gruesome archaeologist. There was really no question about what it was. And when I unearthed a fingernail painted a distinctive poppy-red, no question about *who* it was.

I froze, squeezing the rock in my hand. Nero sat beside me obediently, waiting for further instructions. A shudder went through me as if I'd been hit from behind. I remembered her parting words to me:

The last psychic I went to scared the daylights out of me. Said he saw negative energy around me . . . danger. . .

The memories came unbidden: Natalie's auburn hair blowing in the ocean breeze as she removed her visor and wiped the sweat from her brow; the healthy glow of her suntanned face after the run. I kneeled at her shallow grave, my logical mind arguing that I couldn't be certain who it was, not on the basis of a fingernail. It was a futile argument. I *knew*.

I reached into my purse for my new phone and dialed 911. Since it was coming from a wireless, my call wouldn't be routed directly, and the dispatcher wouldn't see the address on his computer screen. I heard one ring, and a male voice answered.

"Nine-one-one emergency."

"My dog just found a body on the Temecu Reservation. Five forty-six Pala Verde Highway."

"You calling from a cell phone?"

"Yes."

"Where are you now?"

"Sitting right next to the body."

"A human body?"

"Very. Five forty-six Pala Verde, the Temecu Reservation. Please get somebody out here."

I saw no need to give details over the phone, especially knowing I'd have to plod through them all over again when the authorities arrived. I cut the connection and put the phone back in my purse. Staring at Natalie's finger, I felt numbness creeping over me. I welcomed its sweet amnesia. Here was the emotional distance that allowed surgeons to slice open chest cavities and saw through ribs. Blessed detachment.

I sat and thought about what would probably happen next. My call most likely would be routed to the nearest California Highway Patrol. Aquillo's place was a good fifteen miles from Highway 76. I settled into a comfortable position, patting the ground.

"Come 'ere, pup. Might as well make yourself comfortable. We're gonna be here a while."

Nero settled on the ground, but his muscles were still

tense, as if he were ready to spring any minute. I couldn't smell it, but the scent of the body had him riled. I was glad the rain had let up, at least for now.

I heard someone coming and looked up. The approaching vehicle made no cloud of dust today, since showers had settled the dirt road. I couldn't see the make of the vehicle, just a streak of teal speeding my way. I was thinking it didn't have the look of an emergency vehicle when a cold instinct gripped me:

Hide.

I took cover behind the fence that ran along the side of the house, calling my dog in my most commanding voice.

"Nero, heel!"

The dog got to his feet but was reluctant to leave the body. After one last sniff at the grave, he trotted toward me behind the fence. When he reached my side, I jerked his collar and fixed him with a stern glare.

"Stay."

He seemed to take me seriously, for the moment anyway, and sat back on his haunches.

There was a tiny knothole in the fence, just about shoulder level. I peered through it and watched as the approaching vehicle pulled to a stop in Aquillo's driveway. It wasn't an ambulance. Nor was it a police vehicle. It was a teal Geo Metro.

The driver's side door opened, and Wolf got out. The fringe on his leather coat swinging, he walked toward the pepper tree with certainty in his stride, as if he knew exactly what he was going to find when he got there. He stopped at the mound of dirt where Nero had been digging and looked into the hole. He bent down to inspect it more closely.

"Holy shit!"

Whether his voice carried surprise or anger, I couldn't tell. Maybe both. He paced back and forth, as if trying to figure out what had happened here and what to do next. He finally stopped pacing and took a good look around. He began to walk in my direction. For a second I panicked, until I realized he was heading for the tool shed.

The thud of his footsteps coming closer pushed a button in

Nero somewhere. Before I could stop him, the dog jerked from my grip and bounded away. I lunged to catch him, but it was too late. He rounded the fence, barking ferociously.

I ran after him, stopping short at the edge of the fence. I peeked through the wooden slats and saw Wolf turn toward the barking dog. Time went slow-mo. As the Rhodesian ridge-back charged him at full speed, Wolf reached into the pocket of his fringed leather coat. I stepped out from behind the fence just in time to see the flash of the semiauto in his hand.

19

My Glock was out of its holster and aiming for body mass by the time I came around the fence. I had the advantage of surprise, which probably saved Nero's life. In the moment it took for Wolf to register my presence, Nero was on top of him, sinking his fangs into the boy's gun hand. His weapon went off with a blast that echoed across the chaparral, but Nero didn't let go. I'd never heard such ugly, guttural noises coming from the dog's throat. Finally the gun fell to the dirt with a thud. When Wolf reached for it, a snarling Nero went leaping for his jugular.

"Nero, stop!"

To my amazement, the dog backed off and half-crouched, half-stood, training every nerve on his quarry. As for Wolf, he'd turned in my direction and was having a staredown with the eye of my Glock. I heard the blood pounding in my ears.

I was standing there wondering what the hell to do next when I heard another vehicle coming up the road. We both turned our heads to look. This time it was a green Bronco with klieg lights mounted on the roof. Either tribal police or sheriff—from three hundred yards, it was too far away to tell. Wolf looked at his gun in the dirt, then back at me. Anger darkened his eyes.

"What do you say we put the fuckin' guns away before the cop gets here?"

The coldness in his young voice put a chill in my heart. I steadied my Glock with a double-hand grip.

"What do you say we just stay right where we are."

The tattoo on his cheek shifted as he narrowed his eyes.

"What are you doing out here?" His voice accused me of an unspoken crime.

"I might ask you the same thing."

"Hey, I belong here, man. This land belongs to my family. You're the one who's fuckin' trespassing."

He had a point there.

Behind us, the Bronco had come to a stop. A female officer in green khakis got out and racked her shotgun, then raised a megaphone to her face.

"DROP YOUR WEAPON AND GET YOUR HANDS IN THE AIR!"

I dropped my nine and put my hands over my head. Wolf raised his hands in a bored manner. That's when I noticed he was wearing thin kid gloves. He glared at me and spoke under his breath:

"You and your fuckin' dog are gonna get yourself killed if you don't stay away from here."

Behind us, the megaphone blared.

"WALK TOWARD ME NOW, NICE AND SLOW."

I stepped forward, and Nero jumped to my side.

"Please don't hurt the dog," I called out. "He's a trained K-9."

"I WON'T HURT THE DOG IF THE DOG DOESN'T ATTACK ME."

I glanced sideways and spoke urgently under my breath to Nero.

"It's okay, buddy. Now for godssakes, *heel*."

I continued forward, careful not to let Wolf get behind me. We were about thirty feet from the officer now.

"ON THE GROUND, BOTH OF YOU. FACEDOWN."

I lowered myself to the ground and felt Nero lowering himself alongside me. The earth was damp from the morning rain and smelled vaguely metallic.

"NOW TURN YOUR HEAD TO THE LEFT AND STRETCH YOUR HANDS OUT IN FRONT OF YOU."

When I turned my face left, I could see Wolf lying about ten feet away from me. He still had a teenager's body, with bony shoulders and limbs not yet fully developed.

"NOW CROSS YOUR RIGHT LEG OVER YOUR LEFT ANKLE. I'M GOING TO ASSUME THAT BOTH OF YOU ARE ARMED. IF EITHER ONE OF YOU COME OFF THE GROUND, I WILL SHOOT. WE'RE GOING TO BE HERE A WHILE, SO I SUGGEST YOU RELAX. ANY MOVEMENT I WILL TAKE AS A THREAT."

She wasn't taking any chances. Then again, I'd just called in a dead body, and a gun had been drawn when she arrived.

No wonder she was handling this by the book. She came forward, and I watched as she put Wolf in handcuffs. As she stepped toward me to do the same, I reassured my dog.

"It's okay, Nero. She's cool."

As the officer bent down and slapped the handcuff on my wrist, I could hear Nero's tail behind me, thumping the damp earth. She had a pretty face, even when she wasn't smiling. I read the name-tag pinned on her shirt: Deputy Angie Moon. A gold Temecu Tri-bal Police emblem was embroidered on her sleeve.

"They use German Shepherds for K-9s," she said. "This isn't a Shepherd."

"He's a Rhodesian ridgeback. It was an experimental program for the Escondido Police Department a few years back."

She double-checked my handcuffs.

"Uh-huh."

Nero's tail was thumping harder now. He liked Angie.

"You want to tell me what's going on here?" she asked.

In the distance I could hear the sound of a helicopter.

"My dog was digging over there and found a body. I called 911 and while I was waiting for you to show, this guy drove up. I could see his car wasn't a police vehicle, so I took cover. He went right to the grave and cursed. When he started walking toward the tool shed, my dog ran out from behind the fence and charged him. He fired and missed. I pulled my gun to slow things down, and that's about where you came in."

The chopping sound of the helicopter was growing louder. She was patting me down and came across the twenty-two in my ankle holster.

"You always carry two guns?" she asked.

"I'm a PI. Wallet's in my purse by the fence over there. You're welcome to it. Oh, shit. Except my PI license got stolen earlier this week. I'm still waiting for the replacement."

I could imagine what Deputy Moon thought of that one. She pointed in the general direction of Natalie's grave.

"There's a body over there?" she asked.

"Yes, ma'am."

"You have any idea who that is buried over there?"

"Yes, I do." My voice was nearly drowned out now by the chopper directly overhead. I could feel the ground vibrating underneath me in response to the roaring motor.

"That's my airborne backup," she yelled. "They're gonna be my eyes and ears here while we process this scene. Hope you don't have any plans because you're in for a long day."

"I ain't gonna say shit. Not till you get me a lawyer."

Wolf had answered the last five questions in exactly the same manner. The chopper—an SDPD airborne law-enforcement unit—had landed in a clearing on the chaparral and was quiet now. The two pilot officers stood guard as Deputy Moon tried to pry information out of the kid.

"Is that your Geo Metro over there?" she asked.

"I told you, I ain't saying shit. What's the matter, Angie, you hard of hearing?"

I watched for a reaction in her body language and saw none. She calmly walked back to her Bronco, retrieved a clipboard, walked over to Wolf's Geo, and wrote down the license plate number.

A light rain had begun to fall. My toes were starting to feel numb. We'd been on the ground a good twenty minutes now. I could smell the canine stink of Nero's damp coat beside me.

"Okay," she called to the other two officers. "Let's get this one into the car."

She was pointing to me. One of the SDPD pilot officers came over and helped me off the ground. When I'd stomped some blood back into my toes, he escorted me toward the Bronco.

"Can my dog get in, too?" I asked.

"Yeah, okay."

We settled into the Bronco and waited another forty-five minutes, during which time four other vehicles arrived—two sheriffs, a CHP, and the crime-scene tech van. I watched as they marked a perimeter around Natalie's grave and searched the Geo Metro. Nero sat beside me in the back seat of Agent Moon's Bronco, panting happily. He was loving this.

"Just like old times, huh, boy?"

* * *

The Temecu Reservation Area Station was small but warm
and dry, for which I was grateful. I'd liked the tribal detective,
Rubio Valquez, from the moment I'd met him in the linoleum-
floored room that served as his combination reception
area–interview room–office. The crows' feet around his eyes
told me he'd passed up youth long ago, but he had the posture
and build of a much younger man. He flipped over the cassette
in his tape recorder and started into Side B.

"And if you don't mind, can you tell me again what you
were doing out there this morning?"

"I was hired by the defense to look into the murder of Dan
Aquillo. One of the first things I did was to come out and take
a look at Aquillo's place—"

"Why'd you do that?"

"To get a sense of how the victim lived, who he was."

Valquez nodded. He'd run my name through the computer
at the Department of Investigative Services. Once he'd determined I was a legitimate PI with a clean record, our conversation had taken an almost friendly tone.

"So in the course of investigating Aquillo's place, you
found the body."

"My dog found it, actually. He's a tracker."

Nero seemed to understand me and lifted his head from his
paws.

"And you said you think you know the identity of the
body?"

"Yes. Her name is Natalie Hurston. She was the ex-wife of
the suspect they arrested in the Aquillo case. That was the first
thing I did when I took this case, interviewed Ms. Hurston. I
wanted to see what she had to say about her ex."

"Her ex being William Hurston?" he asked.

"That's right," I said patiently.

"And again, you're guessing the identity of the body on the
basis of . . . fingernail color?" There was a suggestion of
doubt in his voice.

Fingernail color, plus a dream about a sky raining blood
and another psychic's warning.

"Yes," I answered. "It's an unusual color."

He took that into consideration, perhaps contemplating the complex nuances of female cosmetics.

"Did you have any prior knowledge of the kid who drove the Geo to Aquillo's this morning?"

"Yes. I met him and his mother, Lucy Aquillo, yesterday."

"Where?"

"Coincidentally or perhaps not so coincidentally, I met him exactly where I encountered him this morning—under the pepper tree at his uncle's house. He and his mom had come to put flowers on Dan Aquillo's gravestone in the cemetery next door."

"So you were at the scene yesterday also."

"But I had no idea at the time that a body was buried there." Not entirely true, I realized, remembering my sense of something human near the spreading roots.

"Maybe the kid didn't have any idea, either."

I sat back in my chair and chewed my thumb knuckle. It was my word against Wolf's. Nobody but me had seen him head knowingly for Natalie's grave. In all fairness, he had fired his gun in self-defense after Nero attacked him. Still, I doubted the weapon was legal.

"You going to keep him on a firearms charge?" I asked.

Valquez shook his head.

"He wasn't armed when we frisked him. As for the twenty-two near the grave, he claims it's yours. The gun's not traceable. You and I both know we won't find any prints on it—he was wearing gloves. We're going to let him go. I'm afraid we have to."

20

My body was spent. The adrenaline rush from this morning's brush with death—and death threats—was long gone, replaced by bone-tiredness. The humble Temecu Area Station was beginning to depress me, and I was ready to get out of there. Valquez reconfirmed my home phone number and told me I could go. I was halfway to the door when I realized that I had no ride. I turned and called back to him.

"Hey, can somebody give me a lift back to Aquillo's? My truck's still out there."

Valquez had gone back to his report writing and looked up with a blank stare. My question took a few seconds to register.

"Your truck's at the crime scene? Afraid you're gonna have to leave it. The techs will be processing the vehicles there till tomorrow. Do you have somebody you can call?"

I thought of calling David, but immediately dismissed the idea. David was a lawyer first, a friend second. He'd want a blow-by-blow accounting of the day's events and would probably be pissed that I hadn't called him earlier. I missed McGowan desperately at that moment, feeling stripped and alone. No boyfriend, no truck—even my damn guns had been bagged as evidence. A lump formed in my throat, and I was coming close to losing it when I felt Nero's wet tongue on my fingers.

"Hey, Buddy." I leaned down, to hide my tears as much as to pet the dog. "I'll bet you're pretty hungry about now, huh, boy?"

Valquez was still looking over at me, waiting for my answer. He gave a hopeful smile.

"You look like the type who has at least a friend or two."

In fact I had several, none of whom I wanted to inconvenience with a long drive to the reservation. I was considering calling my mom when a familiar face popped into my mind.

"Can I use your phone?"

"Sure."

I found Sequoia's number at the back of my weary brain and used Valequez's phone to ring him up. This time he did answer, with a cheerful hello that clashed with my dour mood.

"It's me, Elizabeth."

"I figured I'd be hearing from you about now."

"Why's that?"

"I saw all the commotion down the mountain today. Helicopter, cop cars, news people. Figured you'd be somewhere in the mix. Where are you?"

I hadn't known about the news coverage. The crews must have arrived on the scene after I'd been taken in for questioning. I was glad I'd missed them.

"I'm stranded at the Temecu Area Station without wheels. I'll explain later. Can you come get me?"

"Um-hm."

He hung up without a formal good-bye, as if we were right across the room from one another. Odd guy, Sequoia. But nice. I hung up and walked with Nero to wait by the door. Outside it was raining steadily. I hadn't noticed the rain during my questioning and wondered how long it had been coming down. For Natalie's sake, I hoped that the crime-scene techs had managed to preserve the evidence before the weather got to it.

When Sequoia's old Jeep drove up, I pulled my jacket over my head and jogged out, my dog at my heels. As I came around the passenger side, the door opened and Nero jumped into the back.

"What," I said as I settled into the front seat, "a hellacious day."

The sound of rain was loud on the canvas roof. Sequoia was staying dry in a dark green Goretex jacket. He waited for me to buckle up before he stepped on the gas.

"I didn't have to post bail, so it couldn't have been that bad," he said with a grin.

"I went back to Aquillo's place this morning. I knew something wasn't right out there. Did you get that feeling, too?"

He shrugged slightly and cranked up the speed on the windshield wipers.

"When we got out there, Nero picked up a scent and started digging. He uncovered a body, not far from that pepper tree."

"Your dog uncovered a body?"

"A hand, anyway." The memory of Natalie's finger protruding from the dirt came back, and I shuddered. "It was a woman I interviewed earlier this week. She used to be married to the same guy who's been charged with Aquillo's murder, William Hurston."

"That's the doctor, right?"

"Right. Anyway, just about the time I realized what was in the ground there, Wolf showed up. Guns were drawn, and it was a big mess."

He took his foot off the gas for a moment and looked over at me with surprise.

"Wolf pulled a gun on you?"

"More like on my dog. But the kid had a semiauto, and he was savvy enough to be wearing gloves. Is he involved with that bad element on the res you were telling me about?"

Sequoia shook his head.

"I hadn't thought so," he said. "Now that you tell me this, I'm not so sure. How'd the cops end up getting involved?"

I explained it to him as best I could, from my 911 call to my interview with Rubio Valquez at the area station.

"I'm probably leaving out important details, but that's the gist of it," I finished.

"That's a heck of a day, all right. You hungry?"

"Even if I'm not, I should be. Nero here's starving."

"Just made a batch of fry bread. You like fry bread okay?"

"Never had it before, but it sounds scrumptious."

My wristwatch said four o'clock, but with the rainstorm shutting out the light, the day looked later. I leaned back in my seat, vaguely aware of the scenery going by. The windshield wipers flapped away at full speed, barely keeping up with the downpour. My eyes fell on a sculpture dangling from the rearview mirror. I got a strong vibe from it.

"What's this?" I asked.

Sequoia grinned.

"Indian car insurance."

"What?"

"It's for protection on the road."

"Really. Can I see?"

"Sure." He pulled the thing off and handed it to me.

It was a section of tree branch embellished with objects: a bear carved of deep turquoise, a black talon of some sort, and three spotted quail feathers. The objects were attached to the wood with sinewy ties. The branch itself was pale and smooth, the result of careful sanding. Each totem radiated energy, as if there were more to them than mere material substance.

"Interesting," I said, hanging it back on the rearview.

The totem swung like a pendulum as Sequoia made a hard left, and we headed up the mountain. Eventually sagebrush and rye grass gave way to a mature forest of mountain oak. The road rose at a challenging angle—San Francisco without the sidewalks. Sequoia put the Jeep into low gear and gunned the motor. We lurched forward, and I heard Nero skittering for a foothold in back.

"It's a little rough for a while here, but then we level out," he said.

When we crested the hill, the trees thinned out and I could see the valley below. Even with the low-hung clouds, the vista took in at least forty or fifty miles of backcountry. To the east I could see the rain slanting diagonally onto the desert plains.

"This is spectacular," I said.

Sequoia nodded and pointed.

"Aquillo's is right down there. That's where I saw the commotion earlier. Looks like everyone's gone home now."

I squinted, trying to recognize a landmark—the doubled-trunked pepper tree, perhaps—but I was looking from too far away, in weather too poor, to see much detail. We slowed as Sequoia turned onto a narrow, unpaved road. Fifty yards or so later, he turned again, and we came to a stop in a small clearing.

"We're here."

Sequoia's house sat back against the trees. It was more round than rectangular, with a dome-shaped roof, and con-

structed of materials that blended with the surrounding ter-
rain. I climbed down out of the Jeep, and Nero jumped out after me. Smoke from the chimney commingled with the scent
of rain-soaked oak leaves.

"What a cool place," I said.

"Thanks. I call it my geodesic tepee."

He led me to the entry and opened the front door, which I
noticed was unlocked. The aroma of something freshly baked
hit my nostrils as soon as I stepped across the threshold.

"Yum, whatever that is."

"Fry bread and sweet-potato casserole."

I found myself standing in what looked like a large circular
studio. There was a kitchen to the left and a sitting area to the
right, with a crackling fire as its focal point. Toward the rear
of the studio was a bed and in the very center of the room, a
spiral staircase corkscrewing up through the ceiling.

"What's up the stairs?" I asked.

"That's the guest loft."

The reddish-brown walls, textured and painted like tem-
pura, were hung with an eclectic mix of Indian blankets, photos, and modern art. A thirty-two-inch TV sat near the
fireplace. The sound was muted, and the improbably paired
faces of Woody Allen and Mariel Hemingway filled the
screen.

Sequoia noticed me watching.

"*Manhattan.* I'm taping it," he explained.

"One of my all-time favorites."

"The Gershwin soundtrack alone puts it on my top ten.
Here, have a seat. Food's coming up."

I tossed my purse on the futon and sat at the table while Sequoia busied himself in his tiny kitchen. He pulled something
limp and red from the refrigerator and threw it to the floor, but
Nero gobbled it up before I could even tell what it was. For us
humans, he dished up two plates of fry bread and sweet-
potato casserole and placed them on the table. In spite of the
delicious aroma, I didn't have much of an appetite.

"Thank you," I said as Sequoia took a seat.

He nodded and reached for the butter.

"Thank you, Great Spirit," he said.

On the TV screen, Woody wore a hurt-puppy expression as Mariel's lips moved. This was the final scene, where she was leaving for London and telling him to have a little faith in people. It always made me sad. I picked up my fork and dabbed at the sweet potatoes, feeling the aftershock of the day's events.

"I don't get it about Natalie's death," I said. "Hurston's still in custody, so he didn't kill her—not directly, anyway. What I can't figure out is why anybody else would kill his ex-wife."

Sequoia didn't respond, just chewed slowly. I put down my fork, distracted now.

"I've been thinking about this all afternoon. I've seen Hurston twice, enough to have a sense of the guy. I'm pretty sure he had nothing to do with Aquillo's murder. But now his ex-wife shows up dead. Hurston's the obvious link, but I ca—"

I was stopped short by Sequoia's hand on my arm. The human touch startled me into silence.

"Put your thoughts aside so you can eat in peace." He smiled gently and took his hand away.

The TV had gone to black, the credits rolling by in small white letters. I stared at my plate. After a minute or so, I picked up my fork again. I started to bring it to my mouth, then put it back down.

"I can't do that, put my thoughts aside. I need to figure this out. Two people are dead. This is important."

Sequoia nodded, considering my last statement.

"More important than nourishment?"

"Right now? Yes."

"Your mind is running in circles. You said yourself you've been thinking all afternoon. Maybe what you need to do is stop thinking."

"I don't know if I *can* stop thinking."

"You know why you can't stop thinking?"

"Because I'm being paid to work this case?"

Sequoia ignored my smart-alecky tone.

"No, that's not it. Your mind is running in circles because you're afraid. Seeing that woman's body today made you feel afraid and alone, and you think if you keep your mind running, you can escape your fear and loneliness."

The truth of his words hit me like a bull's-eye. I avoided his eyes.

"Tell me, Elizabeth, are your best insights the ones you figure out by running your mind in circles, or are they the truths that Spirit brings to you?"

"I'll have to think about that," I answered. When he frowned at me I said, "Just kidding, Sequoia."

At that he laughed, a generous, heartsome sound.

＃ 21

Sequoia stood at the sink, rinsing the soap from the last of the
dishes. He'd refused my offer of help, assigning me instead to
fireplace duty. Stepping over Nero, who was stretched out in
front of the fire, I tossed a eucalyptus log onto the dying em-
bers and prodded it with a poker. When I was satisfied it
would burn, I walked over to stare out the window, where the
rain was coming down harder than ever.

"When do you get your truck back?" Sequoia asked.

"They said they'd be processing it until tomorrow."

"You might as well stay here tonight. No point driving you
all the way down the mountain in this weather, especially since
you'll just need a ride back to the res tomorrow morning."

"That does make sense. Thanks for the hospitality." I continued to stare out at the rain, seeing in my mind's eye Nero's
growling charge at Wolf and how quickly the boy had drawn
his gun.

"Hey."

I turned to see Sequoia drying his hands with a dishcloth
and smiling at me.

"You're thinking again," he said.

"Yep."

He picked up something off the kitchen counter.

"Incoming," he said, tossing a missile my way.

I reached up and caught it—a cassette tape.

"That's what I use when I need answers," he said.

"Solo round-frame drumming," I read off the back of the
tape. "What is this?"

"It's a shaman thing. Best used with stereo headphones.
Keep it."

I packed the cassette into my purse.

"Thanks, I guess. So what more can you tell me about that
bad element on the reservation?"

"Not much. I don't know any of those kids. Sure didn't

think Wolf was messed up with them. That's sad news. I don't like what I see happening down the mountain lately. Dan Aquillo's the first murder I can remember on this reservation. Unless you count a couple of drunken fights over the years."

He kneeled down next to Nero in front of the fire and began to rub the sleeping dog's neck.

"Hey, enough of this cop stuff, okay? How about I tell you a story?"

I sat on the futon and smiled.

"I love stories."

"This is about my Aunt Christina. I think I mentioned her before."

"A couple of times. She's the *curandera,* right?"

"That's right. She was always teaching me stuff. One of the most valuable things I learned from her was how to rely on Spirit when I got afraid. It was a hard lesson, but one I never forgot."

"Tell me."

"This happened when I was a kid," he began, stroking the narrow space between Nero's eyes. "I was just on the verge of manhood—about sixteen, I think—and she made me spend the night alone in Diablos Canyon. There was all kinds of talk about how the canyon was haunted and so on. Stories about people who'd been killed or disappeared in there without a trace. So this was a scary thing. Aunt Christina taught me a chant to use and told me that no matter what happened, I must stay wherever I laid my head that night and trust in that chant, trust in Great Spirit."

"Dubious child-rearing tactics."

He ignored my jesting.

"I hiked into the canyon, and I found a spot under a ledge in a little gully. I didn't sleep for most of the night, just lay there with the stars and the night owls as company. Every little sound frightened me."

He paused here, eyes focused inward, remembering.

"Just before dawn I'd almost dozed off when I heard something right behind my head. I was too scared to move a muscle, laid there stiff as a board. I watched as two big rattlesnakes came crawling right into the gully, one on either side of me."

The mention of rattlesnakes brought back a traumatic childhood memory of a coiled rattler I'd inadvertently cornered in our garage. I could still hear the deadly buzzing of its tail. I stared at Sequoia and realized I was holding my breath.

"What happened?" I asked.

"I was scared, I'll tell you that. Shaking even. But I remembered what my Aunt Christina had taught me about contacting Great Spirit. I started to sing my chant. And you know, after a time I understood that those snakes wouldn't harm me. They were my allies. For the rest of the night, they lay beside me, listening to my song to Great Spirit. When the sun rose over the hills, they slid back into the brush."

He rolled up his sleeves and extended his forearms, displaying his snake tattoos.

"That's why I keep them with me today."

I studied the tattoos. They were beautifully rendered, with diamond-patterned skin and lifelike heads.

"So that's what those are about."

"Mm-hm. In the Native American tradition, animals play a big role in the spiritual path. We call it 'animal medicine.' When an animal comes to you, it has a message for you. Do you have an animal?"

"I don't know. I don't think so."

He frowned at that.

"You probably have one that's been hanging around, showing up. You just haven't noticed it yet. You might meditate on that when you go to sleep tonight. The snake is my sacred animal. It's like a guardian that reminds me I'm protected by Great Spirit."

I quoted Psalms.

" 'Yea, though I walk through the valley of the shadow of death, I will fear no evil' . . ."

"You got it."

Without warning, another memory came back. My own valley of the shadow of death—a strawberry field. Gunfire.

Three people down. McGowan in my arms, bleeding. Going into shock. Dying. I shook my head and snapped out of it.

"The Temecu Tribal Police have my guardian," I said dryly.

Sequoia looked puzzled.

"My gun," I clarified. "Both of them."

"Weapons are tools, not guardians," he said.

"Tool, guardian, whatever."

"Not the same." He wasn't going to drop it.

"My boyfriend once told me that guardian angels might protect my soul, but in the detecting business you needed a gun to protect your ass, if you'll pardon the expression. I think he was right."

Sequoia nodded, but his thick brows had come together in a questioning expression.

"This is the boyfriend who died?"

I was taken aback.

"Did Thomasina tell you that?"

"No, but you said you lost someone close to you. I'm sorry. That must have been rough."

"It's okay."

Sequoia looked at me like he didn't believe it was okay at all.

"Don't worry about your guns," he said. "You have strong guardian medicine."

I thought back to this morning's threat from Wolf:

You and your fuckin' dog are gonna get yourself killed if you don't stay away from here.

"Thanks for the positive thoughts, but I'll feel a whole lot better when I get my guns back."

Nero, sensing tension in the room, lifted his head. Sequoia gave him a reassuring pat.

"Your boyfriend had a gun the day he died, right?"

"Yes, he did."

Sequoia hiked his shoulders.

"Didn't protect him."

A curse was on my lips, and it was all I could do to hold my tongue. Pain tore through my heart, and I rose abruptly, knocking my purse off the futon. The bag tipped over, and its contents spilled with a clatter and roll onto the wood floor.

"I'm sorry," Sequoia said quickly. "That was a stupid thing to say. Forgive me."

He leaned down and righted my overturned purse. I squatted down to help him, grateful for something to do.

"I'm still a little sensitive on that topic," I said.

He looked at me tenderly. In that look I saw a fleeting resemblance to Thomasina.

"Who wouldn't be," he said.

He picked up the last few items scattered on the floor. One of them was the envelope I'd snitched from Aquillo's mailbox, the one from the Intertribal Gaming Consortium. He raised an eyebrow as he handed it back to me.

"You didn't have to steal that, you know." He winked to show he was being lighthearted about it. "I can give you mine."

He went to the kitchen and sifted through a basket of mail on the counter. When he returned, he handed me an envelope that was identical to the one I'd cadged from Aquillo's mailbox.

"It's a pledge for funds. The consortium's working to get Indian gaming on next year's ballot."

I opened the envelope and read the flyer inside. Just as he'd said, it was a request for donations. I frowned, puzzled.

"I thought gaming was already legal."

"There's a movement to limit gambling on tribal lands. The consortium's working to keep our casinos from being controlled by the state. I think just about everybody on the res got one of these. Probably not all that significant that Dan Aquillo had one of them in his mailbox."

I remembered the vibe I got when I was flipping through Aquillo's mail. The envelope had felt charged with energy. I'd had enough psi experience to trust my instinct about it.

"What if I have a hunch this envelope is significant?"

"You *think* it's significant, or you have a hunch it's significant?"

"Definitely a hunch."

"Then you better talk to Abel Rivers."

"Who's Abel Rivers?"

"The guy who heads the consortium."

Sequoia let out a yawn and began sorting through a stack of videotapes next to the TV.

"Hey, I'm talked out, and I'm sure you are, too. How about a movie?"

"Sounds good."

He selected tape from the pile and put it into the VCR.

We were about ten minutes into *Annie Hall* when the stress of the day caught up with me, and I began to have trouble keeping my eyelids open. I said good-night and retired to the loft, a cozy space with a generous skylight that must have been glorious on starry nights. I put my head on the pillow and stared through the glass ceiling, thinking about what Sequoia had said about animal medicine and guardians. Sometimes I saw animals in the stars: a ram, a bull, a lion, a goat. There were no stars on this night, however. I drifted into sleep seeing nothing but rain droplets, sliding like tears down the glass.

22

Rubio Valquez took my Glock and snub-nose 22 out of the Zi-plock evidence bags and passed them across his desk.

"Sorry about the inconvenience," he said.

"Hey, at least you didn't seize my dog." I checked the magazine—still loaded—and slipped the gun back into the holster strapped under my windbreaker. The twenty-two's rounds were still chambered, as well. I tucked it into the holster at my ankle. "I'll try not to park at a crime scene next time."

Valquez smiled and slid my truck keys across the desk.

"It's parked out back," he said.

Nero at my side, I walked out and around the building. The truck had been sitting in the sun, and the stuffy air inside had a sharp smell. The crime scene techs had done a so-so job of cleaning up. There were plenty of blue-gray smudges of fingerprint dust left on the dash. I started the engine, wishing that Sequoia hadn't said what he'd said about McGowan's gun not saving him. With a pit in my stomach, I realized that my guns didn't make me feel as safe now as I'd expected them to. I hoped that Sequoia was right about my having good guardian medicine.

I picked up my cell phone and called David's number. He answered with a curt hello.

"I take it you've heard about Natalie Hurston," I said.

"Yes, but I can't talk now. I was preparing a motion to dismiss charges against Bill Hurston, based on insufficient evidence and procedural violations. Then this freakin' disaster falls into my lap. I'm on my way to court now. Can you meet me outside the courthouse at noon?"

"Yeah, sure. Does Hurston know about Natalie?"

"Yes. I told him this morning. That could be what precipitated this disaster."

"What disaster?"

"I'll explain later. Sorry, I've got to run or I'll be late. See you noonish." The phone went dead. I started the truck and pulled out of the area-station driveway, heading west on Highway 76.

Twenty minutes later, I glanced at the directions in my lap. Sequoia had misplaced Abel Rivers's home phone number, but he'd sketched a crude map to the man's house on the back of the Intertribal Gaming Consortium envelope. Rivers's place was in Valley Center, a predominantly white community west of the reservation.

All traces of yesterday's storm were gone and in the bright morning sun the hills glowed like a frame from a Disney movie. I was traveling through one of the rare parts of the county that had escaped the developers. Acres of raw land stretched between spacious, ranch-style houses. The closer I came to Rivers's place, the more spacious they became. *Interesting,* I thought, *that a tribal bigwig chooses to live here, rather than on the reservation.*

I pulled into a long, sloping driveway and slowed as I approached the house. A man wearing sunglasses and an Australian sheepherder hat was emerging from a shiny black Cadillac in the driveway. The back car door opened and a little girl—about four from the looks of her—scrambled out. I pulled the truck alongside them and cut the motor.

"Good morning," I said as I climbed down from the cab. "I'm looking for Mr. Abel Rivers."

The man looked up. A gray mustache contrasted handsomely with his dark, deeply lined skin. The muscles in the man's face tensed.

"I'm Abel Rivers. Who are you?"

I stepped forward and shook his hand.

"Elizabeth Chase, a friend of Sequoia's."

The face muscles relaxed.

"And what's our young shaman up to these days?"

"Making fry bread and watching Woody Allen movies, last I saw."

Rivers laughed.

"I could have guessed."

I leaned down and smiled at the little girl. She was wearing a bathing suit and rubber sandals. In her hands she carried a small portable CD player. The headphone wires hung on her tiny chest like a necklace.

"Hi there. What's your name?"

"Caitlin. What happened to your nose?"

Kids. Such blunt little creatures.

"It bumped against something hard."

She giggled and, in a sudden attack of shyness, ducked behind Rivers's pant leg. He rubbed the shiny brown hair on her head and smiled at me.

"You one of Sequoia's students?"

"No, I'm a private investigator. I'm looking into . . ." I hesitated, not wanting to speak too graphically in front of the child ". . . this recent unpleasantness on the reservation. I have some very general questions, if you have a few minutes."

"I'm going swimming," Caitlin announced proudly. "Granddaddy has a pool."

I felt Rivers sizing me up—a woman in jeans, new hiking boots, and a new if slightly soiled cotton shirt—trustworthy-enough looking if you could ignore the bandage on the nose. He shrugged.

"You wanna come out back while I watch my granddaughter here?"

"Thank you. I'd appreciate that very much."

I followed Rivers along a brick path leading through a thicket of rhododendron to the rear of the house. Caitlin walked between us. She'd donned the headphones and was bobbing her head, singing with abandon to music only she could hear.

"Spice Girls," Rivers explained as he held open a gate for me.

I was vaguely aware of them.

"Man, I feel old."

"Wait'll you reach my age." He laughed easily, as if living to his age were a foregone conclusion.

Around back, a designer swimming pool, complete with lifelike boulders and a waterfall, was built into a south-facing hillside. Acreage stretched below, bordered on the east by a row of towering eucalyptus trees. Rivers and I settled onto chaise longues while Caitlin took off her headphones and rubber sandals.

"Granddaddy, watch!" she cried as she ran and jumped into the pool. Seconds later her gleeful face bobbed to the surface.

"No running, kiddo," Rivers reprimanded gently.

"This is a lovely place," I said.

"I've been fortunate," he said. "So what brings you to me?"

"I understand that Dan Aquillo was working with you on the Intertribal Gaming Consortium." This wasn't the exact truth. I was guessing he had worked with Aquillo.

"Yes, that's right."

"Did you know him well?"

His smile was half-sad, half-amused.

"I knew Dan from the time he was a little fellow, long before he became a casino big shot."

"His girlfriend told me he was like a god to some people because of all the amazing things he'd done for Temecu."

"He wasn't a god. But he was like family."

"Were you surprised when his life ended the way it did?"

"More like shocked. I'm still shocked. I can't imagine who'd do that to him. He was loved by this community. Especially after all he did for the tribe when he got back."

"Back from where?"

"Nevada. Danny was always ambitious. After school, he got fed up with what he called the backwards life on the reservation. Went off to Vegas in his early twenties. Took one of his sisters along. The two of them got jobs and learned about the casino business."

"His sister, Lucy, you mean."

"Yeah. Have you interviewed her?"

"Not officially. Sequoia introduced us."

Rivers grinned knowingly.

"Sequoia still got the hots for her?"

I smiled and shrugged.

"So when did Dan and Lucy move back to Temecu?"

"Oh, Lucy's been back for years. She was gone just a short time. Had a real brief marriage in Vegas, but her husband

passed away before her son was born, and she came on home.
Dan stayed on a while longer, but he'd been back . . . oh, at
least six or seven years now."

"Do you think Dan still had ties to Las Vegas that might
have a bearing on his murder?"

Rivers's graying brows came together, and he looked at me
through narrowed eyes.

"You mean like mob ties? I don't think so. Once he moved
back to the res, he put all his experience into getting Mystic
Mesa up and operating. He turned it into a heck of a profitable
enterprise."

"I understand that Dan and the new manager, Peter Waleta,
owned most of the business."

"Yeah, along with a few others."

"Including yourself?"

He brushed at a fly hovering near his face.

"I have a few shares. Nothing to speak of."

"Aquillo's shares passed on to Waleta when he died, is that
right?"

"I see what you're doing. You're following the money. Unfortunately, I don't think that's going to get you where you
need to go. I've known Peter Waleta since he was a kid, too.
Money's important to him, but it would never be more important than a friend. I don't know what happened that night, but
it seems to me Dan just underestimated Bill Hurston."

"Did Dan know Hurston?" I knew the answer. I just
wanted to see if Rivers did, too. Apparently so, because he
nodded.

"Oh, sure, from way back. Dan met the guy when he
started working in Vegas. Hurston was a high roller back then,
from what I hear."

"When was this again?"

"Oh, let's see . . ." He looked out at the pool, where Caitlin
was splashing her way across the deep end on a plastic sea
horse. He smiled at the sight. "Lucy came back to the res
when Luke was born. So that must have been the late seven-
ties or early eighties sometime."

"Luke?"

"Her son."

"She has two sons?" I asked.

"No, just the one."

"You must mean Wolf, then."

He laughed derisively.

"Oh, yes, I forgot. It's *Wolf* now." He rolled his eyes.

Clearly, Abel Rivers had an issue with the kid. Then I remembered Wolf's diatribe about gaming ruining the Native American people.

"I'll bet Wolf's not real crazy about your consortium," I said.

"Nope." Rivers took his hat off, ran his fingers through his thick, gray hair, and settled the hat on his head again. "The kid's got a lot of growing up to do."

Chances were excellent that Rivers didn't know about Wolf's recent run-in with the law. Although the story about the body discovered on the reservation yesterday had appeared in the morning newspaper, Natalie's name was being withheld until family had been notified. Wolf's name had been withheld because he was a minor.

"Sounds like you know Wolf pretty well," I said.

"Yes. Dan and I tried to talk some sense into the kid. I'm all for preserving Indian rights, but we can't battle the entire white culture without battling ourselves. We're too much a part of that culture now."

From the designer patio furniture to the custom pool to the satellite dish at the edge of the terrace, this appeared to be a family that had melded with the mainstream.

"So tell me about this gaming consortium," I said.

"Our intertribal group? That doesn't have anything to do with Danny's problems, hon."

Hon. How endearing.

"Probably not," I said. "I'm just curious what it's all about."

"Basically, it's just a bunch of us Injuns—" he looked over at me and winked "—putting our heads together to get this initiative on the ballot before Cowan and the governor shut us down."

"Cowan, the assemblyman?"

"The very same," Rivers said dryly.

"Why does he want to shut you down?"

"He and the gov are antigambling, period. But our strongest opposition comes from Las Vegas. Indian gaming in California cuts into Vegas profits by over a quarter of a billion dollars a year. There's a heck of a lot of people in Nevada who would like to see the Indian casinos shut down. So we're banding together to hang onto our rights."

"You said a bunch of you, meaning—?"

"Temecu, Pechanga, Viejas, La Jolla—so far we've got eleven tribes joined up. Our organization gets signatures, sits in on congressional meetings, stuff like that. Politics. Sounds exciting but when it comes right down to it, it's pretty damn boring."

"And you're the chair, huh? You always been the leadership type?"

"I got my Ph.D. from Stanford in political science, so yeah, I suppose this kind of thing has always interested me. Although Dan was the real power behind the Indian gaming movement. I'm just a paper pusher for the consortium."

"What did you do after you got your Ph.D.?"

"Law school. I was a labor-relations lawyer before I retired."

"How about that. I'm a Stanford grad, too." I looked at my watch. "We managed to get through fifteen whole minutes without our alma mater coming up. You know what they say—Stanford alums always have to drop the name within five minutes of meeting someone."

"Is that what they say?"

"Yeah. Pathetic thing is, they're usually right. Anyway, Dan was a fairly high-profile activist, is that right?"

"Very much so. He really galvanized this community to take action. Not just about the gaming issue. About land-use rights, preserving the culture, education—a lot of things. He's going to be sorely missed in this community, I can tell you that."

I heard some frantic cawing and looked over at the eucalyptus trees. Several black crows were swarming around one of the upper limbs. *A murder of crows,* I thought silently.

"Mind if I ask you a nosy question?" I asked.

"That depends on how nosy."

"If you're so concerned about Indian affairs, why don't you live on the reservation?"

"I did, for years. But I think it's time for our people to integrate into the larger culture. I'm an activist, not a separatist."

Above the trees I could now see what the cawing was all about. A huge red-tailed hawk was circling overhead, its outstretched wings tipping against the breeze. Suddenly the wings pinned back, and the bird began losing altitude at an astonishing speed. It dove straight for the eucalyptus where the crows were gathered. The crows dispersed in a burst of jabbering.

"So bottom line, Mr. Rivers, is that you believe William Hurston killed Dan Aquillo."

"I'm no judge or jury, hon. If you want more information, talk to Norm Clapp. He owns the old mine on Mystic Mesa Road. Just about everyone knows Norm. If there's something going on under the surface, he's the one who'll probably have heard about it."

23

The dive-bombing hawk was on my mind as I sat on a cement bench outside the San Diego Courthouse, waiting for David. I scratched Nero's ears and realized I'd been seeing a lot of hawks lately. Sequoia had said that animals could be viewed as guardians or guides. I wondered what hawk medicine meant and made a mental note to find out.

A human stream began to flow from the courthouse. Among the faces I recognized was that of Milton Coben, the deputy DA. I'd seen him briefly on the local morning news at Sequoia's, confirming that no charges had been filed yet in the Natalie Hurston murder. The prominent brow shadowing his eyes gave him a pensive look, even as he chatted amiably with his female companion. My first impression was that he was a decent guy and a dedicated prosecutor.

David came through the doors a couple of minutes later. From the look on his face, it hadn't gone well. He sat down, face flushed, too upset to say hello.

"I take it the judge didn't entertain your motion to dismiss," I said.

"It's worse than that." He let his head fall back and stared into the sky as if appealing to a higher court. "I can't believe they're going to let it in. There's no way Hurston's comments today should be allowed on record. They took this alleged statement without my knowledge, without my presence, and without legal permission."

"What comments? What's going on?"

He let his chin fall forward and slowly blinked at me.

"Hurston confessed."

I wasn't sure I understood.

"Confessed to what?"

"Confessed! To killing Aquillo. When he heard about the death of his ex-wife, he asked to speak with the police. I wasn't there, but supposedly that's when he burst out with this phony confession."

"What makes you so sure it was phony?"

David looked at me as if I'd just said something profane about his mother.

"The confession is inconsistent with the facts of the crime," he said stiffly.

"Let me play devil's advocate here. You've got Aquillo's blood on Hurston's clothes—"

"Hurston took off his clothes before he went to bed. They were piled in a heap on the floor when Aquillo's body fell on them." His voice was rising, and a couple walking past us on the courthouse plaza turned to look.

I paused, waiting for him to calm down.

"You've got Hurston at the scene of the crime with no alibi. There was no sign of forced entry. And now you've got a confession. I don't know, David, *inconsistent* is not the first word that springs to my mind."

"There's no murder weapon! They've checked the hammers being used on the area of the hotel under construction. No blood was found on any of them, nor were Hurston's prints. Coben is trumping up evidence that builds his case against Hurston, but he's brushing aside evidence that suggests another killer."

"What evidence?" I asked.

"You mean apart from the fact that the Mystic Mesa killings haven't stopped now that Hurston's in jail?"

"Let's stick to Aquillo, which is the case at hand. That's what the judge is doing."

"All right. Case at hand. There was no sign of forced entry, true. But only one card key was retrieved from Hurston, and hotel policy is to issue two."

"Hurston could have misplaced the other one," I said. "He was drunk, remember."

"We have shoe prints on the hotel-room balcony that clearly did not belong to Hurston. I knew about that. But now they've found hair in the room and on the body that belonged neither to the victim nor to Hurston. Fibers all over the damn place that did not belong to the victim or Hurston."

I was about to point out that one could expect that kind of evidence from a hotel room that had been open to the public, but I didn't want to rile him further.

"When did this new evidence come in?" I asked.

"Days ago, but did anyone tell me? Apparently these people have never heard of the Brady Rule. I'm supposed to be informed *immediately* when contradictory evidence turns up. I didn't see reports on the hair and fiber evidence until after Hurston blurted his false confession this morning."

I wasn't sure if David was as upset as he appeared, or if this was just part of his defense attorney game face. He looked back at the courthouse.

"The judge doesn't care," he said irately, "that she might be destroying the life of an innocent man."

"I know what Hurston would say to that. He'd say his life has already been destroyed. Face it, David, the man's given up on his life."

"That doesn't diminish the fact that if I'm right, the real killer remains at large. Her honor seems to be forgetting about that part."

"Since Aquillo's nephew was right there when I found Natalie's body yesterday, I'm sure the DA will be giving him a good, hard look."

"Hurston's taking credit for that murder, too."

"What?" Now my voice was on the rise. "How could Hurston have murdered Natalie? He was in jail."

"I doubt Coben or the judge is taking Hurston seriously about Natalie, but I don't want to assume anything. We have to move fast. With a crime this vicious, a jury gets emotional. They jump on a defendant like pack dogs and tear him apart."

"Is Hurston still in central lockup?"

"Yep."

"I want to talk to him. Will you hang onto Nero for awhile?"

* * *

The jail was a few blocks from the courthouse, so I walked over. As before, I checked in and was escorted to one of the seats in the narrow room behind the transparent barrier. When the prison guard led the defendant to the phone behind the glass, I was startled all over again. In just one week, Hurston looked like he'd aged five years. From his prominent skull to his bony hands, his body looked drawn, as if he were sinking into himself. I picked up the phone and got straight to the point.

"I thought you told me you were innocent."

"I'm sorry," he said. "I lied."

"No. You're lying now . . . and I want to know why."

He sighed, as if the very thought of responding to the accusation made him weary.

"You don't know I'm lying," he said.

"You told me to ask anyone. I believe your words were, 'I'm a failure but I'm not a killer.' "

He pondered that before answering.

"How do you know I wasn't lying *then*?"

"I'm psychic."

He gave a half-hearted laugh, thinking I was joking.

"People lie for one basic reason," I continued. "To cover ass. Theirs or someone else's."

He feigned shock.

"Are you always so vulgar?"

"You confess to ripping the skin off a man's head, and you're calling *me* vulgar?"

He looked at me closely.

"Pretty sure of yourself, aren't you?"

"About you, yes. I don't believe you killed Aquillo, and I sure in hell know you didn't kill your ex-wife."

"There's no way you can be certain of that."

"Sure I can. Not even a week ago, while you were sitting in your jail cell, I was jogging with your ex-wife on the beach. Natalie was as healthy as a horse. Do you even know how she died?"

The autopsy report had not been released yet, but I'd gotten the basics from Rubio Valquez that morning. Natalie

Hurston had been dead for at least forty-eight hours before her body was discovered. Cause of death was a .32-caliber bullet that had entered under her breastbone and lodged near her heart. A bullet that did *not* match Wolf's gun. There'd been a defensive wound where a bullet had torn through the webbed skin between her fingers.

"It doesn't matter how she died," he said. "I didn't mean that I killed her with my own hands. I meant that I was the one responsible for her death."

There was conviction in his voice this time, and it gave me pause. He sagged in his chair, looking more like a martyr than a killer.

"Natalie wasn't your biggest fan, but she didn't seem to think you were capable of murder."

He let out a joyless laugh.

"She always did underestimate me."

"Help me out here, Bill. I've been running my mind in circles trying to figure the connection between Natalie and Aquillo."

"Run no farther. *I* am the connection."

"And your motive to kill them would be—?"

"I owed both of them money and couldn't pay up. A radical credit-resolution plan, but there it is."

"Yeah, right." The skepticism in my voice egged him on.

"If you don't think that debtors fantasize about killing their creditors, you're a little naive, detective."

The gulf between fantasizing and doing was a big one, and I didn't believe Hurston had what it took to make that leap.

"I should think that you, as the debtor, would be the one at risk of bodily harm."

He brightened.

"Well, there you go. Another motive. I killed them before they could kill me. Call it proactive self-defense."

"Now you're being absurd. You and Dan Aquillo were old friends, weren't you? I hear you met back in Vegas."

"Friends?" He took off his glasses and rubbed his eyes. "Allow me to clarify. A casino operator is not a gambler's friend. Yes, I met Dan when he was a pit boss at Caesar's

Palace." He shook his head and put his glasses back on. "The eighties. Those were the good old days." The ember of a happy memory lit his eyes, but it died quickly, and he looked at me suspiciously. "How did Natalie know Dan and I were friends? She never even met him."

He'd assumed I'd gotten the information from his ex-wife. I let him go on assuming it.

"She told me you had a time-share in Vegas. Did you entertain Dan and Lucy at your time-share, or were you just chummy with them at the casino?"

He froze as if he'd just seen a ghost. I was about to probe the silence when he pointed to my face.

"You got a rhinoplasty in the middle of an investigation?"

My fingers found the bandage on my nose.

"Someone beat me up after I asked about you at Mystic Mesa last week. I suppose you masterminded that, too?"

For the first time he seemed to come out of himself.

"Who beat you?"

"He didn't introduce himself. Who knows? Maybe it was the same guy who buried your ex-wife. You wouldn't have any idea who beat me, would you?"

"No," he said softly.

If he was acting, he was doing a hell of a job. He looked genuinely concerned.

"Dr. Hurston," I asked sincerely, "what happened to you? Surely this wasn't the life you envisioned for yourself when you went to medical school."

He was counting the coils of the phone cord with his fingers again.

"You've never known a gambler, have you?"

"Not really."

"Find some. Talk to them. Talk to the gamblers at the end of the line, the ones who've wasted fortunes and lives. The ones who'll go right on wasting them because they have no choice. You'll understand me then."

His voice was filled with pain and remorse. It wasn't the voice of a cold-hearted killer.

"So you bludgeoned and scalped Aquillo to get him off your back about a debt. That's your story?"

"Yes. He drove me right out of my mind."

"And Natalie? You just, what . . . had her bumped off? A penniless, down-and-out gambler like you can pull those kind of strings?"

"Sure, why not? Don't forget how manipulative us gamblers can be."

I thought about it a minute.

"I don't think so. For one thing, the night of Aquillo's murder you'd called Natalie to apologize for the pain you'd put her through. Why would you bother if you were planning to have her killed?"

"Maybe I was apologizing for *that*." He sighed deeply and slipped his fingers under his glasses to rub his hollowed eyes again. "Look, I know you're trying to help me. You seem to really care, and I appreciate that. But don't bother trying to save my sorry soul. Just let it go. Let me go."

"The problem," I said, "is that if I let you go, I let the real killer go. You know that, and I know that."

He couldn't hold my gaze. He hung up the phone and rose abruptly, signaling to the guard that the interview was over. I slumped in my chair, feeling defeated. A deputy approached to escort Hurston back to his cell. I looked at his uniform and had to smile. Perched on the top of the deputy's badge, wings proudly outstretched, was a sterling silver hawk.

24

Once again my footsteps creaked on the old wood stairs leading to the Pony Express Mine and Rock Shop. I saw the video camera tucked under the eaves and waved as I walked beneath it. I commanded Nero to sit and stay on the porch. He complied with a happy dog smile, tongue hanging out of his panting mouth. I pushed through the door and called out:

"Hi, Norm!"

But when I walked in, Norm wasn't around.

"Hello?"

My greeting met with silence.

I walked over to the Native American display along the wall and searched among the dream catchers, kachina dolls, turquoise bracelets, and silver belt buckles, at last finding the little cardboard box I'd seen during my last visit. I opened it and shuffled through the animal medicine cards. Midway through the deck I found what I was looking for. The front of the card was printed with an exquisitely detailed drawing of a hawk. With broad shoulders and piercing eyes, it stared at me above text that read:

Messenger

Hawk is akin to Mercury, the messenger of the gods. Hawk medicine teaches you to be observant, to look at your surroundings. Observe the obvious in everything that you do. Life is sending you signals.

"Hey, it's you again."

I turned to see Norm standing behind the counter.

"Where'd you come from?" I asked.

"Doing some work back in the mine. Been chipping away at a little lode of tourmaline I found a few months ago."

"Do you always just leave the shop untended like that?"

"The shop wasn't untended. I got a monitor back in the mine. I saw you walk in."

"You're so high tech, Norm."

He had a smudge on his cheek, which made him look boyish as he grinned.

"You want to see the mine?"

I felt a thrill. I'd never been inside a mine before.

"Yeah, sure."

He motioned me behind the counter and opened the steel-reinforced door. I walked into the tunnel, which was dark and damp and smelled of earth. An occasional timber pillar supported the roof. I was intuitively aware of the tremendous pressure all around me but somehow standing inside the earth didn't frighten me. On the contrary, I felt an almost womblike security. The tunnel got narrower for a time, then widened again. Norm stopped at a rocky alcove lit by work lamps. A fan circulated the dank air.

"You've got electricity back here?" I asked.

"These lights work off a generator, same as the monitor there."

I looked up to a small screen that gave a bird's-eye view of the shop in front. Norm was right—you could see everything from here.

"Here's the lode I'm working on."

He tapped gently at what looked like plain old rock to me.

"How can you tell it's tourmaline?"

"That comes with experience." He picked up a drill from the floor of the mine. It looked like a high-tech version of my trusty cordless at home but with a much longer bit. "Here, mine yourself a chunk."

I found a niche and drilled. In a few seconds a nugget of rock came loose and fell to my feet.

"Wow, that's powerful."

"Diamond-bit drill," Norm explained. He reached down and picked up the nugget. "I think you've got some talent for this work. This is a nice piece." He placed it in my hands. "Keep it, it's yours."

"Thanks." Looking closely, I could see a greenish streak in the rock. "This fascinates me. I expect to see brilliant colors in the sky and garden, but the very crust of the earth comes in rainbow shades. Blows my mind."

Norm nodded, enthusiasm lighting his clear blue eyes.

"Shades you don't see anywhere else, sometimes. You sound like a miner, you know that?" He took the drill out of my hands and put it back into an oversized storage box near the wall of the cave.

"You need all that room for tools?" I asked.

"That's my millennium preparedness kit," he laughed. "I've got everything in there—water, canned goods, flashlights, batteries, you name it."

I looked further down the tunnel.

"How far back does it go?"

"Pretty far. There's a second entrance that opens out the side of the hill there. The mine extends another twenty-five feet beyond that. You ready to go back to the shop?"

"Sure," I said. "You first."

Norm led the way. Light from the working area receded and the tunnel grew dim, lit only by an occasional bulb strung overhead.

"So what brings you around Temecu? You one of Sequoia's students?"

The same question Abel Rivers had asked. I gave a similar answer.

"Not formally. I'm a PI, actually, looking into Dan Aquillo's death."

He laughed.

"A private cop, huh? I figured as much."

"Really? How'd you guess?"

"First thing you noticed was my security system. Makes you either a criminal or a cop. But you have that cop look."

"What look is that?"

He glanced at me over his shoulder.

"Like you've seen one shithead too many."

His remark made me sad, true as it was.

"You weren't fooled by my beguiling beauty?" My voice

was heavy with sarcasm. I was feeling anything but beautiful these days.

"Your beguiling beauty's got nothing to do with it. You keep your eye on the door and don't let people stand behind you. That's always a dead giveaway."

I was uncomfortable talking about myself and changed the subject.

"You used to be with the bureau. What's your take on the Aquillo thing?"

"Looks to me like that guy they arrested just lost it. But I'm not familiar with the facts of the case, and frankly I don't want to be. I turned in my badge years ago and haven't regretted it for a single day. I didn't know Aquillo all that well, personally. Of course he was quite a hero to the Luisenos, after coming back from Las Vegas and getting the casino built."

As we walked, I reached out to touch the wall of the mine. It felt cool under my fingertips.

"You think Aquillo still had ties to Las Vegas?" I asked.

"I think that would be a valid line of questioning. But like I say, I really didn't know the guy too well, personally."

"But you know his nephew, Wolf."

"Yeah, pretty well. He and his mom have been on the reservation a lot longer. She's been a fixture at the mission for years. Everybody knows Lucy. You want to know more about Aquillo, she's the person you want to talk to."

"She works at the mission?"

"Yeah. Real nice lady. She's had a hell of a time raising that kid without a father."

We rounded a bend in the tunnel, and I saw light ahead.

"You hear about the body they found on Aquillo's property yesterday?" I asked.

"Yeah, I heard."

"I was the one who found it. Wolf showed up while I was waiting for the cops. My dog charged him, and he pulled a twenty-two."

Norm turned around and frowned.

"That's not good at all."

"No. If the bullet in the body had matched Wolf's gun, it

would be even worse. I'm not sure what to make of it. Does he run with the kind of guys who tried to rob your place a few months back?"

"Not that I'm aware. He's involved in a political group, that bunch that's trying to shut down the Indian casinos. A gun, huh? That surprises me."

"Can you think of anything—maybe something you've heard—that might shed some light on these murders?"

"Nothing comes to mind. But if you give me your card, I'll keep an ear to the ground for you."

I pulled out my new wallet and handed him a card.

"A miner with his ear to the ground for me. What more can I ask?"

We'd reached the entrance back into the shop. I walked out to the display near the wall and brought the medicine cards over to the cash register.

"I'd like to buy these," I said, fishing a twenty out of my wallet.

Norm let out a hearty laugh.

"Another white customer falls prey to my Native American trappings. Sure you don't want a dream catcher to go with these?"

I could feel the color rising in my cheeks.

"Maybe I'll be back for a feather headdress next week, but no, just the cards today."

He continued to chuckle as he opened the cash register.

"That's not a bad idea, feather headdresses. I could probably make a bundle off those."

I held out my hand to collect my change.

"Thanks, Norm. For everything, I mean."

His eyes were a cool, clear blue, but the look he gave me was as warm as the desert sun.

"Don't mention it. Keep watching that beguiling back of yours, y'hear?"

"You know I will."

25

According to the large brass plaque that marked the entrance, the Temecu Mission had been built in 1816 by Franciscan missionaries with a zeal to convert the local tribe to Christianity. I remember reading somewhere that most of the labor had been done—under force—by the local Indians. I parked in front of the adobe compound, and Nero followed me across the rough brick walkway to the gift shop. Hanging from a rusted nail on the door was a sign reading "Be Back" and beneath that promise, a plastic clock. The clock's movable hands read four-thirty—ten minutes from now.

To pass the time, I took Nero for a walk. The adobe pathway wended under an arch and into a narrow courtyard between the shop and the church. A century plant graced the center garden, its three-foot, white-spiked blossom toppling over like a jester's hat. A statue of a serene Franciscan priest stood next to a fountain lined with azure blue Spanish tiles. Water bubbled gently from the center spout.

The pathway ended at the chapel. The enormous doors, made from thick planks of rough hewn wood, were closed. I pulled one of the massive wrought iron handles and poked my head inside. The interior was nearly black compared to the bright sunshine outside. In the dim light of candles flickering near the altar, I could see that all but one of the antique pews were empty. A woman knelt in the front row. I couldn't see her face, but from the back it looked like Lucy Aquillo.

I quietly backed out and closed the door. Shading my eyes from the glaring western sunlight, I retraced my steps to the gift shop. I found a bench beside the shop door and waited. At four-thirty on the dot, Lucy appeared. Her mind must have been elsewhere because she walked past without recognizing me.

"Lucy?" I asked.

She turned, a question in her face.

"Cokes at Norm's rock shop, remember?"

"Oh, yeah, of course. You're Sequoia's friend." She glanced at Nero. "Nice dog."

"Nice mission," I said, getting up off the bench.

She unlocked the door with a key she wore on a coiled plastic bracelet. It looked like a phone cord wrapped around her wrist. I thought of Bill Hurston, counting the coils like beads in a rosary.

"This mission's one of the area's oldest landmarks. Ever been here before?"

"No. I've heard about it for years. If I'd known it was this gorgeous, I would have visited sooner."

Lucy pushed the door open. I commanded Nero to stay outside.

"Ah, let him in," she said. "It's hot out there." Nero returned her sympathetic smile with a wagging tail.

An assortment of scents rushed to my nostrils as I walked into the shop. Leather, cedar, and something spicy I couldn't identify. A nativity scene made of china and another carved out of wood filled a shelf near the front window. Lithographs of the works of Native American artists shared wall space with traditional Christian images. They came together in a painting of an Indian Christ, complete with halo and long-suffering eyes.

Lucy walked around a glass counter and sat on a wooden stool near the register. Her loose cotton dress fell around her like a drop cloth on a living work of art. Her eyes were large and liquid brown, set above cheekbones remarkably smooth and wide. I could see why the guys fell for her.

"So are you and Sequoia dating, or what?" she asked.

I smiled, amused by how curious people were about my connection to Sequoia.

"He's related to one of my best friends in the whole world, Thomasina. I've been going through a tough time, and she thought Sequoia might be able to help me out."

"Has he been? Helping you out, I mean."

"Yes, very much so."

She nodded as if this didn't surprise her.

"He's a good guy."

Woman to woman, I sensed that Lucy had no sexual interest in him. Platonic affection only. Poor Sequoia. As for me, I was far too raw from my recent loss to have interest in any man.

"Tough times, huh?" she said. "What's going on?"

It took me a few moments to answer.

"Someone very close to me was killed," I said. I had mixed feelings about putting McGowan's death into words. On the one hand, it cemented a painful reality. On the other, sharing the fact somehow made that reality easier to bear. When Lucy nodded sympathetically, I remembered what Abel Rivers had said about her losing a husband years ago. And now only days ago, her brother Dan. "I guess you of all people know what that feels like," I added.

She sighed and lowered her eyes.

"This sounds old-fashioned, but I lean on God to ease my pain. It helps."

There was an awkward silence while I struggled with my own renegade thoughts about how leaning on God hadn't eased my pain nearly enough. Not that I didn't keep leaning.

"I'm sorry about your brother," I said at last. "I heard the man they arrested confessed to killing him."

She nodded, but said nothing. Whatever emotions she was feeling were hidden far from the surface of her smooth brown face. I wondered if she was hiding more than emotions.

"Do you think this man Hurston really did it?" I asked.

She shrugged her fine, strong shoulders.

"How would I know?"

"Someone said you and your brother had known Hurston for a long time. That must be awful, to have an old friend mixed up in this horrible thing."

"I've known Bill a long time, yes, but I don't know him well. I met him many years ago, when I was a waitress in Las Vegas. Never saw much of him, though. He was a weekend gambler."

She'd known Hurston well enough to call him Bill, I noticed.

"Did he seem like the kind of man who'd do something that vicious?"

She shook her head slowly from side to side, looking resigned.

"If he says he did it, maybe he did. Who am I to say? 'Judge not, lest ye be judged.' " The phone next to the cash register rang, and she reached for the receiver. "I've been praying for both their souls, Dan's and Bill's. Excuse me."

I listened as Lucy took the call. It was somebody asking for information. I heard her recite the shop's hours and give directions to the mission. As she talked, I busied myself with the knickknacks displayed at the counter.

I caught the words "thank you for calling" right before Lucy hung up.

"Were you looking for anything in particular?"

"Yeah, actually. I'm interested in hawk medicine. You know anything about that?"

"Not a whole lot. We've got some Zuni fetishes here, if that's what you're after." She pushed a basket filled with small, carved animals across the counter to me.

I sorted through the little animals—marble buffaloes, frogs and turtles carved from malachite, a swan made of quartz. I'd almost given up when I saw it—a bird fashioned out of dark brown agate. It reminded me very much of a miniature Maltese Falcon.

"Ah-ha," I said. "Just what I need." I turned it over and was shocked by the price sticker—thirty-two bucks. I handed over my credit card just the same.

"So you're into animal medicine," she said as she put the fetish into a blue cellophane bag. "You ought to talk to my son."

"Wolf's into this stuff, too?"

She nodded and ran my card through the register.

"That's not his real name, you know. His birth name is Luke, after my favorite book in the New Testament. So what does he do? Changes his name to Wolf."

I wondered if Wolf had told his mother about our encounter under the pepper tree yesterday. From her casual air, it didn't seem that she was aware of it or, in any event, aware that I'd been a part of it.

"How is Wolf?" I asked lightly.

"Don't ask." There was a tense silence as Lucy waited for the purchase to clear.

"What's the significance of wolf medicine?" I asked.

"Supposed to be about loyalty to Indian ways or something," she said as she handed me a pen and the credit card slip. "But I say he's more like a lone wolf, howling at the moon. I worry about my son sometimes."

It looked like she worried about him a lot.

"Teenage boys can be difficult," I said as I signed my name. I was hoping she'd elaborate, and she did.

"He's had a couple of run-ins with the law this year."

"Anything serious?"

Lucy frowned as she returned my card and handed me the cellophane bag.

"No, but he's so angry and political. He's got all these crazy ideas. Now he's caught up in that antigaming group. I don't like some of those casino-hating people."

Someone shouted outside the window, and we both turned to look. A red pickup loaded with teenagers was pulling to a stop along the road. Amidst a chorus of yells, a body leaped off the truck bed. The truck gunned it, fishtailing as it sped away. A moving picture of reckless youth.

"That your boy coming now?" I asked.

"Speak of the devil," she said.

Wolf burst into the shop like a gale-force wind, the fringe at the edges of his leather coat swinging as he walked. Nero jumped to his feet and began to growl. When Wolf realized who I was, his defiant face froze. After a shocked pause, he found his voice again.

"What are you doing here?" he said angrily.

"Luke!" Lucy reproached him with a stern look. "Where are your manners?"

I got the answer to one of my questions—she was obviously clueless about our encounter at Natalie's grave yesterday. He ignored her question.

"I need a ride to my meeting tonight, Mom."

Lucy shook her head.

"Can't tonight. I need the car. I've got bingo with the girls."

"Fuckin' bingo! What kind of bullshit excuse is that?"

I saw an opportunity and ventured into the fray.

"What time's your meeting?" I asked. "Maybe I can take you." A calculated risk, but one I felt I could handle.

Wolf cast a sideways glance at his mother, as if uncomfortable talking in her presence.

"You can take me now," he said.

I looked to his mother. "That okay with you, Lucy?"

"Sure, I guess so."

Wolf spun around and walked out without saying goodbye. When he was gone, Lucy gave me an embarrassed look.

"You see what I mean by angry?"

"It's a rough age," I said, motioning Nero to heel. "Good luck at bingo tonight."

"Thanks."

When I reached the door, I turned around to wave goodbye. She was looking out the window, watching Wolf, a dark look on her lovely face. I didn't blame her for worrying about her son.

26

Wolf was standing by my truck smoking a cigarette when Nero and I came out of the Mission Gift Shop. I walked over and unlocked the doors with my remote. He reached for the door handle.

"Not so fast," I said.

He turned and glared at me.

"New truck," I said. "I have a no smoking policy."

He rolled his eyes, sucked a long drag, and tossed the rest of his cigarette onto the white gravel parking lot.

"Thank you," I said. "I also have a no weapons policy. I need to see your jacket."

He turned to me with a wounded look, as if I'd offended his dignity.

"Fuck you." He said it quietly, sounding almost stunned.

"It's not like I'm being unreasonable here. You pulled a gun on me yesterday, remember?"

"I pulled a gun on your dog, man, after he attacked me."

"You and my dog are going to have to kiss and make up if we're all going to ride in this truck together. Please just give me your jacket so we can get on the road, okay?"

He removed the fringed coat, revealing angular shoulders and bony arms under a thin white T-shirt. Without his leather armor he looked almost fragile. No concealed weapon bulged in either his waistband or pant pockets. I took the coat and felt something heavy in the right pocket. I reached in and pulled out a good-sized Buck knife.

"Why the heavy weapons, Wolf?"

"Maybe I don't feel safe around here."

"You're safe with me." I held up the knife. "I'm going to hang onto this until I drop you off." I put the knife in my pocket and handed Wolf's coat back.

He shook his head in silent reproach. I led Nero over to him.

"Put out your hand," I said.

Nero sniffed Wolf's fingers. He didn't growl, but he looked like he was reserving judgment. I walked around and climbed in behind the wheel. Wolf got in the passenger side, the dog sitting between us. The air was hot and stuffy inside the cab. I rolled down my window and looked at Wolf, who was popping a stick of gum into his mouth.

"Did you kill Natalie Hurston?" I asked bluntly.

He stared straight ahead. The *W* tattoo on his left cheek lengthened and shortened as he chewed.

"I didn't even know the woman, man."

"I don't believe in coincidences. There's no way you just happened to show up at her grave yesterday morning with a loaded gun in your pocket."

"I don't have to talk to you. The cops already asked me all this shit. That's my uncle's property out there. If anyone's out of line, it's you, man. That's a special place you don't know nothin' about."

"I know a little," I said. "I know that tree is a Temecu landmark. Sequoia told me the branches were bent when it was a sapling, the limbs marking the northern boundary of the res. I get a really heavy vibe from that tree."

He looked at me intently.

"Who *are* you?"

"I'm a private investigator. I don't think Bill Hurston killed your uncle, and I'm trying to find out who did. What were you doing on his property yesterday, Wolf?"

"I was going to have a private ceremony."

"For your uncle?"

"For my people." He chewed his gum defiantly, but a slight tic in the muscle near his left eye gave him away. Wolf was afraid.

"What kind of ceremony?"

"It's personal and private, man."

"So you're saying you were there by total coincidence and have absolutely no knowledge of who killed Natalie Hurston, is that it?"

"That body was a total fucking surprise to me. I had no idea it was there, and I have no idea how it got there."

Some kids can't lie to save their souls. Some are pathologically good at it. I wondered if Wolf fell into this second camp because I found myself believing him.

I put the key in the ignition and started the truck. Maybe his lips would loosen up as we drove.

"Which way?"

"Make a right at the highway," he said. "I have to stop home and change before the meeting." Then, in the gentlest tone I'd heard from him yet: "If you don't mind."

We rode without talking for a few miles. I was waiting him out, hoping he'd find the silence uncomfortable. Finally, I was the one to break it.

"Why don't you feel safe around here?" I asked.

"It's not a safe world," he said easily, as if the answer were obvious. He pointed to the right. "Turn in here, right past this fence."

I braked, looking for a driveway. All I saw was a dirt road, hardly more than a bare stretch between sparse clumps of saltbush and tumbleweeds bleached white by the desert sun.

"Here?" I asked.

"That's what I said."

I ignored the attitude and followed the dirt road around a pile of boulders and past a tangle of sagebrush, stopping abruptly where it ended in front of a small house with a tin roof. I put the truck in park, and Wolf bailed out before I'd even stopped the engine. I parked, and Nero and I followed him across the sandy soil. When he heard my footsteps behind him, he turned and frowned.

"Where do you think you're going? Stay in the truck."

I let out a laugh.

"I don't think so, Wolfman. You ride with me, you treat me like a human being. *Capice?*"

He stared me down, and I wondered if he was hiding something in the house. When he could see that I wasn't intimidated by his puffed-out chest and hateful glare, he turned his back to me and walked to the small front porch. He tipped a cactus planter and retrieved a key, which he used to open the front door. I left Nero outside and followed Wolf into a small

living room furnished with inexpensive but tasteful pieces—
Montgomery Ward's best, in southwestern colors. A rawhide
rug stretched under a low glass-topped coffee table, where an
ashtray overflowed with Marlboro butts. The air was stale
with smoke.

He muttered something under his breath that sounded like
"out in a minute" and disappeared into the short hallway that
led to the rear of the house. I was restraining myself from emp-
tying the ashtray when I saw a business card with the Temecu
Tribal Police logo sitting on the glass tabletop. I picked it up
and recognized the name: Rubio Valquez, Detective.

An entertainment center cluttered with audio-video equipment and tapes dominated the far wall. I could see a few
books on the shelves and walked over to read the spines. *Joy
of Cooking, Webster's New Collegiate Dictionary,* and a King
James Bible. Remembering Lucy's comment about naming
her son after her favorite book in the New Testament, I pulled
the Bible off the shelf. It opened to the book of St. Luke,
where a color photograph had been wedged into chapter fifteen. The header at the top of the page read, "The Prodigal
Son."

The subject of the photo was a small boy. Though the child
was not more than four years old, I recognized Wolf immediately. It wasn't so much the blue-green eyes and brown skin,
but more the petulant slant of his eyebrows, even at that young
age. He was wearing a pint-sized pair of denim overalls, tiny
high-top sneakers, and a striped shirt. I looked at the page beneath the picture and read randomly from the text, Luke 15:4.

"What man of you, having an hundred sheep, if he lose
one of them, doth not leave the ninety and nine in the
wilderness, and go after that which is lost, until he find it?
And when he hath found it, he layeth it on his shoulders,
rejoicing."

I heard a door slamming and footsteps coming down the
hall. Wolf came out dressed in a beaded suede tunic. Most of
the Luisenos I'd seen dressed like Sequoia, favoring jeans and

T-shirts. Wolf was the only local I knew who regularly wore traditional Native American clothes.

I held up the business card.

"Did Valquez come here and interview your mom about your uncle's murder?"

"Kind of looks that way, doesn't it?"

"Is that a yes?"

"Yes-s-s." He drew out the S, turning his reply into a hiss.

Again the attitude.

"Must be pretty upsetting, the way your uncle Dan was killed."

He shrugged and leaned over to pick up the Marlboros off the coffee table.

"Some people think he had it coming."

I was shocked but tried not to show it.

"What people?"

"The people who think he betrayed his tribe."

"How did he betray his tribe?"

"I told you. He learned the white man's greed and brought it to our res with his casino."

"Are you telling me that you actually believe your uncle deserved to have his head ripped off just because he made it possible for people to play video poker?"

When I looked back at Wolf, tears had sprung to his eyes.

"I'm sorry," I said. "That was a little harsh."

"Maybe he didn't deserve to die, but he was messing with forces he didn't understand."

"What forces? Political forces?"

He rolled his eyes as if I'd asked the most moronic question in the world.

"No, unseen forces." He waved his cigarette at me. "Forget it. You wouldn't understand. Sorry, but you're just too white."

Nothing like being judged by the color of your skin. Not that I didn't notice color, too. I just didn't do it in the usual way. The colors I looked for were in people's auras. Sometimes the hues jump out at me without prompting, but most times I have to make a conscious effort to see them. A friend once gave me a page filled with multicolored dots of no particular pattern and told me that if I stared at it long enough, eyes slightly out of focus, a three-dimensional image would pop out. For me, reading auras is a little like that. I keep my subject in soft focus and soon the colors of the aura reveal themselves.

I tuned into Wolf's aura now and was surprised by what I saw. Where I'd expected angry shades of red, I saw only murky gray. Most auras radiate outward, like stars. The energy field around Wolf pulled in and down, like a black hole. I'd seen this once before, when I was a practicing psychologist. The aura belonged to a woman who confessed to me that she'd purchased a gun and several times had considered putting it in her mouth and pulling the trigger. She dropped out of therapy soon after that. A few years later I heard that she'd jumped to her death from the Coronado Bridge.

"Maybe I would understand about the forces," I said. "Try me. You might be surprised."

Wolf looked at me through wary eyes.

"I've had my share of experience with unseen forces," I assured him. "Which ones was your uncle messing with?"

"My uncle left our tribe a long time ago. He lived in the white world and when he came back he brought their sickness with him. People can't keep taking from the sacred tribe and the sacred earth, man. There's consequences for that shit."

"Consequences, meaning the forces of nature will get back at you?"

"Kind of like, yeah."

"Are you saying that you think the person who killed your uncle was being used as a vehicle by the forces of nature?"

"Maybe."

Something was being left unsaid, hidden deep inside him. I tried to find what it was in his blue-green eyes but saw only confusion.

"Who killed your uncle, Wolf?"

He shook his head and walked over to the entertainment center. With his back to me, he pawed through the CDs, making quite a clatter.

"I think Hurston did," he said. I could hear pain under the

tough-guy voice. "That guy's a walking, talking example of what can happen when you turn a deaf ear to nature's ways. It's pitiful, man."

"You know Bill Hurston?"

He nodded, which surprised me. His mom had said that she hardly knew Hurston at all. I presumed Hurston had spent most of his time in Temecu gambling at the casino—not a place an underage kid like Wolf would or should hang out. I didn't imagine it was a place Wolf had wanted to hang around, anyway.

"Where did you meet him?" I asked.

He turned back to me, a stash of CDs in his hand.

"He started coming around Ed's a couple years ago."

"Ed's."

"The restaurant. Used to come in and promise everybody he was never going back to the casino. It was pitiful, man. Then that white bitch would come in and tell him they missed him at the tables, and it would start all over again."

I cocked an eyebrow.

"Which bitch was this?"

"Trish somebody."

"The blackjack dealer?"

"You ask a lot of questions, man." He looked at the clock on the wall. "I gotta go. Meeting starts in twenty minutes."

27

We climbed back into the truck—a boy, a dog, and me.

"Mind if I listen to music?" Wolf asked.

I started the ignition.

"Why not? Go ahead." I was curious to hear what kind of music spoke to him.

Wolf popped one of his CDs into the dashboard stereo. As I turned onto Highway 76, the truck cab filled with the strong backbeat of gangsta rap and its rhythmic, rhyming profanity. It seemed odd that someone who so disdained the larger culture would respond to American pop music. Perhaps the language of disillusionment and despair crossed Wolf's barriers. Perhaps Wolf was more inculturated than he wanted to believe.

I'd been driving for ten minutes when Wolf turned the volume down.

"It's in that church up ahead," he said.

"What's the name of this organization again?" I asked.

"Citizens Against Gambling or something."

I nodded and turned into the blacktop parking lot. As I slowed, Wolf reached for the door handle.

"You can just drop me off here," he said. "I can get a ride home."

I parked in a spot near the back and cut the engine.

"I thought I might stay and hear what these guys have to say."

He shrugged.

"Suit yourself. Can you give me my knife back?"

I hated to turn it over, but it really wasn't mine to keep. I found the folded Buck knife in my pocket and passed it across the seat, hoping he wouldn't find a use for it. He scooped it out of my hand and hurried inside.

The sun had gone down, so I left Nero in the truck and joined the crowd filing into the building. The group was medium-sized, perhaps twenty-five people. Most of them were dressed down in jeans and casual shirts. Men and women were represented about equally, but the crowd was mostly white.

I stopped at the back of the room, where a laminated table was spread with dry-looking store-bought cookies, a cheap chrome coffeemaker, and Styrofoam cups. As I helped myself to coffee, a tall, middle-aged woman standing to my right talked heatedly to a man in a cowboy hat.

"It's exactly what we've been saying would happen. Two murders in the last two weeks. Now, you tell me that casino's not a harmful influence on our community."

The man in the hat stood with his legs slightly apart, hands thrust into his jeans pockets.

"No human involved in that first murder, anyway," he said.

I took a sip from my cup. The coffee managed to be bitter and watery at the same time. A white-haired man joined their conversation, gesturing with a densely sun-spotted hand.

"They're killing themselves out there now. Scrambling for each other's money. Serves them right."

If that was all there was to it, I wondered silently, *why had a white woman from the coast been murdered on the reservation?*

The man in the cowboy hat shook his head.

"I've been watching this country go to hell in a handbasket ever since I got back from Vietnam. Now the damn Indians are taking their profits and buying up all the property that rightly belongs to U.S. citizens."

Never mind that the U.S. had ripped the land off from the Indians in the first place.

He turned around midrant and noticed me standing behind him. "You a registered voter in this county?" he asked. His face looked familiar.

"Yes," I said.

"Like you to sign our petition." He reached for a clipboard on the table. As he offered it up, I noticed the way his stomach bulged against his plaid shirt. I looked more closely at his face.

"You work at the restaurant right outside Mystic Mesa, don't you?"

"I own that restaurant," he said proudly.

"You must be Ed."

"That's right."

"Has the casino hurt your business?"

"I can't say that it has, no. But what really burns me up is the goddamn place takes in millions every year and don't pay taxes on a dime of it. Where's the justice in that, huh?"

His flushed face demanded an answer. I shrugged without uttering a word, fearing anything I said might fan his flaming convictions. I thought about Wolf, the super Indian, and Ed here, the cowboy entrepreneur. Talk about politics making strange bedfellows.

"But us taxpayers have to keep up the goddamn road to the casino," he said angrily, "and pay for all the law-enforcement problems it's creating."

The tall woman chimed in.

"It's not even the taxes that bother me so much," she said in a shrill voice. "It's what they're doing to our natural resources." She spoke more loudly than was necessary, perhaps hoping those standing around would overhear. "Tribal casinos operate outside environmental laws. They can pollute all the air and water they want, and we can't do a thing about it."

This was hyperbole. The tribal government had strict environmental regulations of its own. At the front of the room, a ruddy-faced woman with broad hips walked to the podium and cleared her throat.

"We're about to begin, people, so please take your seats."

I handed the unsigned petition back to Ed and found an empty seat near the door.

"Is this taken?" I asked the clean-cut man sitting to the right.

"No," he whispered. "Have a seat."

"Good evening," said the woman at the podium, "and welcome to Citizens Against Unregulated Gambling. As I'm sure most of you are aware, we've got a very special guest speaker tonight. This man has served our district in all kinds of capacities for over twenty years. He understands this community; he understands our issues and our concerns. He's committed to preserving our environment, our economy, and a way of life that works for all of us. Ladies and gentlemen, Assemblyman Russell Cowan."

The room burst into enthusiastic applause.

With short, purposeful strides a pudgy man in a too-tight brown suit approached the podium. His red hair was thinning and cut in an old-fashioned style that emphasized the fact. He smiled politely at his audience and waved down the applause.

"Good evening, folks. We're gathered here tonight to address a situation that could have far-reaching consequences, not just for us, but for our children and our children's children. As you may know, the California Native American tribes are gathering together signatures to put the legalization of Indian gambling to the California voters. That means they can build casinos anywhere they want to, regardless of their impact on our great state. Now, I'm all for helping Native Americans . . ." he paused for a patronizing smile ". . . but what they're asking will have a dangerous impact, not only on our society, but on the California constitution itself."

I listened for the next ten minutes as Cowan laid out what sounded like an updated version of "the Red Menace." Across the room, Wolf sat low in his chair, arms crossed over his chest. When it was over, the man sitting next to me applauded as he rose to his feet. He was small in stature, with a well-formed physique and fresh-faced good looks.

"Hope you'll join us again," he said. He didn't fit in with the rest of the crowd. He exuded city-boy intelligence and ambition and dressed the part. He carried off his ensemble of loafers, chinos, and unstructured jacket with panache that communicated he was a player.

"We're meeting again in about three weeks," he said. "Meantime, here's some information about our campaign." He handed me a brochure.

I glanced at the flyer. The front was printed with a photograph of Cowan wearing a tight smile. *"We all want to help Native Americans,"* the letter under his picture began, *"but enacting flawed legislation is the wrong approach."*

He leaned toward me and lowered his voice.

"Listen," he said, "I overheard that ugly conversation at the back of the room tonight. I just want you to know, our campaign is not about bigotry. I work for Russell Cowan, and he's a really sweet guy." He held out his hand. "My name's Steven Hawking. And no, I'm not the world-renowned physicist or even related to him. But I do envy his brains."

He managed to be charming without being unctuous, a tough act.

"Do you know if there's anything to this talk that the Temecus are killing each other?" I asked.

He shook his head.

"No, I think that's just knee-jerk racism. Unfortunately our antigambling position does attract a certain bigoted element. I'm a third-year law student, working as an assistant on the assemblyman's campaign. The pro-gaming movement is unconstitutional, which is why I'm opposing it. I try to ignore the yokels in our camp. That's politics. Inevitably you have to join forces with people you don't entirely agree with in order to reach a common goal. Here," he said, reaching into his pocket, "give me a call if you want to know more."

I took the business card he offered.

Steven *Hawk*-ing. The four letters stood out like an omen. I immediately remembered the message on the medicine cards. *Observe the obvious.* I knew I needed to talk to this man.

"Thank you." I handed him one of my own cards. "Listen, I'd like to stay in touch." As he read the card, I explained: "I'm investigating those murders on the reservation. If you hear anything, call me, would you?"

He looked up at me with earnest hazel eyes.

"I'll do that."

I looked around for Wolf and saw him through the open door, heading into the parking lot. The assemblyman was stationed at the exit, shaking hands as people left the meeting. As I neared the man, I caught a faint whiff of his Old Spice cologne. He thrust his freckled hand toward mine, pumped it mechanically, and flashed me his practiced smile.

"Russell Cowan. Glad you could come. Hope you can join us again."

I stepped out into the parking lot. Behind me I could hear the assemblyman giving the very same treatment to the next person in line, like a fleshy robot. I looked around, but it appeared that Wolf had already left.

My cell phone rang on the drive home.

"I wish you'd carry a pager," David said. "I've been trying to reach you all day."

"What's up?" I said, slowing for a silver Porsche Boxter merging none-too-politely into my lane.

"Hurston's confession is sticking. This is going all the way now. The judge set a preliminary trial date. Time is running out. Do you have anything for me at this point?"

"Not yet," I sighed. So many leads, so few certainties.

"Well, I have something for you. I got my hands on Aquillo's will today and found out where his shares in the casino went."

"And?"

"Half went to his sister, Lucy. The other half went to the girlfriend, Trish Brown. Waleta didn't get squat."

I remembered the way Trish had averted her eyes when I'd asked her about her relationship with Waleta. Suppose Trish and Waleta were lovers? With Trish inheriting Aquillo's casino shares, that would give either or both of them motive to kill him.

"I think it's time you reinterviewed Trish," David said.

"I think a formal interview will put her on guard. I've got to cozy up to her somehow."

"I'll leave that to your subversive genius," he deadpanned. "Talk to you later."

I hung up and checked my watch. Nine-fifteen. I pulled into the nearest gas station to fill my tank and consult a battered Yellow Pages for the number of the Mystic Mesa Casino. The husky voice that answered my call assured me that Trish was working until two that night. My next call was to Thomasina.

"What are you doing tonight?" I asked.

"I'm in heaven. I'm reading that new Toni Morrison novel."

"Heaven can wait. It's time we had a girls' night *out*."

28

"There, you're done."

I breathed a sigh of relief as Thomasina finished painting my face with the last of what felt like twenty coats of makeup. I stared in the mirror and gasped. My long brown hair was gone, hidden under a smart blonde wig reminiscent of Princess Di. My nose bandage was gone, revealing features rendered unrecognizable by eye shadows, blushers, and lip paint. Gone were my beloved jeans and long-sleeved T-shirt, replaced by a form-fitting, sequined, white minidress that made me look cheaper than a plastic cup. But what did me in were the shoes—four-inch white spike heels. I turned around to check the view from the back. It was even more alarming than the front.

"I don't know about this. I feel like Elvis in drag. Where do you *find* this stuff? These shoes are obscene."

Thomasina laughed—with me, or at me? I wasn't sure.

"The shoes double as weapons," she said. "Here, give me."

She leaned down and held her palm out. I wriggled out of one of the pumps and placed it in her hand. She thrust the stiletto heel close to my face and gave me an evil grin.

"That'll put an eye out, don't you think it won't."

"Be that as it may . . ." I let the sentence drift as I donned my leather bomber jacket, which was a little bulky around the hem due to the semiauto tucked in a holster I'd sewn into the lining.

"No way," she said. "That jacket completely ruins the look."

"Tough. If I'm going to the game rooms in that casino, I'm not going unarmed. Last time I did that, my face was beat in. Talk about a ruined look."

I checked my weapon, making sure the clip was locked in tight and the chamber loaded. Once again I remembered what

Sequoia had said about McGowan's gun not saving him. Thomasina caught my anxious look.

"Don't worry, Elizabeth. Even I wouldn't recognize you. Nothing's going to happen. We're just a couple of nice girls out for a good time."

I glanced enviously at Thomasina's siren red dress, which looked downright subdued next to my sequined monstrosity. Maybe it was the way she carried herself—shoulders back, head held high on a long, elegant neck. I smiled at my friend. It was good to be with her.

"You look like a nice girl, anyway. As for me . . ." I turned to view my body in profile and sighed.

She pulled me away from the mirror.

"Come on, get over yourself. We've got work to do."

We took Thomasina's BMW 323i, a recent purchase. I'm not one for fancy cars, but I have to admit that the ride was smooth and quiet as Thomasina negotiated the winding road to the reservation.

"So," she said, "we're looking to make nice with the victim's girlfriend tonight. What's her name?"

"Trish Brown. A pleasingly proportioned blonde."

"Ah. Trish, the Dish."

"When I interviewed her a couple days ago, she failed to mention that her murdered boyfriend left her his shares in the casino. She also got defensive and squirrely when I brought up the subject of her boyfriend's partner, Peter Waleta."

"You think something's going on between Trish the Dish and the murdered guy's partner, is that it?"

"It's crossed my mind." I looked for the moon outside the car window but couldn't see it. "Maybe that's what Rosemary meant by Trish not treating Dan with enough respect," I added, more to myself than to Thomasina.

Thomasina looked me over from my wig-covered head to my spike-pump-clad toes.

"So if Trish had something to do with you getting beat up after your last trip to the casino, your costume is pointless."

"She wasn't even there that night. It's Waleta I'm worried about. If anyone sent someone after me, it most likely was him."

Thomasina tensed her brows and focused on the road ahead.

"Where'd your incident happen, anyway?"

"You mean the tire blowout and one-two punch?" I looked out the window. The climbing road was leveling out, approaching the mesa. "Right about here, actually."

"Anyone tries that tonight, they're going to have to deal with me."

"God help the sorry suckers."

The glow of the dashboard gave off just enough light for me to see Thomasina's eyes sparkling in the dark.

"You're in a lot better shape than the last time I saw you," she said.

"Yeah, Sequoia really worked wonders on my face."

"Not just your face. Inside. I think it's been good for you to get back to work. It seems like you're getting to the other side of your grieving over McGowan's death now."

"I just hide it better these days," I said.

She reached across the seat and gave my hand a squeeze.

"Has Sequoia been any help on the res?" she asked, gently pulling her hand away to negotiate a turn in the road.

"He made a couple of interesting introductions for me. Tell me about you guys. How close were you growing up?"

"Not close in terms of how much time we spent together, but we've always been tight. As little kids we used to play together at the spring powwow the family had every year in Temecu."

"So how are you and Sequoia related again?"

"We had the same great-grandfather, remember? That picture I showed you of Night Cloud. He was a full-blooded Luiseno. He died when we were real small."

"I still don't quite get how you and Sequoia are second or fifth or tenth cousins or whatever you are."

Thomasina chuckled.

"Second cousins. Night Cloud married my great-grandmother, Shoshena—a black woman. I've heard different versions of how they met, but in any case their marriage was a major scandal. They had two sons, Samuel and William.

Samuel married into the Temecu tribe—he's Sequoia's grandfather. William married into an African American family—
he's my grandfather."

Thomasina paused as she dimmed her lights for an oncoming car.

"We still have our spring powwows with the Temecu side
of the family. Our family got integrated long before it became
the thing to do."

"It must feel like walking between two worlds," I said.

"Funny you mention that. I often think that way about you,
how you walk between two worlds, the seen and the unseen."

"It does feel that way."

"You and Sequoia both. He calls it the shaman's way."

The term sounded too lofty to describe me.

"I'd hardly call myself a shaman. This is our turn, right
here."

Thomasina spun the wheel, and the BMW glided onto
Mystic Mesa Road.

Minutes later we pulled into the circular drive in front of
the casino. Thomasina flirted shamelessly with the valet as we
got out of the car. We walked into the place with about a million eyes on us. I leaned over and whispered in her ear.

"Great idea, buddy. I've never felt so inconspicuous."

"It's called hiding in plain sight. If anybody's looking,
they're looking for a sensible brunette, not a flashy blonde. If
you can avoid waving your PI license around and just be cool,
this will be simple."

"Yeah, as long as I don't get arrested for hooking."

We made our way into the blackjack room, and I scanned
the tables. I pointed my chin toward a game table near the bar.

"That's her, over there."

Trish stood in the pit, shelling out cards and wearing a
bored expression. She looked more like a showgirl than a card
dealer tonight. Her blonde hair was piled artfully onto her
head, playing up her large blue eyes. Her ample body was fit-
ted with a dress that emphasized every generous curve.

We wandered over and waited for a couple of seats to open

up. After a few minutes an elderly couple left, and Thomasina and I slid in to fill their seats.

"You look great tonight," I said to Trish as I sat down.

"Thank you," she answered in a perfunctory tone. She obviously didn't recognize me yet.

The cards flew onto the table, and the betting began. Unlike the other night, I had no idea what would happen next. I tried to get a sense of who'd win and lose, but my hunches had gone AWOL. Within ten minutes I was down forty dollars. I hated the feeling of losing, and it was all I could do to stay seated.

A skinny man with a pointed goatee and sharply pointed sideburns to match wheeled a locked steel box up to our table. The action stopped while he collected Trish's cash. As he worked, I studied her. Was it possible that she and Peter had conspired to murder Dan? I tried to get a sense of what she might be hiding.

As if feeling my eyes on her, Trish looked over at me and smiled.

"You guys having fun?"

"I sure am," Thomasina said. "Can't work all the time."

"What do you two do?"

"I'm in public relations," Thomasina said. "Not a bad job, but not as exciting as hers." She nudged my arm. "My friend here's a psychic."

Trish glanced at me dubiously, taking in my sequined dress and overdone makeup.

"Oh, yeah?" she said, her tone mildly amused. Then she did a double take on my face, her eyes going wide. "Hey, I know you."

"I was wondering when you were going to recognize me. Did you mean it the other day about needing a psychic reading? I get the sense you have a heavy load on your mind."

"I thought you were an investigator." There was caution in her voice. "You're really a psychic, too?"

"Obviously not an infallible one," I laughed. "I just lost forty bucks here." She smiled and I felt her relax.

The play started up again. I began winning more often than

not. As if we were the two sides of a single pair of scales, Thomasina started to lose. Before the house cut too deeply into my friend's stash, the play stopped and Trish signaled for a replacement. When Trish stepped back to let the new dealer in, Thomasina and I tossed in our cards.

"Leaving so soon?" Trish asked me.

"Quit while you're breaking even, I always say."

She glanced at my sequined frock, one pale eyebrow arched high.

"Love your dress."

"Really? You don't think I look like RuPaul?"

At the mention of the famous transvestite, she let out a laugh.

"I met her once, you know."

"*Her*?" Thomasina asked.

"Him, whatever. I've got a picture if you don't believe me."

"No way," I said. "Really?"

"Come here, I'll show you."

She led us to the bar and pulled a black-framed photo from the wall. Sure enough, the lovely RuPaul towered over Trish, with one long arm around her shoulders and the other around the shoulders of Dan Aquillo.

"Who's that?" Thomasina asked, pointing to Aquillo.

"That's Dan," she said, the smile leaving her face.

"Where was this taken?" I asked.

"Caesar's Palace. We went back for a long weekend last year."

Thomasina was staring at the photo.

"RuPaul! That's so cool. You must meet a lot of famous people in this business."

"More like infamous," Trish said. "Bunch of sociopaths, a lot of them." She hung the framed photo back on the wall and turned to me. "So you'll really give me a reading, huh?"

"Sure, if you want one." I kept my tone nonchalant.

"I'd need this to be completely confidential."

"Of course. I use the astrological chart in my readings, so I'm going to need your exact birth date. If you know the time, that's even better."

She reached behind the bar for a pen and a cocktail napkin and was writing her birth data when a man called out her name. The three of us turned to see who'd spoken. I recognized the linebacker-sized frame of Peter Waleta. His eyes locked on Trish, and he gave no sign of recognizing me.

"The number 9 table is unmanned." His tone was harsh and scolding.

"In a minute." Trish's tone was equally abrupt. She pushed the napkin across the bar to me. "Can we do this tomorrow morning, say nine or so? I start work at noon. You remember how to get there, right?"

I folded the napkin into my purse.

"Right. I'll see you tomorrow at nine."

29

The next morning I turned onto East Washington Avenue and chewed my lip, realizing that I might have to do my interview without the benefit of background information on Trish. I could do the astrological reading with just the birth chart, of course. But I'd been hoping for some down-to-earth data to guide my questioning. Just as I was approaching her neighborhood, my car phone rang.

"Patricia Ann Brown," Joanne began without saying hello, "also known as Trish Brown, was born in San Antonio, Texas. Maiden name Ford. Arrested at the tender age of twenty-one for bad-check writing."

Joanne, high up on the food chain in the world of consumer finance, has access to the kind of databases most people don't even know exist. In her constant press to cram more than humanly possible into each twenty-four-hour period, she's dropped niceties like "hello" and "good-bye" from her repertoire. Those who can't take her abrupt friendship style fall away; those of us who value her directness hang in. Joanne's an armchair detective and gets a huge kick out of helping me in my exploits, but I used her so often during my last case that my guilt finally reached critical mass. She's now on my payroll.

"Otherwise, she's a perfectly good girl, as far as public records go. You see that in her chart?"

I pulled to a stop and waited for a green arrow.

"Matter of fact, I do."

"I love it when you can give me the birth date with the name," Joanne said. "Lets me hack into all kinds of interesting stuff."

"You hacked for this info?"

"More like breached protocol, but you didn't hear that."

I slowed in the eighteen-hundred block and pulled to a stop in front of Palm Vista Apartments.

"Hear what?"

She laughed and we signed off.

Spaces were scarce along the street, and I had to park down the block. A portable sprinkler was watering one of the lawn's bald spots. Once again I climbed the outside stairs to Apartment 207. I rang the bell and waited. Below me, a compact, middle-aged man was walking past the pool. From my perch on the balcony I became fascinated with the circular bald spot on the top of his head. I heard the door open behind me.

"Good morning," Trish said. "Come in."

"How are you?" I said as I stepped inside. There was no odor of Italian food today, just the faint traces of a chemical disinfectant. An upright vacuum cleaner stood in the middle of the living room. Trish, clad in pink sweats, closed the door behind me.

"Sorry I'm not dressed," she said as she ushered me in. "Doing some chores, and I don't dress up for that."

The room was dark, save for a weak lamp in the corner. I took a seat on the sturdy plaid sofa and pulled her astrological chart out of my handbag. She stood before me clasping her hands, as if she weren't quite sure what to do next.

"This is great that you could come today."

"Hope I can help," I said.

She crossed her arms over her chest and went to the window. The curtains were already drawn, but she pulled them together so that even the sliver of light between them disappeared.

"I've never been to a psychic before," she said.

"People often feel the need after they've lost a loved one."

She maintained her position at the closed window.

"It's not that. Well, it sort of is. I've got something eating me up inside."

My spirits rose at the prospect that whatever was troubling her might lead to a break in the case.

"Why don't you have a seat," I suggested, "and we'll get started."

I placed her chart in the center of the coffee table between the two candleholders. With uncertain steps, Trish walked over and sat down.

"Can we light one of these candles?" I asked.

"We can light both."

She found some matches and ignited the wicks of the long, blue candles. The darkness of the room receded a bit, and I felt myself breathe easier. Not magic—just the comfort of ritual. I said a silent prayer, asking that whatever transpired here would be in the service of the highest good. When I looked up, Trish was watching me.

"You're not religious, are you?" she asked warily.

"Depends on how you define religious." I leaned closer over her chart and studied where the planets had been on the day of her birth.

She stared at the zodiac wheel with uncomprehending eyes.

"So that's my birth chart, huh? What are all those red lines?"

"I'll get to that in a few minutes," I said.

Trish's anxiety filled the room. For a psychic reader, dealing with that kind of energy can be like trying to fly a plane in high winds.

"I want you to get comfortable," I said. "Sit back and take a deep breath. I'll be able to help you more if you relax. Imagine you're surrounded by peaceful, loving white light."

"Oh, shit. You are religious."

She was so mortified at that prospect that I had to laugh.

"Just shut up and do it, okay?"

She sat back and sighed heavily.

"When someone comes to me for a reading," I continued, "it usually means they're at a crossroads in their life. Is that true for you?"

"I don't get what you mean."

"You're at a choice point. A place where the decision you make today could have a profound effect on your future."

"Yeah, you're right, now that I think about it."

I was studying the chart, looking for a place to begin, when she blurted out:

"I don't know what the right thing to do is."

The muscles in her jaw worked silently. I waited several

moments, giving her a chance to articulate whatever it was that she was chewing on. In the end, she decided not to share it.

"Why don't you let me read what I see here and maybe the answer will come to you." I looked at the part of the chart that had interested me from the moment I'd seen it. "I see a complicated love life," I began.

Her pretty blue eyes widened.

"How can you tell that?"

I'd already suspected a romance between Trish and Peter Waleta, and now I saw supporting evidence of it in her birth chart.

"Right here," I said, pointing to the lower-right quadrant. "You have four planets in Gemini, two of them in the fifth house of romance. I'm seeing more than one lover."

Her eyes darted from the chart to me.

"What else do you see?"

"First, tell me about your lovers. There was Dan and then . . . who's this?" I pointed to the second planet in Gemini.

She bit her lower lip.

"I'm afraid that if I say what I'm thinking and I'm wrong, it will hurt innocent people."

I nodded in what I hoped was a reassuring gesture.

"The facts are friendly, Trish."

"What?"

"It's a slogan I like to use when I'm afraid to look at difficult situations in my own life. It means that whatever is, *is*. Avoiding reality—even if it's an unpleasant reality—rarely makes a troublesome situation go away. Facing the facts is the first step to solving the problem. Ergo, the facts are friendly."

She wasn't comforted but looked even more unhappy.

"Can't you just tell me what to do?"

I shook my head.

"I can tell you what I see, but I can't tell you what to do. A reading isn't about getting answers from outside, Trish. The answers must come from within you. Is there something you want to tell me about these men in your life?"

She stared at the carpet and nodded.

"It has to do with—" She put her fingers to her mouth and shook her head. "This is confidential, right?"

"Right."

"I think Peter might be involved in Dan's death." She looked up and added, "Peter Waleta, his partner."

"What gives you that idea?"

"Dan and I had dated on and off for years, I think I told you that. Well, during some of those off times, Peter and I had been together. But that was history, I swear it was. Anyway, someone had started a rumor that I was seeing Peter again behind Dan's back. It wasn't true. That's what Dan and I were arguing about in his office that night."

"What argument?" I asked.

"I saw Dan in his office that night, after my shift ended at eleven. I didn't want to tell the police, for obvious reasons."

"Did you work it out?"

"No. We were in the middle of it when his phone rang. Dan took the call and when he hung up, he walked out. That's the last time I saw him."

I remembered the hotel phone record from Hurston's room and the call made to Aquillo's office at 11:30—shortly before the murder.

"Did Dan say who was on the phone?"

"No, he just said something had come up at the hotel and he had to go. After he left, I went to talk to Peter. I wanted Peter to tell Dan that the rumor wasn't true."

"You told me earlier that Dan and Peter worked well together."

"They did. You've got to understand, we'd all known each other for years. I mean, Dan and Peter knew each other as kids, long before Dan met me in Las Vegas. They respected each other. At least I thought they did."

"But?"

"That's what's troubling me. After I talked to Peter that night, he went to the hotel to work it out with Dan. I didn't tell the police about that either. I mean, I didn't want them to jump to the conclusion that Peter killed Dan."

Geminis are notorious liars. Looking at the preponderance

of Gemini planets in Trish's chart, I couldn't help but wonder if she was fabricating this story. I thought back to the harsh exchange between Trish and Peter Waleta the night before. The part about the phone call from the hotel to Aquillo's office jibed with the phone record. But suppose Trish were making up the part about Peter Waleta? That would make her the last one to see Aquillo alive.

Rather than confront her, I moved on with her reading. I didn't give her answers but did give her some insights, like the job change I saw in her near future. When I was through, she offered me a check.

"No," I said, "this one's on me. I do hope you'll consider telling the police what you told me today."

"I'll think about it," she said. "Just talking to you has made me feel much better."

We rose and she led me to the door. I stepped onto the cement balcony and looked down at the pool. Dozens of shefflera leaves had sunk to a greenish-brown heap on the bottom, giving the courtyard a decaying look.

"Thanks again," she said.

I turned back as she was shutting the door.

"Let me just leave you with this," I said, and she poked her head out again. "The most valuable thing you have is your word. In the end, our words and actions are all any of us take from this life. Choose them wisely."

"Okay, I'll do that." She sounded so sincere. Geminis are good at that.

30

The Temecu Reservation Area Station, a flat-roofed, cinder-block structure desperately in need of landscaping, was not an attractive building by any stretch. Still, it looked a lot better to me now that I was walking into it a free woman rather than under arrest.

Rubio Valquez was reading the newspaper when I approached his desk. I felt a touch of envy. Between my late girls' night out with Thomasina and my morning appointment with Trish, I hadn't had time to read my own paper. I took the chair in front of him, where I'd spent the entire afternoon the day Natalie Hurston's body had been found. He looked up, a puzzled expression on his face.

"What brings you back?"

"How would you feel about comparing notes on the Aquillo-Hurston case? I'm not getting anywhere."

"Don't know how much help I'm going to be to you. I'm just a lowly tribal cop, you know. I can process drunks and barking dogs, but if it's something interesting, like homicide, well . . . that goes to Milt Coben and the San Diego PD."

"Do I hear a touch of sour grapes?" I asked.

The crows' feet at the corners of his eyes wrinkled in amusement.

"Na, not really. We don't have the resources to do an investigation like that. I'm just a little jealous, is all." He picked a card up off his desk and handed it to me. "That's the SDPD detective in charge of the Aquillo case, if you want to give him a call."

I memorized the name—Karl McKenna—and handed the card back.

"No, Detective Valquez—"

"Call me Rubio, please."

"No, Rubio, I don't want to talk to the SDPD. I want to talk to you. I think you're more likely to know what's going on around here than the city cops."

A lot of small-town detectives would have let that get to their egos. Not Valquez.

"I'll give you what I've got," he said with a shrug.

"Let's start with the Aquillo murder. What do you make of that? Honest opinion."

"I think they're on the right track with Hurston. From everything I've learned, he and Aquillo went way back, met in Las Vegas twenty-some years ago. That's a lot of history. Friendships that old are like marriages—things can look fine from the outside, but inside all hell's breaking loose."

"And what about Natalie Hurston?" I asked.

"That's a toughie. We got a soil match between the grave and the shovel in the tool shed at Aquillo's, but no prints off the shovel or the body to link Aquillo's nephew or anybody else to the crime." He narrowed his eyes. "Can you keep something under your hat?"

"Sure."

"We found Natalie Hurston's Volvo at the bottom of a ravine about a quarter mile off-road from Aquillo's place. When we questioned the family, her sister told us that Natalie had mentioned she was going out to Aquillo's to pick up some valuables Hurston had given to him as collateral for some bets. A Rolex or something."

"You mean Natalie met someone out there?"

"Looks like it. Who she met, nobody knows."

"What about the bullet that killed her?"

"Couldn't trace it."

"Have you found any link between the two murders?"

"Only Hurston, who's taking credit for them. I'm sure you're aware of that." He chuckled. "You picked yourself a hell of a defendant."

"I'm loving the challenge," I said sardonically. "I talked to Aquillo's girlfriend, Trish Brown. I guess you have, too."

"Several times."

"She doesn't think Hurston's guilty. Did she tell you that?"

"Nope. She limited her comments to yes, no, and I-don't-know. Don't think we haven't looked real hard at her."

"And?"

"She was dealing blackjack the night of the murder. She went home when her shift ended at eleven o'clock, a half hour before Aquillo's earliest estimated time of death."

"What if she didn't go right home?"

"That would contradict the testimony of the night manager, Peter Waleta."

I decided to keep Trish's confession about her fight with Dan confidential. For the time being, anyway.

"Speaking of Peter Waleta, what about him?"

Valquez turned the page of his newspaper.

"Oh, we turned Waleta inside out. He made the call to 911, and we always look at that person the hardest. He's clean. First of all, his employees stated that he was on the job at the casino all night. Second of all, a lot of witnesses remember him wearing the same clothes all night. Those clothes came back from the lab without a microdrop of blood on them. If you'd seen that crime scene, you'd know how impossible it would have been. Whoever killed Aquillo got messy. Third, Waleta agreed to a lie detector test and passed it with flying colors."

"He wouldn't be the first killer to do so."

Valquez frowned. "I saw Waleta at the scene. He was broken up. He and Aquillo had been friends since they were little kids."

"You said yourself that old friendships are deceptive from the outside. I also know they dated the same woman."

"Trish Brown, you mean. We grilled him about that. Waleta said it was old news, and the girlfriend said the same thing. I just don't see Waleta as the doer, myself."

"How do you see Aquillo's temperamental nephew?"

"Who, Wolf? We've got several witnesses who say he was playing billiards at Ed's on the night of the murder."

"What witnesses? His thug friends?"

Valquez let that one pass.

"As for the gun he pulled on you at the Natalie Hurston crime scene, the ballistics didn't match up."

"Believe me, I remember."

We lapsed into a thoughtful silence. After a few moments, I stood to go.

"Speaking of Ed's, how about some lunch?"

Valquez looked at his watch. "It's only quarter past eleven. Thanks anyway, but I'd better stick around."

"So not only are you humble, but you're dedicated as well."

Valquez grinned and returned his attention to his newspaper.

"Actually, I'm just not hungry yet."

"If anything else comes up, will you call me?"

"Sure. You got a business card?"

I rummaged in my purse in search of my business-card holder.

"What earth-shattering news is the *North County Times* reporting today?" I asked as I pawed through the contents of my bag. If World War III had started, at least I'd have heard about it.

"Nothing of major interest. Let's see," he read, " 'Water Rates Likely To Increase', 'President To Unveil Budget Plans.' Oh, here we go: 'Indian Tribes Lose Ground in Casino Battle.' "

As my fingers searched, they found a small cellophane bag near the bottom of my purse. I pulled out the little hawk fetish I'd purchased at the mission last week—the one I thought of as my miniature Maltese Falcon. It reminded me of the medicine-card message. What did hawk medicine mean again? Something about observing your surroundings, although that wasn't quite it. I'd have to look it up again.

"Looks like the governor's moving closer to putting a cap on the amount of gambling we can do on the res," Valquez said with a sigh. "The tribes lost a good leader in Dan Aquillo." He looked up as I handed him a card.

"Thanks for the update," I said. "Sure I can't interest you in lunch? My treat."

He smiled warmly. "Another time."

I was halfway to the door when he called after me.

"Hey, you're going to Ed's to double-check on Wolf's alibi, aren't you?"

"Humble, dedicated, *and* perceptive," I said on my way through the door.

31

My cell phone rang just as I was pulling out of the area-station driveway.

"I can hear your mind going in circles all the way up here."

Sequoia. I looked out the window, up toward Palomar Mountain.

"I suppose you can see me going in circles, too. I drove out here this morning to talk to Rubio Valquez, the tribal cop. Now I'm on my way to lunch, just pulling out of the area station."

"I had a feeling you were around. Want to come up here for lunch? I've got some arugula and feta-cheese salad going here."

How could I resist? The best I could expect at Ed's would be a greasy grilled cheese sandwich.

"Can't say no to arugula. You're going to have to give me directions again, 'cause there's no way I can remember."

"It's not like there're street signs. Why don't you just keep driving, tell me what you see, and I'll tell you where to turn."

The plan worked pretty well, and I arrived at Sequoia's geo-odesic tepee without a hitch. I drove into the clearing to see him standing out front to meet me.

"How was your vision quest?" I asked as I walked to the door.

"Fine. How's your investigation going?"

"Let's just say I'm preparing for defeat," I said, stepping inside. The TV was on, and I recognized another Woody film, *Crimes and Misdemeanors*. I was instantly hooked.

"You ever seen this one?" he asked.

"Of course I have. I believe it's Woody Allen's masterpiece."

Sequoia smiled and paused the movie.

"In that case, don't forget the famous words that haunted the Martin Landau character here." He nodded toward the TV, where Landau's conscience-stricken face was frozen on the screen.

I thought about it a minute.

" 'Murder will out,' " I quoted.

He nodded, obviously pleased that I'd made the connection.

"But Sequoia, the whole point of this film is that murder *doesn't* always out. The Landau character gets away with it."

"Yeah, but Dan Aquillo's murderer won't. Not with you tracking him down."

"You sound like my mother. Nothing but boundless faith in my abilities."

"She must be a wise woman."

He turned off the TV and went into the kitchen. I drifted around the small house, nosing around his things.

"What's this?" I asked, pointing toward an instrument by the futon.

"That's my drum."

"Is that a shaman thing, too?"

"Yeah," he laughed. "My prop. Got to have a drum for my shaman act."

He walked over and sat cross-legged on the floor, the drum in front of him. He began pounding against the skin that was stretched taut over the top. It made a hollow, low noise with a slight ping at the end.

"That's a strangely pleasing sound," I said.

Sequoia beat the drum more quietly.

"Sit down and close your eyes. Travel where it takes you."

I did as he said, all the while struggling with an urge to hurry through lunch and be on my way. I wanted to inform David about my meetings with Trish Brown and Rubio Valquez. I figured I'd be polite and play audience to Sequoia—for a few minutes, anyway. I looked at my watch. I'd give him five.

Pong-pong-pong-pong-pong-pong-pong . . .

I felt the vibration of the drum, literally, through my skin. I leaned against the back of the futon and closed my eyes.

At first, I experienced just the monotonous beating sound. My thoughts rambled. I don't know when it happened, exactly, but eventually time seemed to drop away. My thoughts ceased, retreating in deference to the sound. In the darkness behind my eyes, I saw an opening in front of me, dark and hollow. I was drawn to it, though at the same time it filled me with apprehension. As the drum continued to beat, I drew closer to the dark opening. It turned into a cave, and I felt myself being sucked down.

I was falling into a cave, tunneling deep into the earth. Just as it seemed that I would be falling forever, I saw an opening up ahead. It was the other end of the cave. I crawled through the space and found myself in another world.

All the while, I was aware of myself sitting on Sequoia's futon, listening to the beating of his drum.

In the other world, I emerged from a pile of boulders at the edge of a meadow. I could see blue sky above me; I could feel the wind on my face. A trail ran directly past me, winding toward a hill bordering the meadow. Curious, I followed the trail to the right and up the hill.

Pong, pong, pong, pong, pong, pong, pong . . .

The trail became narrower as I climbed. The grasses at my feet turned to brush. Soon the trail was only big enough for rabbits and other small animals. I tried to push through the dense brush and felt the branches scratching my skin. Further progress was impossible. I stopped struggling and turned around, following the trail down a long slope, where it opened onto a vast expanse of chaparral.

Sequoia's drum beat on.

I recognized the chaparral. It seemed to me to be a parallel universe of the Temecu Reservation. I could see the cemetery by Aquillo's and beyond it, the double-trunked pepper tree. A man was standing near the edge of the cemetery. I jogged to catch up to him, my footsteps beating a rhythm on the packed dirt. I could see that the man was Dan Aquillo, but when I reached the cemetery, he was gone. I heard a screech and looked up.

A hawk soared down from a high limb of the pepper tree. As it floated to the ground, it turned into a wolf and ran away. I sprinted, but by the time I reached the tree, the wolf had vanished. I stood under the tree's leafy canopy, looking out in every direction, but the wolf was nowhere to be seen.

I felt drops on my skin. I looked up, confused. It was a perfectly sunny day—nothing but blue sky peeking through the leaves. And something else—a bird's nest, cradled in a branch over my head. A sudden gust of wind came up and pushed the nest out of the tree. As the small bundle fell toward the earth, I reached up to catch it. Closing my fingers around the falling object, I realized it wasn't a bird's nest at all.

It was a bloody scalp.

32

"I'm just suggesting that you take a look at the tree, is all."

Rubio Valquez responded with silence and a look that could have wilted plastic flowers. I'd just given him a blow-by-blow description of my vision about the scalp in the pepper tree. I could only imagine what he might be thinking.

"I like you, Elizabeth. I think you know that. But with all due respect, this happened in your imagination."

"There's a distinction between imagination and visions, and I'm trained to know the difference. I'm a psychic investigator, Rubio. This is what I do, professionally. If you want to check me out with the SDPD or FBI, I'll be happy to give you references."

He exhaled audibly.

"You realize that those crime-scene techs went over that area with about a hundred fine-tooth combs."

"Of course. But do you think they looked in the tree?"

This time there was a little groan with the exhale.

"I could be way off," I said evenly, "but if I'm not, this investigation will be taking an entirely new turn, don't you think?"

"In what way?"

"Given the victim's time of death and Bill Hurston's comatose condition, there's no way he could have killed and scalped Aquillo, driven out to the edge of the reservation, climbed a tree to hide the scalp, driven all the way back to the casino hotel, and collapsed into unconsciousness. I don't think even Johnnie Cochran could make that scenario fly."

Valquez's eyes crinkled, and he chuckled under his breath.

"No, I guess not. *If* there was a scalp in the tree. I can't believe I'm doing this, but . . ." He let the sentence drift, picked up his keys off his desk, and walked me out.

"I don't want you breathing a word of this to Angie Moon," he said as we approached his Bronco.

"Okay, no breathing."

We pulled out of the area-station driveway and headed to Aquillo's. I enjoyed being a passenger for a change. Along the way, we passed by some ugly prefabricated structures I hadn't noticed before. If it weren't for the windows, I would have thought they were storage garages, not houses.

"What is that?" I asked.

"You can blame the Department of Housing and Urban Development for that blight," he said. "HUD housing: Hot, Ugly, and Depressing."

"I'm inclined to agree."

The comment led to a conversation about architecture—a subject in which Valquez was delightfully versed. The discussion lasted for the duration of our ride to the north end of the reservation. When the cemetery came into view, my stomach knotted. Valquez slowed as we passed the headstones, and I began to second-guess myself. Sequoia had assured me that I was a natural shaman. He said I'd been called to journey into the underworld by Aquillo's spirit, who was helping me. He'd insisted that I return to the area station and get Valquez to look at the tree.

It had seemed like such a good idea, up on the mountain. But now that I was riding with Valquez, I was having doubts. What if the scalp in my vision was symbolic, not literal? Too late now. The pepper tree appeared ahead, demanding attention like an insistent suitor.

As Valquez pulled the Bronco to a stop in Aquillo's driveway, I could feel darkness clinging to the spot, the way odor clings to soiled clothing. Darkness, I realized now, that had been pulling me here from the beginning.

Valquez cut the ignition.

"It's been two weeks since Aquillo's murder. If the top of his head is up here, what hasn't been eaten by the vultures is bound to be pretty well disintegrated."

"Maybe we should call in the forensic team," I suggested.

He grabbed a pair of gloves off the seat and shook his head.

"I'm willing to entertain your notions—anything to solve a

case, right? But I'm not about to risk my reputation with the San Diego team on a psychic's hunch. Hope you don't take that personally."

"Not at all."

We got out and walked to the tree. Valquez wriggled his fingers into the gloves, eyeing the trunk doubtfully.

"I can give you a leg up," I said.

"Thanks."

I twined my fingers and made a stirrup for his foot with my palms. He stepped into my hands and pushed off, grabbing the east-facing trunk and pulling himself up. Bits of bark fluttered to the ground as he swung his left leg over and straddled the broad branch.

As Rubio shimmied higher into the tree, I pulled a few bright red berries from between its leaves, crushing them under my nose. The peppery aroma reminded me of my childhood. Rubio's voice came down from above.

"Temperature sure dropped all of a sudden, didn't it?"

I looked up into his face. Gravity had pulled a shank of hair into his eyes. He brushed it away with a gloved hand and peered into the tree.

"I should have worn a jacket," he said. "I can already feel the days getting shor—holy shit. Mary Mother of Jesus!"

Valquez was staring, open mouthed, at something on the branch in front of him.

"Son of a bitch." His voice was soft now and a little awed. "Someone took a hammer and nail and pounded the thing right into the tree."

I thought back to my shamanic journey, remembering the hawk that had flown down from the tree—the one that had turned into a wolf and run away. I didn't say it out loud, but I had a pretty good idea whose handiwork this was.

33

The sun was sinking toward the foothills, and the shadows were long by the time I pulled into Ed's Country Cafe on Highway 76. I'd arrived here by a process of elimination. The first place I'd looked had been the house, then the mission, and finally the mine, where I'd asked Norm for his bright ideas about where to search next. He was the one who suggested that I look for Wolf at Ed's.

I parked my truck in front of the hitching post between the gravel parking lot and the restaurant. The place had been reroofed since my last visit, the new shingles looking raw in the orange light of late day. I pulled open a new screen door that didn't squeak to announce my arrival. Someone had the remodeling bug around here. Ed was behind the bar and looked up as I walked in.

"Hi, Ed. How you doing?"

He squinted, trying to place me.

"We met the other night at the antigambling thing," I said. I remembered Ed's offensive remark—*"No human involved in that first murder anyway"*—and tried to keep the disdain off my face. "Is Wolf here?" I asked.

"In the other room."

I walked past the booths and into the back room, where the object of my search was playing pool with a heavy-set kid in baggy clothes. I leaned against the wall and watched as Wolf sank the remaining three balls.

"One more?" he asked his opponent.

"No, I gotta go, man."

The kid shuffled out without even a glance at me. I watched him leave and then turned back to Wolf, who greeted me with his patented scowl.

"What do you want?" he asked.

"How about a game?"

He didn't say anything, just racked the balls. I picked up a cue and chalked the tip.

"You a stripe man or a solid man?" I asked.

"Stripes. Always. You can break."

I lined up my cue ball and focused on the lower right corner of the triangular stack. I hit the outside ball with authority, sinking my yellow number one in the corner pocket. I studied the table, looking for my next shot.

"It's time to start talking, Wolf."

"Don't feel like talking," he said. "I don't talk when I play."

"Is that so?"

For the hell of it, I attempted a tricky rail shot and missed the side pocket by a hair. Wolf showed no emotion as he walked around the table. He leaned over, fixed his eyes on the white ball, and made a few gentle practice strokes with his cue.

"The police found your uncle's scalp in the tree this morning," I said.

His cue froze in midstroke.

"It's amazing what forensic technicians can do these days," I went on. "Who'd think you could get enough of a fingerprint from a little old nail to make an identification?" I was bluffing, but I could see that he was worried.

He tossed his cue onto the table with a clatter and bolted for the door. I jumped sideways and held my cue horizontally across the doorway, blocking his exit.

"Look, I know you didn't kill your uncle. But I'm the only one who's going to believe that until you start talking to me. You've got to trust me on this one."

He pushed my cue aside and walked out.

"You don't know shit."

"I do know shit," I called after him. "I know lots of shit. I know that you're angry and depressed, and the only person you've ever seriously considered killing is yourself. And I don't want that to happen."

He stopped in his tracks. When he turned to look at me, I saw the eyes of a frightened animal. I leaned my pool cue against the wall and picked up my purse.

"Come on. Let's take a drive."

Wolf consented wordlessly, following me through the restaurant and out to the parking lot. We didn't speak as we got into my truck. I pulled onto Mystic Mesa Road and headed into the reservation.

The silence lasted for a good fifteen minutes. I spent the time thinking about what to say—and praying that whatever I said came out right. The truth was, I had nothing on Wolf and neither would the police. I was flying on pure intuition here, and everything depended on whether or not I could get him to open up. I broke the ice with a story.

"When I was a little girl in grade school," I began, "the other kids wouldn't play with me."

Wolf didn't move a muscle, just continued to stare out the window.

"That hurt for a long time. It wasn't fair, the way they treated me. I used to fantasize about all kinds of terrible things happening to those little creeps. But the truth was I just wanted them to like me."

Still no response.

"You know why they wouldn't play with me? Just because I was different. To this day it bugs the shit out of me when people won't accept anyone or anything that doesn't match their idea of normal. Whatever the hell normal is."

Wolf shifted in his seat. I could feel his eyes on my face, but I kept my concentration on the road ahead.

"What was so different about you?" he mumbled.

"I knew things they didn't know. Saw things they couldn't see."

"Like what?" Wolf asked.

From the side of the road, a squirrel darted onto the pavement and stood up, stiff with fear. I eased my foot on the brake, and the rodent scampered back into the weeds.

"In second grade, I dreamed our school principal was going to be killed in a car accident. It scared me, so I told my teacher about it. She said it was just a nightmare, but three months later it happened. She must have told people because word got around. Kids started avoiding me and calling me names. 'Witch,' 'devil's girl,' all that kind of stuff. I scared them, I can see that now. But when I was eight, it just seemed like the whole world was against me."

I swallowed a lump in my throat. After all these years, I could still feel the pain of that rejection.

"Dreams and visions are sacred to my tribe," he said.

"I know. I think I was born into the wrong tribe."

I looked over, hoping that might have cracked a smile, but Wolf's lips were set in a straight line, and he continued to stare out the window.

We were getting closer to my destination. I was pretty sure I could remember how to get there, but I made an effort now to watch for the turn that led up the mountain.

"Would you believe me if I told you I saw your uncle's killer in a vision?"

This time Wolf did take his eyes off the road.

"You did?" he asked, staring into my face.

"Yes. Your uncle's killer was lying in wait inside the closet. He had this murder carefully planned. He was filled with hate, all right, but this was no spur-of-the-moment crime of passion. That's how I know it wasn't you. You may be angry—filled with hate, even—but premeditated murder? Don't think so. You're no calculating killer."

He unconsciously fingered the tattoo on his cheek but didn't say anything.

"When you cut the scalp from your uncle's head, he was already dead. I know that."

I felt him tense up and hold his breath.

"What I don't know," I went on, "is why you did such a drastic thing. Or why you cut his tongue in two. I don't think it was your uncle's politics or this business about him bringing gambling to the reservation. I think your rage went deeper than that. What did he do, Wolf? What made you hate him that much?"

My stomach was churning—in sympathy, I think, with the war going on inside the young man next to me, struggling to keep it all inside.

He didn't answer, and I didn't press him.

Minutes later, I reached the turnoff, and we began to climb the mountain. The truck ground into low gear where the road became steep. I hit an unexpected rut, and we lurched to the left. I shifted into four-wheel drive. The valley stretched out below us; the sky above it glowing deep orange along the horizon. At the crest of the mountain, I pulled off the road and onto the ridge that overlooked the valley. I cut the engine and reached into the storage box behind the seat, retrieving my binoculars.

"Come on," I said. "There's something I want you to see."

I got out of the truck and went to the edge of the cliff. The drop was steep. Scrappy little shrubs clung to the cliff face. Another twenty minutes and it would have been too dark, but as I looked through the binoculars, I was able to make out the double-trunked tree. Yellow crime-scene tape circled it like a Maypole. I heard Wolf come up behind me. I turned to hand him the binoculars.

"Take a look," I said.

He shook his head, refusing the offer.

"I don't need to see it," he said. "I see it everyday, over and over in my head."

The admission seemed to sap his strength, and he lowered himself onto a nearby boulder. He slumped his shoulders and stared at the ground.

I found my own boulder at a safe distance. Defeated as he appeared, Wolf was volatile. His depression could turn to rage in a heartbeat.

"You see what?" I asked.

He looked up now, taking in the vista.

"The bodies of my uncle and father in that horrible hotel room. I thought both of them were dead. Swear to God, I did."

It took a moment for his words to sink in. When they did, my mouth fell open.

"Your *father*?"

34

The colors of Temecu Valley faded to gray as the sun dropped below the horizon. Wolf stared beyond the mountain ridge in the direction of the pepper tree, the scowl never leaving his face.

"Bill Hurston is your father?" I was shocked and couldn't keep the surprise out of my voice.

Wolf nodded. I remembered the story of Lucy Aquillo's brief marriage in Las Vegas to a man who had lived just long enough to father her son. A myth, apparently.

"Is this a secret?" I asked.

He picked up a stone and tossed it over the cliff's edge, where it disappeared without a sound.

"Not my secret," he said.

"Who knows about this?"

"Hardly anybody. Just my mom and him, I guess, now that my uncle's dead."

"You've kept this quiet your whole life?"

"I only found out two years ago. That's when he started showing up in Mystic Mesa, after his wife dumped him. Guess he wanted to woo my mom back or something."

Now I could see the resemblance to Hurston. He had his mother's full lips and warm brown skin, but the narrow face and long nose were his father's. I tried to remember if the eyes underneath Hurston's glasses were the same blue-green as Wolf's.

"How did you find out that he was your father?"

"He came out to the house one day. I didn't even know who the fuck he was, man. He started giving my mom this sob story about how sorry he was. Promised her he was going to straighten out his life, stop gambling, all this shit. I didn't know what the fuck was going on. I thought he was crazy, man. I started to kick him out, but he pulled a picture out of this Bible. It was me, as a little kid. Guess my Uncle Dan gave it to him or something. He said he'd been carrying it around in that Bible for ten years."

I remembered the picture of the scowling young Wolf.

"That must have been quite a shock."

"Yeah." His tone said I'd never know what a shock.

"Did you get to know him?" I asked.

"A little. He promised my mom and me he'd stop gambling, and he did stop. Several times." He laughed, but his sadness was palpable. "He didn't gamble for almost a month, that last time."

"But he started again."

"Yeah, about a month ago Uncle Dan told me about it. Said my father'd been gambling and passing out every night at the casino hotel. I hated my asshole uncle. Our great tribal leader—yeah, right. He gave that hotel room to my father, encouraged his sickness. He ruined people, but he didn't even care, long as it made him rich."

In the chilly silence that followed I wondered if my hunch about Wolf's innocence was wrong. Was it possible he *had* killed his uncle? I took care in framing my next question.

"So you went to the casino to confront your uncle?"

"No. I went to the hotel to get my dad out of there."

"How did you know where to find him?"

"It was common knowledge by then. If he wasn't winning, he'd be passed out by midnight in the room at the end of the hotel." He stopped, lost in thought.

"So you went to the room—" I prodded.

"I knocked, but nobody answered. I went around back to see if I could look inside. The balcony door wasn't locked, so I walked in and turned on a lamp. My uncle was facedown on the floor with all this blood around his head." His voice had become quieter and quieter, so that I could barely hear him now. "My dad was on the bed. I tried to wake him up, but he wouldn't open his eyes."

"And you thought that he was dead."

"His mouth was hanging open, and his hands were cold. I was sure he was dead, man."

I believed him. I also began to understand his torment. After seventeen years without his father, Wolf had finally won him back—only to lose him again. Or so he thought.

"Weren't you afraid that a killer might be hanging around?"

"It didn't even cross my mind. I figured they'd killed each other. It looked to me like my greedy fuckin' uncle had been hassling my dad for money, and they got in a fight. I thought Dan killed my dad. Do you know how much I hated him that moment?" Wolf's voice shook with anger. "You don't know what hate is; you don't even know."

The night creatures were coming alive. I could hear the insistent rhythm of crickets all around us. Somewhere overhead an owl hooted.

"I cut him," he said. "And I'm glad I cut him."

I sat in the twilight, stunned by what I'd just heard. And a little frightened. I wrapped my arms around my chest and slid my fingers under my jacket, touching the butt of my gun.

"So you scalped him out of hate."

"It was more than that. You wouldn't understand."

"I think I do understand. You made a sacrifice. What was the meaning of nailing his scalp to that tree?"

Wolf took his time responding.

"It was a sacrifice to the four winds," he said at last. "I did it so that the evil he brought to our tribe would go away. Most of all, I wanted to lift the curse on the Aquillo family."

"You cut his tongue in half, too." My palms were sweating, but I tried to keep my voice matter-of-fact. "Why?"

"All those years I'd had a father, and Dan knew. He lied to me."

Wolf's heinous acts made a gruesome kind of sense. I looked over to study his face, but it was too dark now to see clearly. His silhouette was as still as the stone on which he sat.

In my mind's eye I was back in my vision, standing under the tree where the sky rained blood. Natalie Hurston's body had been buried under that tree, too.

"Did you kill your father's ex-wife and sacrifice her for the tribe, too?"

His dark form turned toward me.

"No way. I didn't even know that woman. Never met her in my life. I wouldn't even know how to find her. Besides, I don't believe in killing."

"Then what were you doing there that day when I found her body?"

"I'd had time to think things over. I'd seen cop cars at my uncle's, and I began to get worried that someone would find the scalp. I was going to take it down and burn it."

"Did you use your knife to cut off your uncle's scalp?"

He didn't answer. I was wondering how I might persuade him to give up the weapon when he spoke again.

"I thought my father killed my uncle. You don't think he did?" I heard a small note of hope in his voice.

"No, I don't. But when I find out who did, you're going to have to come forward with your knife. Will you do that?"

"I'll think about it."

I stood up and dusted off the butt of my pants.

"Come on, let's go," I said.

"Where?"

"I'm not turning you in," I said. "You're going to have to trust me. There's someone I need you to talk to."

"Where are we going?"

"You'll see when we get there."

35

The high-rises of downtown San Diego glittered against the midnight-blue bay. Wolf shifted in the passenger seat as I exited at First Street and slowed into city traffic. If I'd told him we were going to Central Jail, he never would have agreed to come along. He didn't figure it out until we were walking toward the building. When he saw the official seal of the State of California on the north wall, he balked and his eyes got wide. I put my hand on his arm.

"If I were going to turn you in, I would have done it by now. Should have done it by now. But I need your help here. I want you to talk to your father."

His feet remained planted on the sidewalk.

"Why should I believe you?"

"My goal is to find out the truth of what happened that night. I think you talking to your dad is the only way I'm going to do that." I squeezed his arm until his eyes met mine. "Please?"

He nodded and followed me into the building.

Deputy Capshaw was on duty again. She remembered me.

"Evening visiting hours are almost over. I'm gonna need to see his driver's license," she said, nodding toward Wolf.

"Doesn't have it with him. He's a minor. He's with me," I added reassuringly.

She made a note on her clipboard and led us to the narrow visitors' room behind the glass. As we waited, Wolf's nervousness vanished, replaced by a steely calm. It seemed to be taking longer than usual for the guard to bring Hurston out, and my own nerves began to get edgy. Seven minutes passed before the prisoner appeared. He was almost fully seated before he realized who was sitting next to me.

Shock froze Hurston's face muscles. Staring at Wolf in disbelief, he slowly picked up the telephone. The knuckles on his hand had gone white. I picked up the phone on our side and spoke first.

"Wolf has already told me what he did," I said, keeping my voice down. "The police found the scalp this afternoon, and it's only a matter of time until an arrest will be made. So please, Dr. Hurston, talk to me. If not for your sake, for your son's. Juries aren't so soft on minors anymore."

Hurston sagged. He was the picture of a man whose worst nightmare had just come true. He covered his face with his free hand.

"God help me," he mumbled.

Wolf grabbed the phone out of my hand.

"Why did you kill him?" he demanded in a harsh whisper.

The father and son locked eyes, the son looking angry, the father looking confused. He shook his head, and I read his lips:

"I didn't." He pointed to Wolf. *"I thought you did."*

"No way," Wolf said. "He was already dead when I came into your room."

I reached for the phone.

"May I? I need to hear what he has to say." Wolf relinquished the phone. When I put my ear to the receiver, Hurston was speaking.

"Dan was dead when Wolf came in?"

"That's what he says, and I believe him. He came into your hotel room and found his uncle on the floor with a bloody head. When he couldn't revive you, he thought the two of you had gotten in a fight and killed each other."

Wolf sat beside me, nodding in agreement with this version of events. He held out his hand, asking for the phone again. I gave it to him, and he spoke into the mouthpiece.

"I thought he'd killed you, man. I went into a rage."

Hurston sat back, looking quite blown away. Gently, I took the phone from Wolf's hand and spoke to Hurston in a calm, low voice.

"Just tell me exactly what you did and what you saw."

"I guess there's no point in protecting him anymore."

"No," I said. "At this point you're hurting him more than you're protecting him."

He sighed.

"Saturday night I gambled my last hundred dollars at Trish's table. I was real down and pretty drunk. I'd already planned what I was going to do. I went back to my hotel room and gave myself what I thought was a fatal dose of Versed. That's the truth."

"And that much I've already heard," I said. "Let's get to the part you left out."

The pain in his face wasn't self-pity now, it was parental agony. Perhaps it always had been. It made me like him more.

"All right," he said. "Somewhere in my delirium—and I do mean delirium—I heard a horrible noise. Understand that I was pretty far gone by this time. Versed's a hell of a tranquilizer, so I can't even be sure that any of this is accurate. I didn't even think it was real at the time."

His eyes stared inward. His mind was in another time, another place.

"You thought what wasn't real?" I prodded.

"It sounded like an animal growling. I forced my eyes open—I could barely muster the strength to lift my eyelids. I saw my son at the foot of the bed, a knife in one hand and something bloody in the other. I thought it was a hallucination brought on by the Versed. Or that I'd died and gone to hell."

Wolf sat beside me, watching Hurston talk into the phone. I was glad he wasn't hearing this.

"Then what?" I asked.

"I passed out again."

"So what was the next thing you remember after that?"

His forehead wrinkled as he strained to remember.

"The cops were hauling me out of bed. I saw Dan's corpse as they dragged me out of the room. I was going in and out of consciousness at that point. When they stabilized me in the ambulance, I realized it hadn't been a hallucination. It was real. It was all too real."

"Who killed Dan Aquillo, Dr. Hurston?"

He met my eyes dead on.

"If it wasn't Wolf, I don't know. I've told you everything. If someone else killed Dan, I didn't see it or hear it. That's the truth." He looked at his son. "I wanted to take the fall for him. I wish I could do at least that much for him."

"The last thing your son needs is to have his father imprisoned and possibly executed for a murder he didn't commit."

"You really don't think he killed Dan?"

"No," I said firmly, adding for Wolf's benefit, "I really don't believe your son killed Dan Aquillo."

"Or Natalie?" he asked.

"Or Natalie," I said. "Is that why you confessed when Natalie's body was found? Because you thought Wolf had killed her, too, and you wanted to divert attention from him?"

Hurston nodded.

"Wolf didn't ever know Natalie, but I thought that maybe he resented . . ." He didn't finish the thought. "What happens now?" he asked.

"I find the real killer. But I need your help. Take me through what led up to that night and what happened, step by step. The truth this time."

Hurston stared down at the countertop, remembering.

"I've told you everything now. Again, I'd gone for over a month without gambling. I thought I'd finally kicked the habit. When I fell back that weekend, I decided I'd rather die than live that way again. I went to my room and took the drug. The last thing I did was call my ex-wife. I'd gambled a lifetime of savings away during our marriage, so I felt I owed her an apology before I died. That's it—that's the last thing I remember. Until . . ." He looked up at Wolf and let the rest go unspoken.

"You also made a phone call to Dan Aquillo's office," I said. "It's on the hotel phone record."

Hurston's forehead wrinkled.

"I don't remember that at all. I suppose I must have."

We both thought about that for a minute.

"Either you did, or the killer did." I remembered the room as Peter Waleta had shown it to me. "Do you remember the

ight switch by the front door not working that night?" I
asked.

Hurston shook his head.

"No, everything seemed to be working fine. Of course my
memory about that may be faulty. I was somewhat inebriated
when I came in that night."

It was possible that someone had entered Hurston's room
after he passed out. Someone who knew Hurston's habit of
drinking himself into a stupor each night. They could have
loosened the light bulb, used the phone to summon Dan
Aquillo, and waited for him in the darkness, ready with the
hammer.

"The clerk in the registration office said she saw Natalie at
the hotel that night. Did Natalie come to see you?"

He shook his head.

"Again, if she did, I don't remember. All I remember is—"

"Seeing Wolf in the room," I said.

He nodded and stared at Wolf, his face a mixture of hope
and fear.

"You haven't told the police yet about my son?"

"Not yet," I said.

36

I didn't hear a word out of Wolf until we'd traveled out of the city and were headed into the long freeway stretch north to the reservation.

"He thought *I* killed Uncle Dan." His words came out haltingly, in a shocked tone. It was finally sinking in that his father was not his uncle's killer. I sensed the pieces falling into place for Wolf, rearranging his turbulent emotions. "My father was standing by me. He confessed so that I wouldn't go to jail." For the first time, I heard appreciation in his voice.

"That's what I think," I said. "You believe him, too?"

Wolf nodded. "Yeah, I do."

We traveled another five minutes in silence.

"If my father didn't kill Uncle Dan, who did?"

I turned to look at his mystified face.

"Exactly," I said. "That's where you come in, my friend. Help me here. You know the reservation better than I do. What about those gang kids you play billiards with? Was there something going on between them and your uncle? Something they thought he deserved to die for?"

"No way. The worst those guys do is hijack cars on the highway, roll tourists for money—stuff like that."

"Hijack cars? You mean that's who shot out my front tire and beat me up on the side of Mystic Mesa Road?"

"Could be." He kept his focus on the cars in the lane to our right.

"Could be, or it was?"

He didn't answer.

"If it was your friends, I need to know. Your future may depend on it."

"All right, all right. They rolled you like they rolled the others, man. It wasn't personal. They do it for money and the rush. It had nothing to do with my uncle."

I winced, feeling the sting of betrayal.

"Well, that clears up one mystery." It also explained his attitude toward me from the beginning. Guilt breeds defensiveness.

"What about your father's ex-wife, Natalie?" I asked. "Rosemary in the registration office saw her at the hotel that night. Would your father's ex have any reason to kill your uncle? And if she did, would someone kill her in retaliation, maybe?"

"I told you before, I didn't even know her. Swear to God."

"Do you know *anybody* who might have wanted your uncle dead? How about his business partner, Peter Waleta? Or his girlfriend, Trish Brown?"

Wolf shook his head. "I don't know those guys very well but from what I know, huh-uh. I don't think so. I guess you never know, though."

I heard humility in his voice and ventured a difficult question.

"Have you ever done anything before like you did to your uncle?"

He hung his head and shook it slowly.

We passed the restaurant and turned onto Mystic Mesa Road. The neon lights of the casino complex stood out against the dark land like a fireworks display fallen to earth. Once past the Pony Express Mine and Rock Shop, my high beams became the only sources of light. I followed the dusty road to Wolf's house, where a lone porch light was on. I pulled to a stop, the engine running. In the dim light, Wolf's face was worried.

"The cops are going to be coming for me, aren't they?"

I'd been bluffing about his fingerprint evidence linking him to the scalp, but I didn't tell him that.

"It'll take a couple of weeks for the test results to come in," I said. "You're okay for a while. Meanwhile, I'm releasing you on your own recognizance." As he stepped down, I said, "It's going to be okay."

I watched him walk into his house, hoping I was doing the right thing. If I went to Valquez with what I knew at this point, the SDPD would bring the focus of the entire investigation down on the boy. He'd make a horrible witness. Justice would not be served.

I drove home on autopilot, too tired to think. I searched for an inspiring tune on the FM dial, found nothing but recycled hits, and snapped it off. That's when I became aware that I'd been seeing a face in my mind's eye all evening, unrelated to any thoughts of my own. A message from my subconscious. I finally paid attention to it and pulled to the side of the road. I found his business card in my wallet and called from my car phone. It must have been a residential number because he answered on the second ring.

"Steve Hawking?" I asked.

"Yes."

"I know it's late, but this could be important. This is Elizabeth Chase. I met you at the Citizens Against Unregulated Gambling meeting."

"Yes," he said, so quietly that I almost couldn't hear. "This is weird. I was just thinking about you."

"That happens to me a lot," I said. "There must be a reason I need to talk to you."

"Yeah." There was a long pause, as if some kind of decision were being made.

"Not over the phone," he said finally. "Can I meet you somewhere? It has to be tonight because I catch a plane to Sacramento first thing tomorrow morning."

"Where are you staying?" I asked.

"This isn't a good spot," he answered quickly. "No restaurants, either—I can't take the chance of being recognized. There's a walkway along Carlsbad State Beach. Do you know where that is?"

"Yes."

"I can meet you there in forty minutes."

I looked at the dashboard clock. It was already closing in on eleven.

"All right. I'll see you there in forty minutes."

I hung up the phone and pulled back onto the highway. Forty minutes would give me time to stop home and pick up

Nero. I wasn't about to take a meeting on a dark stretch of beach without my backup.

The marine layer was thick as I parked in the lot at Carlsbad State Beach. A chilly gray mist clung to the cliffs. *Crawling Eye weather,* I thought with a smile. There were a few vehicles parked in the lot, but I saw no one as I walked Nero down the cement ramp toward the beach. We stepped onto the walkway running parallel to the ocean. A long white wave broke onto the sand with a roar and retreated into the fog like a chorus line disappearing behind a stage curtain. Nero stopped in his tracks, and his ears went up. Just ahead, a man appeared out of the fog, wearing a hat and windbreaker. As he came closer, I recognized Steve Hawking's small form and even features. The law student–political activist approached cautiously, as if dogs made him nervous.

"Thank you for coming," I said.

"I'd been thinking about calling you anyway. I've been having a hard time sleeping."

"Why?"

"At first, I passed this off as coincidence. And it may sound that way to you when I tell you. But when it happened the second time, I couldn't ignore it anymore." He looked toward the parking lot with a wary face. "Do you mind if we walk?"

"My dog would love to. But you're going to have to slow down your story because I'm already lost, counselor."

"Oh, sorry. I'll try to put some semblance of order to this. Let's see—I think I mentioned the night we met that I was working for Assemblyman Cowan. One of my duties is to collect campaign contributions and distribute funds—you know, for flyers, bumper stickers, that kind of thing."

"Sounds exciting."

"It isn't, ordinarily." My irony had been lost on him. "But there's been a confluence of events that's perhaps too exciting. Unnerving, if you want to know the truth."

A confluence of events. Poor guy talked like a third-year

law student. Before I could ask what he meant by that, he rambled on:

"We pass the hat at meetings like the one you attended the other night, so we do get some cash contributions. But it's always small potatoes. Our biggest contributors send checks, naturally. I'm telling you all this because it seemed strange to me at the time that I was given the funds in cash."

"What funds?"

"Russell—Mr. Cowan—asked me to deliver a package to one of our supporters out in east San Diego County. That's what he called it at the time, east San Diego County. But the delivery was actually on the Temecu Reservation. I thought that was a little strange since, after all, the reservation was enemy territory. Not to make a bad pun."

I grimaced at the unfunny pun.

"I'm not understanding yet why you're losing sleep," I said.

"Okay, okay. You need a little more background. One thing that bothers me—that's always bothered me—is that a good deal of our support comes from Las Vegas gambling casinos. They've poured huge amounts of money into our campaign. Which is understandable, since the Indian casinos are cutting into their profits."

"Substantially?"

"About a quarter billion dollars a year by some counts. I don't like the idea that I'm politically aligned with Las Vegas, but that's politics, you know. I'm supporting the antigambling coalition from a legal perspective. The precedents being set by these tribes are damaging to the California constitution."

"You mentioned that at the meeting," I said. "I still don't see what any of this has to do with Dan Aquillo's murder."

"I'm getting to that. See, I think the money I delivered came from one of Russell's supporters in Las Vegas, Andy Bello. His visit with Russell coincided with a sharp increase in the campaign's cash contribution fund. That in itself isn't illegal, of course. But what's bothering me is the other coincidence. Russell had me deliver a package to Temecu just two days before that casino manager was murdered."

"What was in the package?"

"A thousand dollars. I took the liberty of looking in the package to see what I was delivering. I almost wish I hadn't."

"So you're thinking that this was hit money, is that what you're getting at?"

He nodded.

"Isn't that a little low for a murder-for-hire?"

"Of course. Which is why I thought nothing of it at the time. But when I delivered the second package just days before the woman was murdered, that's when I started losing sleep. It was just too coincidental."

Nero had trotted ahead, and I couldn't see him through the mist. I whistled for him to come back.

"How much in the second package?" I asked.

"I don't know. I didn't look."

I wasn't sure that I believed him, but I let it go and went on to the next question.

"Why would someone pay to have Dan Aquillo killed?"

"There's a grass-roots drive to put the issue of Indian gambling to the California voters. Dan Aquillo was a leader in that movement. And I keep thinking about this offhand comment Russell made about Aquillo one day. He said something to the effect that there were powerful people who would be happy to see him drop dead."

"Are you implying that Assemblyman Cowan was involved in an execution?"

"I'm saying that I don't know what those two packages of cash bought, but I doubt very sincerely that it was bumper stickers."

"Where did you deliver this money? Who was your contact?"

"I dropped the packages at a place called the Pony Express Mine and Rock Shop, way out on Mystic Mesa Road."

My heart sank. *Please,* I prayed, *don't let Norm be involved.*

"And the contact?"

"The owner out there, a guy named Norman Clapp."

With a sick feeling in my stomach, I realized that it made sense. Norm was a former FBI agent. He had the training. He had the weapons. I tasted something bitter at the back of my tongue.

The information was coming from Steve Hawk-ing. *Observe the obvious.*

"I'm leaving Cowan's campaign," he said. "Whatever's going on here, I don't want any part of it. I have a very bad feeling about all this. I'm not too proud to admit I'm scared. I don't know if it's paranoia or what, but there've been times over the last two weeks when I thought I was being followed."

I couldn't suppress an urge to look back over my shoulder.

"Why haven't you gone to the police?"

"If I'm wrong about all this, coming out with it could end my career before it's even started." Now he looked behind his shoulder, too. "If I'm right about this, coming out with it could end my *life.*"

"But you came to me."

"All day I've been thinking about the way you looked at me at the meeting last night, when you told me to keep in touch. I'm not a superstitious person, but I couldn't ignore that encounter. Then when you called . . . My conscience couldn't handle that doctor getting a lethal injection from the state for something he might not have done. Can you investigate this and keep my name out of it?"

"If I look into this and it pans out, we're going to need your testimony."

He pursed his lips and made no comment. I got the feeling he might not be a willing witness.

"Do you have any evidence that this cash exchange took place?" I asked.

"Like what? A receipt? No, nothing like that."

"Without your testimony, it wouldn't stand up in court. That's not going to help Bill Hurston."

We'd reached the end of the cement walkway. From this point, a wave-soaked rock pier stretched out to sea and disappeared into the fog.

"I have an idea," I said. "I'm going to need your cooperation, though."

"I told you, I don't want to go to the police."

"You don't have to go anywhere. All you have to do is set up a lunch meeting with Cowan. Can you do that for me?"

"No," he said with an emphatic shake of his head. "I told you, I'm out of here. I don't want to see Russell. Especially now."

"You don't have to see him," I said. "I'm going to stand in for you."

37

The next morning I pulled into the parking lot of the small office complex that housed Chatfield's Value-Added Investigations, hoping against hope that Chatfield was back in town. I had a game plan but wasn't sure it was a sound one. I could trust Chatfield to be the voice of reason. I'd seen that when I worked with him during my last case. The case he'd been smart enough to drop, and I'd paid such a high price for taking on.

The door of the agency was slightly ajar. I pulled it open and walked into an empty office.

"Hello?"

The reception area was roped off with crime-scene tape. Sitting in the center of the off-limits zone was what looked like an ordinary beverage cooler. It was a bizarre tableau, but then this was Chatfield's, where one could expect the bizarre.

I was peeking over the yellow-and-black tape to see what the deal was when I heard a friendly voice call out from the back.

"Hey, it's the psychic detective."

Chatfield came forward on a lilting step, dressed in shorts, sandals, and a T-shirt with a giant moose on it.

"Oh," he said casually, "don't go near that. It might be radioactive."

Holding my breath and willing my pores shut, I began backing out of the office. He waved me back in.

"Just kidding. It's only toxic if you lift the lid."

"What is it?"

He glared at the cooler and lowered his voice.

"Evidence for this case I'm on. Someone was paid to dump illegal chemicals. Talk about instant karma—the guy died of toxic fumes. Welcome to the wonderful world of environmental homicide." Suddenly he brightened and gave me an enthusiastic smile. "How are you? How's your case going?"

"Okay, all things considered. Do you have a few minutes?"

"Yeah." He summoned me into his office with a wide, sweeping gesture, as if he were on an airstrip directing a 747. "Come on back."

For all his wacky humor, Chatfield kept a ship-shape office. In striking contrast to David's office, Chatfield's place had no dust, no spots on the windows. One wall was lined with file cabinets and state-of-the-art electronic equipment. On the opposite wall, several years' worth of penal codes, legal references, and investigation manuals lined up on shelves that nearly reached the ceiling. I took my seat, coveting his library.

"So what's up?" he said. "David's been too busy to fill me in, but I've been reading what I can in the papers. It's a puzzler." He pushed his glasses down onto the tip of his nose and lapsed into his feisty old-geezer imitation. "What'n the Sam Hill's going on out at that reservation, anyways?"

"I'm not sure," I said, unable to suppress a smile, "but it's possible that the casino manager got whacked on orders from Las Vegas."

Chatfield's green eyes bulged behind his glasses.

"Whoa," he said, dead serious.

"Either that or he got whacked on orders from an elected California official."

"Are you kidding? Like who?"

"Do you know Russell Cowan?"

"Mr. All-American Assemblyman? Our Knight from the Seventy-Seventh District? Now you are kidding, right?"

"No, I'm not. A young guy who was working on Cowan's antigambling campaign came to me with information that significant cash was delivered to a supporter on the reservation shortly before Aquillo's murder."

Chatfield's red brows furrowed dubiously.

"Could be a coincidence, don't you think?"

"Another unspecified amount of cash was delivered to the same place shortly before the second murder."

Now the eyebrows went up.

"Hmm. Maybe not a coincidence. Motive?"

"It has to do with the drive to put the Indian gambling issue to the California voters. Dan Aquillo was a very influential leader in that movement. Las Vegas casinos are losing hundreds of millions to the Indian casinos, so there's a huge amount of Vegas money pouring into the campaign to limit Indian gambling."

"So this guy who was working for Cowan thinks that he was the unwitting accomplice to a political assassination, is that the idea?"

"That's about it."

"Who'd he deliver this money to?"

"A man named Norm Clapp. He owns an old gold mine on the reservation. No gold in it anymore, but his security system rivals Fort Knox."

"He's a big antigambler, is he?"

"I didn't think so." My voice sounded sad. "He used to be an FBI agent. He's a really nice guy."

"That's what they kept saying about Ted Bundy. Has the unwitting accomplice—what's his name?"

"Hawking."

"Has Hawking told this to the police or deputy DA?"

"No. He's running scared. Afraid to go to the cops, but even more scared that he's being watched."

"He's thinking that the same person who hit Aquillo might hit him?"

"That's my impression."

Chatfield picked up a memo pad and pencil and scratched out some notes. I took a peek at his handiwork. Boxes, lines, letters, and senseless squiggles. He tapped his pen on a cluster of wiggly lines.

"What about this scalping thing? Tearing someone's head off is not exactly the standard MO of a professional hit man."

I opened, then shut, my mouth. To bring up Wolf's part in the crime now would only complicate things.

"Maybe it was a frustrated hit man," I said.

Chatfield looked doubtful.

"Not to put too fine a point on it, but don't you think scalping is a Native American thing? Sounds like something a pissed-off Indian would do."

"Could be," I said vaguely.

He drew some arrows on his pad and looked up.

"There's a huge piece missing here. What about that other body they found on the reservation? Wasn't that Hurston's ex-wife? Hurston's got to be involved. Otherwise, how do you explain the fact that his ex was murdered and dumped on Aquillo's property?"

"I've been thinking about that. One, Hurston called his ex, Natalie, from his hotel room before he passed out. Two, Natalie Hurston was seen at the hotel the night of the murder. Putting those two things together, I think she was worried about him and came to the hotel to see if he was all right. She didn't admit that when I interviewed her. She was scared that day. I think she was afraid to admit she'd gone to see Hurston, afraid she'd be implicated in Aquillo's murder. But I think she was afraid of something else, too. I think she saw the killer when she went to Hurston's room. Maybe the killer saw her, too, and shot her before she could talk."

"Yeah, but why would she end up buried out at Aquillo's place?"

"I think the killer got her out there on a ruse. Her sister told the tribal cops that Natalie had mentioned that she was going to go out to Aquillo's to pick up some of the valuables Hurston had given him as collateral for some bets."

Chatfield made another arrow on the pad.

"Remote location, out of eyeshot and earshot . . . yeah, I guess that makes sense." He shaded one of the doodles on his pad. The pencil made a soft hissing sound as he worked. "Now, how do you find the killer?"

"I'm not sure, but I'll bet Russell Cowan can lead the way. But first we have to get him talking. That's where you come in."

He gave me as serious a look as I'd ever seen on his freckled face.

"I don't know, Elizabeth. Vegas money, high-ranking public official, murder-for-hire—I think this is where the FBI comes in."

Bad vibes sprang up like so many red flags. I'd had negative feelings about the bureau ever since they'd refused to give McGowan and me backup during a critical point in the investigation that resulted in his death. Maybe it was irrational, but I blamed the FBI for McGowan, at least in part. Then there was the fact that Norm Clapp was a former FBI agent.

"Not yet," I said. "I have a plan. Hear me out, and then tell me if you think it'll work."

For the next several minutes I laid out my scheme and made Chatfield a cash offer for his help in carrying it out. His face was impassive as he listened—so impassive that at one point I worried he might be speculating whether or not I was on drugs.

"Well, what do you think?" I asked when I was through.

He sprang to his feet and threw his hands in the air.

"I think you're mad!" he shouted. He sat back down, smiling sheepishly, and said in a normal tone of voice, "I think you have a hell of lot more guts than I do, that's what I think."

38

A large cube of ice escaped the water pitcher and plunged into my glass, sending droplets onto my place setting. The busboy apologized, but I hardly noticed as I glanced at my watch. Russell Cowan was due to arrive any minute. I hadn't been nervous at all up to this point, but the plan that had seemed so doable at Chatfield's suddenly felt risky, reckless even, with too many variables beyond my control.

Too late to do anything about that now. I glanced out the window at the cars parked along the street. Chatfield sat behind the tinted windows of a Dodge Caravan, ready with recording equipment and cameras. Hawking had come through for me, setting up the lunch meeting with the assemblyman and making the one o'clock reservation under his own name. He'd picked the assemblyman's favorite spot: Croce's in downtown San Diego, a restaurant owned by the wife of the late, great folk singer Jim Croce. I'd arrived twenty minutes early to be sure I got a table by the window. Nineteen of those minutes were up.

Across the room, the hostess was heading toward me followed by a chubby man shuffling through the tables. The hairs stood up on my forearm. My woo-woo friend Linda, who gives psychic readings for a living, might call it a confirmation chill—the body's response to an important connection. Cowan reached the table and stared at me, confusion muddling his features. I hurried to put him at ease.

"Hi," I said, extending my hand.

He gave it a half-hearted shake.

"I'm standing in for Steve Hawking," I said. "My name's Merry." I was giving him my middle name, which was fitting at the moment: Merry Chase.

"Where's Steve?" Cowan polished the question with a concerned veneer, but I saw right through it to the suspicion beneath.

"He's going through a lot of stress right now. He asked me if I could come and talk to you about it."

The politician frowned as he settled in across the table from me. His eyes searched my face.

"You look familiar. Haven't I met you before?"

I smiled, doing my best to look delighted to be recognized. I wasn't. I'd put up my hair and changed my makeup in the hope that I wouldn't be recognized. Apparently this transformation wasn't as effective as the Elvis-in-drag disguise Thomasina had cooked up for me.

"Yes, we did meet. Very briefly, at a political meeting earlier this week. I'm amazed you remember. Especially since I'm wearing my glasses today."

The glasses were on loan from Chatfield. The nose frame housed a micro-minicamera, and the video was feeding into his van as I spoke.

Cowan's lips curled into a fake smile.

"I never forget a face. So you're a friend of Steve Hawking's. What a bright young man he is. Top of his class at Hastings Law School, did you know that?" He flicked a pudgy hand. "I'm sure you did. Anyway, we certainly feel fortunate to have Steve on our team. Terrific young man." The phony smile disappeared. "Steve's all right, isn't he?"

"He's okay. He wanted me to give you a message for him."

A waiter came forward, but Cowan waved him away.

"We need a few more minutes, thank you."

The waiter backed away with a subservient nod, and Cowan turned back to me.

"What message?" he asked.

"Well, first he wants you to know that he thinks the world of you. He says you're a great man. 'Outstanding statesman' he called you."

The praise didn't appear to be soothing him as much as I'd hoped it would.

"Why couldn't he tell me this himself?"

I took a sip from my water glass. My throat was going dry.

"He's afraid to face you, I think. It's a very emotional time for him. That murder at the casino really freaked him out."

He shook his head and put on an indignant face.

"That's the problem with this damn Indian gaming. It invites all kinds of bad elements. Organized crime, violence . . ."

I nearly choked on my water. *Freaking hypocrite.*

"I imagine Steve's nervous about the bar exam, too," Cowan said. "Isn't that coming up for him soon? He doesn't need to worry. He'll pass that old thing with flying colors. Is that why he's afraid to face me?"

"Not exactly." I adjusted the heavy glasses on the bridge of my nose. "He's been doing some soul searching."

Cowan looked concerned—for himself.

"I hope he's all right. Mentally, I mean."

"I think he'll be okay. I did a psychic reading for him recently. He's looking deeply at his life right now."

He pursed his lips, as if the mere mention of a psychic reading was distasteful.

"Some unresolved issues came up during Steve's reading," I continued. "I told him he should talk directly to you about this, but—"

"About what?"

"Look, I don't know the details, and frankly I don't want to know. But apparently he feels that he wronged you."

Cowan's face was unreadable.

"He says he has some money," I continued, "that rightly belongs to the campaign."

He stiffened. I had the sense of an animal who'd just smelled danger on the wind and was freezing until it knew the source of the threat.

"I can't imagine what he's talking about," he said.

"He didn't go into details with me. He just said that he'd violated the trust of a good man, and this money he took from your campaign is really bothering his conscience."

Now Cowan was interested.

"What money? I'm sure it wasn't a significant amount. I know Steve. I'm sure he'll be willing to make restitution."

"Well, you're right, he is. But it was quite a bit of money, he said. I guess he was supposed to deliver campaign funds to a supporter out in east San Diego County. Over a thousand dollars, Steve said. He stole the money and padded the packages with counterfeit bills."

The blood was draining from Cowan's face. I cast my eyes down as if ashamed for Steve.

"Like I said, he can't face you right now, but he asked me to give you this. He says he'll pay the rest back in monthly installments." I took a folded piece of paper from my purse and handed it across the table. It was a thousand-dollar check, printed from Chatfield's check-writing software and filled out in Hawking's own hand. Cowan stared at it quietly. I hoped that the familiar handwriting would lend credibility to my story.

"Is this making sense to you?" I asked. "I mean, I'm kind of in the dark here."

He handed the check back.

"I don't know what he's talking about. Tell him to give me a call."

My mind raced to find words that would draw him out without raising his suspicions even higher. In the end, I could only think of one thing to say.

"Okay, I'll tell him."

Cowan pushed up his sleeve and glanced at his watch.

"I don't want to be rude," he said, rising from his chair, "but I have a two o'clock. Enjoy your meal." He turned and walked out.

So much for getting incriminating statements on tape. As soon as I saw him disappear through the front entrance, I grabbed my purse, tossed some crumpled one-dollar bills onto the table, and hurried to the exit at the side of the restaurant.

39

I charged like a quarterback on 'roids through the narrow spaces between the restaurant tables. Lunch diners looked up at me with silent reproach. Pushing through Croce's side exit, I found myself on F Street. Chatfield's van was already waiting at the curb, motor running. I climbed in, feeling shaken and slightly out of breath.

"Man, what a dick that guy is," Chatfield said as I buckled up.

"Hawking called him a sweet guy."

"He is sweet. Sweet as Jonestown Kool-Aid."

He pulled away from the curb, made a left at the light, and merged with the traffic heading north on Fifth Avenue.

"Where'd he go?" I asked.

"The blue Cadillac a block up. See it?"

I followed Chatfield's finger until I spotted Cowan's car. Traffic was heavy, and we idled at the red light. Pedestrians and jaywalkers flowed like water past our front and rear bumpers. I sat back in my seat and looked around. From the outside, Chatfield's van appeared perfectly ordinary. Inside it looked like the production room at a television station. A camera sat on a tripod mounted to the window. A deck of monitoring equipment flanked both sides of the van.

"This vehicle is really something," I said. "There must be fifty grand worth of equipment in here."

Chatfield changed lanes to follow the Caddy.

"My 'Super SurveillanceMobile.' All just one more benefit of Scott Chatfield's—"

" 'Value-Added Investigations,' " we finished in unison.

We were now three cars behind the Cadillac.

"Quiet for a sec, okay?" he said.

He fiddled with the dial on a black box between the seats. Out of a small speaker I heard a phone ringing. Chatfield smiled.

"We gotcha now, buddy."

"What—?" I began, but he held up a hand to silence me.

Out of the speaker came the sound of a message machine picking up. *"Hi, you've reached my voice mail. Please leave a message."* I heard the familiar beep of an answering machine.

"The voice on that machine sounded like Steve Hawking," I said. "Are we catching Cowan's cell-phone calls?"

Chatfield nodded.

The sound of a dial tone came through the black box. Cowan had hung up without leaving a message for Hawking.

"What is that thing?" I asked.

"A portable cellular relay station," he answered. "It picks up the cell-phone signal and locks in the ESN."

"ESN?"

"Electronic signal number." He turned to me and made a smiley face. "Now his cell phone thinks that *we're* his cell site. Isn't that cool?"

The Cadillac made a left on Ash. Cowan was heading for the freeway. A few seconds later we heard another ring coming through the speaker on the black box. This time there was an answer.

"Citizens Against Unregulated Gambling."

The voice was male, matter-of-fact, and efficient.

"This is Russell Cowan. Put me through to Steve Hawking."

"I'm sorry, Mr. Cowan. Steve hasn't come in yet today. Shall I leave a message?"

"No, never mind."

Click.

"He's trying to get in touch with Hawking to check out your story about the money," Chatfield said.

"I don't think he's going to succeed. Hawking told me last night he was catching a plane to Sacramento this morning."

Cowan turned onto First, took the on-ramp to Highway 5, and entered the freeway. He settled into the second lane at a cruising speed of seventy. The black box picked up the sound of another phone ringing and again a man answered.

"Andy Bello." The voice was abrupt.

"Andy, it's Russ. We have a problem."

"What's going on?"

"Hawking didn't show."

There was a pause.

"Hawking's the one who called the urgent meeting," Bello said. "What do you mean he didn't show?"

"I mean he didn't show. Some friend of his came instead."

"What friend's this?"

"I don't know. Some woman. A goddamn palm reader or something."

"Sonofabitch." There was a tense pause. "You think somebody tipped him off?"

"I certainly hope not." Cowan's voice climbed angrily as he speeded up and weaved into lane one.

The man called Bello asked:

"You get a name for the palm reader?"

"She said her name was Mary. A friend from the campaign, I guess. I saw her at a meeting."

"I don't like it."

"I don't either. She said Hawking wanted to return some money he owed us."

"Yeah, right. That's bullshit. Stinks from a mile away."

"It's worse than that. She said Hawking took the cash and delivered counterfeit instead."

Bello's pause this time had an ominous undertone.

"Describe this palm reader." His voice was not happy.

"I didn't get much of a look at her."

"Tall? Short?"

"I don't know. She was already sitting down when I got there."

"Hair color? Distinguishing features?"

"Brown hair. Ugly glasses. But she doesn't always wear the glasses."

"That's just fuckin' great. What's she drive?"

"I didn't see. The whole thing makes me very nervous."

"Don't worry, I'll handle it. We'll find Hawking first and deal with the palm reader later. Hey, counterfeit or not, it got the job done, right?"

"Unless it comes back and smacks us in the face." Cowan's voice was grim.

There was a click. I looked over at Chatfield, and Chatfield looked at me.

"I think we'd better call David," he said.

40

David sat at a back table in Chatfield's office, chewing the end of a pen and frowning at the TV monitor. Russell Cowan's guarded expression filled the screen.

"I don't know what he's talking about. Tell him to give me a call."

Then came my voice, off-camera.

"Okay, I'll tell him."

The camera panned to Cowan's wrist as he checked his watch, then up abruptly as he rose from his chair.

"I don't want to be rude, but I have a two o'clock. Enjoy your meal."

He turned the back of his wrinkled brown suit to the camera and walked away. The screen went black.

David brushed his hair off his forehead and tossed his pen onto the tabletop.

"I don't know what you're so excited about, Elizabeth. So far it looks to me like you acted on flimsy information—without my knowledge or consent—and have succeeded in pissing off a prominent politician."

I felt my mouth drop open.

"Didn't you see the way his face blanched when I told him about Hawking stealing the money and delivering counterfeit bills?"

David threw his hands into the air.

"So what? I'd blanch too if someone told me an employee was ripping me off. You're assuming this cash Hawking allegedly delivered was used for illicit purposes. But what have we really got here? Just this guy Steve Hawking speculating that the money had something to do with murder. That's coincidence, Elizabeth. That's not evidence." David looked over at Chatfield. "Am I right or am I right?"

Chatfield held up a finger and rolled his chair over to the electronic equipment against the wall.

"I'm going to delay answering that question until you've heard my greatest-hits tape here." He pushed a button and a reel-to-reel tape recorder began to spin. The room was filled with the sounds of the cell-phone conversation we'd picked up from Cowan's car.

"Hawking didn't show."

"Hawking's the one who called the urgent meeting. What do you mean he didn't show?"

"I mean he didn't show. Some friend of his came instead."

"What friend's this?"

"I don't know. Some woman. A goddamn palm reader or something."

"Sonofabitch. You think somebody tipped him off?"

"I certainly hope not."

Chatfield stopped the tape and rolled his chair around to face David.

"This begs a question here: Tipped Hawking off about *what*?" He paused to let us consider, then rolled more tape. We listened to the part where Cowan described me and up to the point where Bello said:

"We'll find Hawking first and deal with the palm reader later. Hey, counterfeit or not, it got the job done, right?"

Chatfield stopped the tape again and looked at David.

"What do you think now?"

David lifted his shoulders, hands turned up.

"Okay, the cash got the job done. What job? How do we know he wasn't talking about printing leaflets?"

"Because," I answered, "Hawking told me that Andy Bello is one of Cowan's supporters from Las Vegas. He thinks the money came from him."

David was unimpressed.

"So?"

"So I *know* Hawking is the key to this case. I'll go out on a limb here and say I have it on psychic authority."

"Psychic authority," David said, "won't cut it in court. I'm sorry, but I just don't share your enthusiasm about this. I'm not saying we won't pursue this new information; I'm just telling you I'm not going to risk coming forward with it now.

When it comes right down to it, the statements aren't specifically incriminating. There's nothing concrete here, nothing actionable."

"We've got Hawking's testimony."

"*Do* we?" David asked. "You said he caught a plane to Sacramento. For all we know his plane was headed to Timbuktu. Hell, for all we know he could be trying to set Cowan up. Isn't that right, Scott?"

"Yeah, maybe," Chatfield said. "But what I keep wondering is why Bello asked who tipped off Hawking. Tipped him off about what? Printing leaflets? Seems like there's something a little more sinister going on there."

David conceded the point with a nod.

"Yeah, but the fact remains that all we have are an inconclusive videotape and an illegally tapped cell-phone call. A snotty-nosed law student testifying against a popular California politician? Shaky, to say the least. If we're going to the DA to build a murder-for-hire case against an assemblyman, we'd better make damn sure of what we're doing, or we'll never work in this state again."

I slumped in my chair. I'd expected more enthusiasm from David. When I looked up, he was smiling.

"Cheer up. There's been another development, and I've got to say it looks a lot more promising than your Cowan theory. Remember the kid you ran into when you found Natalie Hurston's body?"

My stomach did a flip-flop. I knew what was coming next.

"Yeah, Wolf Aquillo."

"I think he's our killer. The cops leaned on the clerk in the hotel office, and the old woman admitted the kid was at the hotel that night. It's a well-known fact around Temecu that he was hostile toward his uncle."

"So what real evidence do you have?" I asked, perhaps a little defensively.

"We're working on that. But since Natalie Hurston's body was buried near the tree where they found Aquillo's scalp, it stands to reason that the same person was involved in both deaths. And the kid has showed up at both crime scenes."

"That's just as speculative as my Cowan theory," I said.

"It won't be when the physical evidence is confirmed."

"What physical evidence?"

"They finally got a match on a partial footprint in the dirt behind the balcony. Plus we'll have preliminary results this week on hair and fiber evidence. Too soon for the full DNA analysis, but as soon as the final results are in, I expect they'll be making an arrest." He gathered up his briefcase. "I've got to run. I'm meeting the forensic pathologist at four. Scott . . ." he walked over and shook Chatfield's hand ". . . see you later, buddy. And careful with that electronic surveillance stuff. You can get fined for that, you know." When David walked out the door, Chatfield rolled his eyes.

I felt sick inside. Wolf was going to think I'd betrayed him. Chatfield's fax machine began to sing, and he scooted his chair over to see what was coming through.

"What do *you* think Hawking's cash deliveries were used for?" I asked.

He pulled the paper out of the fax and looked over his glasses at me.

"If I had to guess, I'd say the two deliveries were some-now, the-rest-when-the-job's-done payments for Aquillo's murder. But that's me guessing. You're the one who has to find out."

"What I need to do is interview Norm Clapp at the mine." I pressed my palms together in a prayerful gesture and made my humble plea. "What are my chances of persuading you to come along? Three out of four, two out of three, one out of two?"

"Zero out of infinity, I'm afraid. I've got to be back in Barstow later tonight."

"No problem," I said.

"What do you mean, no problem? You're not planning on going out there alone, are you?"

"Probably not."

He looked at me sternly.

"You tell me this guy Clapp is a former FBI agent with a gold mine and a Waco, Texas–type arsenal. And you're proposing to have a casual chat with him about his role in a murder-for-hire? You're a detective, Elizabeth, not a kamikaze. Remember that."

"I'll get one of the tribal cops to go with me."

"Or go *for* you. I'd like to see you become wrinkled, fat, and gray. Your chances of getting that way are a lot better if you chicken out of assignments like these."

"Quite a pep talk," I joked.

"See why they kicked me off the police force?"

"You were with the police?"

"One of the finest of 'The World's Finest City.' It's amazing I lived through my three years in patrol. I was a violence magnet."

"A violence magnet," I repeated with a laugh.

Chatfield's face was serious. "Kidding aside, I see the same quality in you."

He was right, but I didn't want to dwell on that now.

"Can I take the video and tape?"

"The unlawfully procured electronic surveillance, you mean? Sure," he said with a smile, "have at it."

"Thanks for getting me this far," I said as he gathered the tapes from the equipment bay.

We said our good-byes at the door of his office, and I walked out into the orange glow of another late afternoon. When I was halfway to my truck, Chatfield called after me.

"Elizabeth?"

I turned around.

"Remember this is just a job, okay? The fate of the world isn't resting on your shoulders. I mean . . ." he looked up at the sky, squinted at a crow flying overhead, then looked back. "Don't do anything stupid. I'm getting pretty darn fond of you."

I turned around and walked back to him, surprising him with a hug.

"Don't worry so much," I said.

Chatfield didn't make his customary witty rejoinder, and when I pulled away, his face was somber.

"I'll be careful," I promised.

41

The September days were getting shorter, and this one had nearly slipped away. The espionage with Chatfield and subsequent meeting with David had eaten up most of the afternoon. It would be late by the time I reached the reservation.

I called the Temecu Area Station from my car phone as I headed east. Rubio Valquez picked up, sounding weary.

"Wondered if you might be willing to check out another lead I've got," I said. "Since our last rendezvous proved so fruitful and all."

"Like when?"

"How about this afternoon?" I asked hopefully.

"This afternoon's almost over. I'm off duty in a half hour, and I'm hungry as a bear. I can wait until five, but not a minute past."

"I'll be there."

I made good time until I reached the winding, uphill climb on Highway 76 and got behind the inevitable tractor-trailer chugging along at twenty miles under the speed limit. As we climbed to two thousand feet above sea level, I could feel my blood pressure rising as steadily as the elevation. By the time I turned onto Mystic Mesa, I had ten minutes to get to the area station. I put a heavy foot on the gas, hoping to beat the clock. My speedometer inched toward sixty, about the limit for what was legal on this road.

I passed the mine, closing in on eighty miles per. It would be a shame to miss Valquez now, but I had no intention of driving recklessly. When the needle hit eighty-five, I dropped back. I was a minute too late. As I crested a small rise and raced down the other side, I saw a problem waiting for me on the side of the road: A stealthy green Bronco with klieg lights on top.

Tribal Police.

I braked hard, but even so I passed the Bronco doing at

least seventy-five. The siren went on, and I saw lights flashing in my rearview.

Shit.

I pulled over, seriously annoyed. I watched my outside rearview mirror. When the Bronco's door opened, I recognized Angie Moon's compact figure walking toward me along the road. I rolled down my window, and she peered in.

"You again," she said without enthusiasm.

"Hi."

"License and registration, please."

I scared up the required documents and handed them through the window. Agent Moon secured them to her clipboard and walked back to her Bronco. I sat and waited, hoping she'd skip the part about writing up a ticket. Those hopes died when she came back and handed me a long piece of paper printed in colorful triplicate.

"Sign at the bottom, please," she said.

"Is this really necessary?"

"We don't condone speed racing on the reservation."

"This happened in the course of my investigation. I was hoping to get to the area station to see Valquez before his shift ended." Worth a try.

"You're not a peace officer, Ms. Chase. You have no authority to take the law into your own hands. It's behavior like yours that gives private investigators a bad reputation."

My annoyance got upgraded to anger, but I kept my lip buttoned.

"Where's your dog today?" I think this was her attempt to lighten things up.

"Home," I said sullenly.

"You still carrying that Glock?"

"Yes."

"May I see your firearms permit, please?"

"My wallet was stolen last week, if you might recall. I'm still waiting for the replacement permit from the CSIS."

"May I see the replacement application, please?"

I opened my wallet with a sinking feeling. I'd intended to make a copy and tuck it in my wallet. The application was still on my desk at home. I did have a Xerox of my PI license, though.

"Look, here's a copy of my PI license, right here."

"A PI license isn't a permit to carry a firearm. Do you have the paperwork for the gun or not?"

I smiled feebly.

"I think my dog ate my homework."

Nero had charmed her; my joke about him didn't. Her face remained stony.

"Would it be possible for us to work something out here?" I asked. "I can fax you a copy of the gun-permit paperwork as soon as I get home. It's got my registration number and the whole nine yards. Honest."

She considered it for a moment.

"Okay. You get a copy of the replacement application to me, and I'll give you a break on the firearms violation. In the meantime, I'll just need to have your gun."

Tears stung my eyes, and I let out an exasperated breath.

"Mind if I ask you something?"

She lifted her brows, waiting.

"Why are you so determined to bust my chops?"

"My job is to uphold the law. That's all I'm doing." There was no malice in her voice—or any other emotion, for that matter.

I reached into my holster and withdrew my Glock. I was pissed. At myself, mostly, for being disorganized. She took the gun.

"How about the ankle weapon?"

I was hoping she'd have forgotten about that. I reached down and slipped the twenty-two from the ankle holster under my pant leg.

She took that gun, too, and handed my copy of the ticket through the window.

"I'll hang onto your weapons at the area station and turn them over when I see your paperwork. I'll be on duty until ten tonight."

I stared straight ahead. Another Bronco was coming toward us, heading west. As it passed, Valquez tooted his horn at Agent Moon.

"Could you do me a favor, please?"

She didn't say yes or no, just waited for me to speak.

"Could you radio Valquez and see where he's headed?"

"I don't need to," she said. "I know where he's headed. He's going to eat fried chicken at Ed's restaurant."

"Thank you," I said, not sounding grateful in the least.

For several minutes after Angie Moon's Bronco drove away, I leaned back against the headrest, feeling hungry, angry, and tired. It was getting close to dinner time; I could use a meal myself. I started up the truck, made a legal U-turn, and drove at a geriatric pace, the way one tends to do after a speeding citation.

When I pulled into the gravel lot at Ed's Country Cafe, Valquez's Bronco was among the cars parked out front. In the warm evening air, the odor of fried chicken mingled with the smell of hamburgers. I walked in and spotted Valquez at a booth near the far wall. I walked past the curious eyes at the bar and up to his ta-ble. He was nursing a frosty mug of beer and smiled up at me apologetically.

"I waited till quarter after."

"I know, I'm sorry. I had a little trouble on the road. May I join you?"

"Be my guest. This must be important if you took the trouble to track me down after hours."

I spent the next five minutes bringing him up-to-speed on Hawking's confession about the cash deliveries to the mine just before the murders.

"I need to question Norm about those deliveries, and I don't want to do it alone."

Crow's feet fanned out from Valquez's eyes as he smiled.

"Relax. I've known Norm Clapp for twelve years. He's helped me out on more cases than I can count around here." Valquez paused, looking up with happy anticipation as Ed approached our table with his dinner. "Maybe this kid Hawking delivered some packages, but I doubt very highly they had anything to do with your case. Norm's the last person to be involved in something of that nature."

The restaurateur slid a plate of golden fried chicken in front of him.

"Thanks," Valquez said. He looked across the steaming plate at me. "I'll go out there with you, but I'm telling you there's no way he's involved. No way."

Ed turned to me.

"You want some supper, too?" he asked.

"Just something quick, thanks. How about some salad and mashed potatoes?"

"Coming right up."

"How could Norm not be involved?" I asked when the man walked away.

Valquez picked up a thigh piece and crunched down on a generous bite.

"For one thing, he runs a small delivery service out there. That's why it's called the Pony Express Mine and Rock Shop."

The thought that Norm might be innocent heartened me as I sat back and waited for my food. The restaurant was as crowded as I'd ever seen it. Shortly after Ed served my order, a familiar face came through the door and took a table near the bar.

"Don't look now," I said to Valquez, "but Peter Waleta just walked in."

Valquez dabbed his lips with a napkin.

"Not exactly front page news. Everybody eats here Wednesday nights. Ed makes the best fried chicken for miles."

As a waitress cleared our plates, Valquez tossed a few bills on the table.

"Dinner's on me. I'm ready when you are."

"Thanks."

He looked at his watch.

"No big deal. I go right by Norm's mine on my way home anyway. I'll stop and talk, but as far as I'm concerned, this is a social visit."

42

The horizon was glowing with the day's last light by the time we left Ed's restaurant. I followed Valquez's Bronco back onto Mystic Mesa Road and jostled over the cattle crossing into the reservation. A mile later the casino's prodigious tepee loomed up from the chaparral like some giant upside-down ice cream cone against an orange sherbet sky. Soon we were rounding the bend and approaching the brush-covered hillside that harbored the mine. As we pulled into the dusty parking area in front of the rock shop, Norm was standing on the porch outside. He welcomed us at the top of the steps with a big, easy smile.

"Evening, folks."

"Hey, Norm," Valquez said. "Got a minute?"

"I was just locking up here, but sure, come on in." He said hello to me, and I returned the greeting. When he caught my reserved vibe, his smile faded. "Everything okay here?"

Valquez waved a carefree hand.

"Yeah, fine. We just need to check something out."

Norm held the door open and turned on the light. I followed Valquez into the shop and heard Norm behind me.

"How are you, Elizabeth? You watching that back?"

I glanced over my shoulder.

"As much as I can, thanks." I looked to Valquez for a place to begin, and his brows went up as if to say, '*go ahead, this is your deal.*' I faced Norm. "I'm just wondering. . . Does the name Steve Hawking ring a bell?"

The name didn't just register, it lit up Norm's face like a Broadway marquee.

"Of course it does. Let's see . . ." he snapped his fingers ". . . *A Brief History of Time*. Ordered it from the Quality Paperback Book Club. I confess I only read half of it, but even that was enough to blow my mind."

"Not *that* Steve Hawking," I said. "The one I'm interested

in is a young guy, on the small side, good looking, dresses kind of preppy."

I was watching for signs of nervousness in Norm's body language but didn't see any.

"The description's familiar," Norm said. "He may have passed through the shop as a customer. Why?"

"Did he bring you something?"

"Not that I recall."

"A large envelope, perhaps?"

The lights went on again in Norm's eyes, quietly this time.

"Oh, yeah. I think I can help you out here. I remember now. Young guy, clean cut . . . this one was dressed in jeans, though. He came through a couple times, actually."

"And gave you packages or thick envelopes?"

"Yes, he did."

Norm was utterly at ease, with no defensiveness in his voice at all.

"Can you tell me more about the envelopes?"

"That I don't remember. I just put them in the appropriate boxes."

"What boxes?"

He turned and nodded toward the wall.

"The Pony Express boxes."

Valquez gave me an *I told you so* look.

"I don't suppose," I said to Norm, "that you remember which box Hawking was delivering the packages to."

"No, sorry. Then again, we've only got twelve of 'em here. It's an old Temecu tradition. This place actually used to be a southern outpost of the 1860 Pony Express route that went from Missouri to Sacramento. Let's see, who has boxes? The school's got one, the fire and water departments each have a box, the local cafe's got one . . ." His voice trailed off and his brows wrinkled. "You mind telling me what this is all about?"

There was a rap, like a bird hitting the glass, on the window to my left. I turned and saw a long-haired man waving me forward. I blinked and he was gone. Not quite sure I'd even seen him, I stepped toward the glass.

A crash like a thousand plates hitting cement split my ears

and shook the room. *Earthquake,* I thought as I gasped and spun toward the noise. The front window was exploding inward, shards of glass flying into the shop like a fleet of clear, sharp missiles. Valquez hurtled forward headfirst, his body shattering the glass display case as it landed. The back of his uniform turned from khaki to an ugly, wet red-brown.

I'd never heard machine-gun fire before, and the sound rattled my nerves to the point of paralysis. I wanted to help Valquez, but my muscles were frozen. Norm lunged from behind the counter, grabbing my arm and pulling me down with such force that my forehead hit the floor. The shooting stopped for a few seconds. Bending to stay low, he dragged me behind the counter and along the wall, then reached up with one hand and unlatched the door to the mine.

"Crawl in. I'll lock it from the outside."

"What about you?" Another explosion of bullets rained into the shop, pelting the walls with a deadly rhythm.

Norm's intense blue eyes were as commanding as his shout. "Don't worry about me. Go!"

I wasn't about to argue. I crawled into the dark space, and the door locked me in. I was enveloped in silence.

In safety.

I rose from my hands and knees. My fingers crawled along the rocky wall until they found the light switch. I flipped it on, and the string of bulbs along the ceiling of the mine glowed dimly. I moved further in, propelled by the irrational fear that I'd somehow be safer deep in the earth. I reached the area where Norm had been mining the tourmaline. The CCTV monitor was on, and I had a clear view of what was happening on the other side of the door.

The image was shocking, even in low resolution black-and-white. The display tables in the front of the shop had been blasted apart. Merchandise neatly arranged just seconds ago now littered the floor. I couldn't see Norm anywhere, and that worried me. On the monitor, the front door jerked open, kicked from behind. A man walked in, an M16 jutting above his pot belly. As I watched the shooter advance into the shop, things began to make sense.

He must have overheard Valquez and me talking over dinner and figured he was about to be found out. I ran through everything I knew about him and it all fit. His career in Vietnam. His hostile talk about Indians and their casinos at the Citizens Against Unregulated Gambling meeting. He'd recently found money to put a new roof on his restaurant—a restaurant that had been a local landmark long enough to warrant a Pony Express box of its own. The murder-for-hire was an ingenious arrangement, really. The money had been delivered here anonymously by an unsuspecting middle man. Cowan most likely never saw who took the cash, and Ed probably never saw who paid him. But as Andy Bello had said: *"It got the job done, right?"*

Ed moved through the shop with his M16 in firing position. I said a prayer for Norm. *He must be on the floor behind the counter, hiding or wounded—or worse,* I thought. Crossing the shop floor with a hunter's halting steps, Ed looked as if he were stalking something. Me, I realized with a lump in my throat. The camera lens was mounted above the door to the mine, and Ed's body loomed on the screen as he moved closer. He reached out and tried the handle. When the door didn't budge, he raised his machine gun and unloaded several seconds' worth of rounds into the lock. I could hear the muffled gunfire pummeling the steel-reinforced door.

Thwarted by the steel door, Ed looked up straight into the camera. His eyes were dull and stupid. He aimed the eye of the barrel at the lens, and the CCTV monitor went black.

Fear started as coldness in my feet and crawled up my legs like a rising flood. I felt blind without the monitor and defenseless without my guns. There was a way to open the door to the mine, and Ed was bound to find it sooner or later.

Think!

I remembered the big storage box Norm had shown me on our tour of the mine. Knowing Norm, he'd have a weapon stashed in there with the flashlights and canned goods. I hurried to the box and searched through the supplies inside. Nothing. To the right of the box was a long, weather-proof plastic case. I opened it and smiled with relief. The gun was three feet long with a sight rail along the top of the barrel and a monster-sized magazine jutting down in front of the grip. I pulled it out with some difficulty. I could handle the thing, but its weight made it more suitable for someone with Arnold Schwarzenegger's upper-body strength. I saw a box of No. 1 buckshot in the case, so I assumed the weapon was a shotgun. But I honestly wasn't even sure. It looked like a tommy gun from an old gangster movie. I checked the magazine, which was loaded. Thank you, Norm.

Gun in firing position, I wandered deeper into the mine until I found the second exit. I removed the lock and unfastened the latch, hoping that Ed wasn't aware of this entrance and waiting for me on the other side. Stepping out barrel first, I emerged from the side of the hill.

The earth had spun into the dark side. The scent of sage was strong in the night air. I stood under the early stars, uncertain of my next move. I thought about what Chatfield had said about me being a violence magnet, and the world not resting on my shoulders. Rubio Valquez and Norm Clapp might well be bleeding to death in the shop, but my getting dead wasn't going to help them. I headed up the hill in the opposite direction from the shop, hoping to loop through the brush to the road and get help. The climb quickly became steeper, the sagebrush denser, and the trail narrower. Soon the passage was wide enough for nothing larger than a rabbit. I couldn't push through no matter how hard I tried.

Déjà vu. The sound of Sequoia's drumming came back to me, and my vision of the dense, impassable brush trail. I turned around and headed back down. The heavy gun threw me off balance, and my feet slipped on the pebbly path. The trail widened and ended up in a patch of bone-dry weeds behind Norm's shop.

There was no way to get to the road without going past the shop. I moved step by step along the outside wall, straining to keep my feet from making crackling sounds in the dry undergrowth.

Twenty feet away, the porch steps creaked. I saw Ed's silhouette moving down the stairs. I hoped he was leaving, but when he reached the bottom, he veered left and his dark form headed in my direction.

I raised the shotgun shoulder-level and fired. The gun kicked hard, and the butt slammed into my collarbone. It felt like the shot went wide, but I heard him cry out. He backed away, firing off a stuttering battery of rounds. The staccato gunfire echoed into the night. I flattened myself against the wall and froze. Footsteps pattered across the parking lot. I heard an engine come to life with a roar and came forward in time to see the headlights of a dark Suburban swinging onto Mystic Mesa Road. I lowered the weapon and wiped my forehead. My hand came back wet, and I realized I was bleeding.

43

The blood was running in a slow trickle from a cut above my right eye. The pain was familiar as I probed the wound with my fingertips. It was the old cut on my brow bone from my mugging last week, reopened. Probably happened when Norm pulled me to safety, and my head hit the floor. I decided I'd live. I took a deep breath and headed up the porch steps.

Inside the shop, shattered glass and ruined merchandise covered every square foot of the floor. In the naked overhead light, crystals and semiprecious stones glimmered like dangerous treasures among shards of glass. Rubio Valquez remained where he'd fallen, facedown in the ruined display case. I took his wrist in my hand and felt a pulse so weak I couldn't be sure that I wasn't imagining it.

I rushed to the phone behind the counter and dialed 911. When the dispatcher came on the line, I explained the situation in a quaking voice.

"Hang in there," she said. "We've already got someone on the way."

She wanted to keep me on the phone, but I was anxious to find Norm and hung up. I scanned the floor with searching eyes and began to wonder what the dispatcher had meant about someone already being on the way. Had someone else called? If so, who? I checked behind the overturned tables, steeling myself against the inevitable shock of finding Norm's body. It was nowhere in sight. I walked behind the demolished counter where I'd last seen him. I picked up a shard of glass and held the jagged edge to the light. It was covered in bright red blood. I swallowed hard.

A siren wailed in the distance, the volume rising to a scream. Headlights bounced into the parking lot, and I recognized Angie Moon's Bronco. She jumped out, pistol drawn. I put the shotgun down on the floor behind the counter and met her at the door.

"Valquez is down; I don't know where Norm is." My words came out in a frantic tumble, and I made an effort to slow down. "Ed shot this place up like it was My Lai village. He took off in a dark Suburban about five minutes ago. It's—" my voice caught and tears sprang to my eyes "—bad in here."

She rushed past me to Valquez's side. I followed and stood by as she went through the same motions I had, feeling for his pulse.

"Ambulance is on its way," I said, "but I don't know where Norm is, and it's scaring me. He was right here when he pushed me into the mine. He locked me in and told me not to worry."

She got to her feet, a dazed expression on her face.

"What?"

"I don't know what happened to Norm," I repeated. "When the shooting started, he pulled me down and pushed me into the mine—" I pointed to the steel-reinforced door "—and that's the last I've seen of him. He was right here."

She frowned and retraced my steps, searching the shop.

"He couldn't have disappeared into thin air," she said. "Maybe he was wounded and crawled outside."

She took a step toward the door, and a scratching sound came up from the floor near our feet. Both of us jumped. Moon drew her gun and pointed the weapon at the floor. We heard a muffled chink and a thump. A two-foot-square section of the floorboard raised up an inch or two. The trapdoor flipped open, and Norm's head appeared.

"It's me, Angie. I'm the one who pushed the alarm. Put that thing down."

She lowered her weapon, and Norm climbed out of the crawl space under the floor. He got to his feet, rocking slightly on his heels. A nasty wound had made a bloody mess of his hand, but other than that he seemed all right. His eyes scanned the destruction. He turned to me, and we shared the intimate gaze of two people who'd just escaped death.

"Rubio's still got a pulse," I said hopefully.

"Where's the shooter?" he asked.

I pointed toward the road.

"He tore out of here in a Suburban. It was Ed, from the restaurant."

"We'll have that on videotape." He glanced up at the camera above the mine door. The mounting assembly had been blown apart, and the camera dangled uselessly from a single screw. "At least I hope we will."

"I saw him from inside the mine, before he blew out the lens."

"You found my USAS-12 shotgun, I see." He picked the gun up off the floor.

"So that's what that is," I said.

"Did you fire that weapon?" Moon asked, glaring at me suspiciously.

"Yes, and for the most part, I missed. Although I do think he caught a pellet or two."

A night breeze rushed through the blown-out windows of the shop. It carried another sound: the faint wail of more sirens.

The ambulance arrived minutes later, though it seemed like those proverbial hours. The medics wrapped an oxygen mask on Rubio Valquez's face and whisked him away, sirens screaming. An EMT with bright red hair and a handlebar mustache stayed behind to swab my brow cut with antiseptic and wrap it in a bandage. He didn't think more stitches would be necessary. Within half an hour, at least a dozen vehicles arrived from a half-dozen agencies: U.S. Marshal, Sheriff, Fire Department, SDPD, CHP, ABLE. An APB went out, and roadblocks were set up at the east and west entrances to the reservation. So far there'd been no sign of Ed.

When I finished making my statements to Karl McKenna, the SDPD detective in charge, Angie Moon touched my arm.

"Let's get you out of here," she said.

I climbed into the passenger seat of her Bronco, feeling oddly disconnected from my body. She jumped behind the wheel and started the engine.

"Not a good night to be without a gun. I'm sorry," she said, as she pulled out.

I fastened my seat belt.

"I don't think my little handguns would have made a peanut's difference in there. But I appreciate the thought."

We picked up speed and I stared at the lines zooming toward us in the middle of the black asphalt. Sometimes broken and white, sometimes solid and yellow. Two miles down the road, I started to cry.

"There's Kleenex in the glove compartment," Moon said.

It wasn't what she thought, but I didn't bother explaining it to her. I wasn't crying because I was sad. I was crying because I was so happy that Nero hadn't been with me tonight; that he was safe at home, waiting for me. I skipped the tissue and wiped my eyes with the back of my hand.

We came to a bend in the road and something tugged at me, off to the right. I *felt* Ed again, out on the chaparral. I recognized his presence as surely as if I'd seen and heard him.

"Stop," I said.

Moon lifted her foot from the gas and glanced across the front seat.

"You okay?"

"Stop the car."

"Are you going to be sick?" she asked.

"No, nothing like that. I felt Ed back there. I'm not kidding. Go back."

"You *felt* Ed?"

That wasn't going to be good enough for her.

"I saw something," I lied. "Ed's back there, I know it. Check it out."

Moon slowed into a turnout and pulled a U-turn on the deserted road. Our headlights revealed only the blacktop in front of us. To the left and right the chaparral disappeared into darkness.

"Where?"

I tuned in.

"Pull over up there and see if you can aim your headlights across the road."

The way she looked at me let me know she'd lost faith

again. I could practically hear her wondering if I were delusional. I sat up straight in my seat, straining to see.

"Look, look, look," I said excitedly. "Over there, that bizarre light."

From this direction something was visible. She saw it, too, and pulled to a stop. On the opposite side of the road, about forty feet from the shoulder, a sword of light was raised toward heaven.

"What the hell is that?" I said.

Moon pulled closer and cut her lights.

When our eyes adjusted to the dark, what it was became evident. On a slight rise, smashed into a pile of boulders, was the Suburban. It rested at an angle, the impact having sent its nose into the air. One headlight was still on, throwing a white beam at an eerie slant into the sky.

The lock in my door thumped as Moon pressed the Bronco's autolock switch. She radioed our location into her dashboard micro-phone.

"Probable suspect in a wrecked brown Suburban approximately two miles east of Mystic Mesa Casino, fifty feet off the road. One headlight visible. Code 10. Repeat: Code 10."

Code 10. She was calling for SWAT assistance.

"Can you see from your side if he's in the car?" she asked.

I strained to see, but the Suburban was too far away and the night too dark.

"No," I said.

Moon drew her service revolver and sat stiffly, scanning the blackness outside the windshield. The minutes stretched. I realized I was holding my breath again and reminded myself to breathe. At last we heard the chopping of helicopter blades. Lights appeared from the west, swooping down to the ground like bright arms feeling their way in the night. The Life Flight helicopter landed in a clearing about a hundred yards from the Suburban. Minutes later it was joined by the SDPD Air Borne Law Enforcement copter.

Moon and I watched from the safety of the Bronco. Like a platoon of fireflies, flashlights converged on the wreck. Several minutes later, two of the flashlights broke away from the others and bobbed toward us through the darkness. Moon rolled down the window, and McKenna peered in.

"Better get out here," he said. "I want you to hear the doctor explain this."

"The situation is this," the doctor began. His face looked ghoulish in the upward light of the flashlight, but his voice was gentle and sad. "The suspect is alive and conscious. The bullet wound in his shoulder is negligible, but he's trapped in wreckage below the waist. He's relatively comfortable because he's numb from the mid-lumbar area down, but there's been massive, irreparable soft-tissue and organ damage. We can extract him with metal cutters and the Jaws of Life, but his compression injuries are such that when he gets pulled out, he's going to die."

The doctor let that sink in.

"For certain?" Moon asked.

The doctor nodded.

"I'm afraid so. Right now the pressure from the metal is what's keeping his blood circulating, but as soon as he's extricated, he's going to suffer catastrophic blood loss. Absolutely fatal, no way around it. He could remain conscious, as long as we don't move him, for up to half an hour, maybe longer. In situations like these I usually ask if the victim would like us to call his family so that he can say any last words. Or perhaps he'd like to speak with a priest or pastor."

"Maybe he'll make a dying declaration," I said, looking to Moon. "He had accomplices in this crime. May I question him?"

Moon looked to Detective McKenna.

"What have we got to lose?" McKenna said. "I'll go ahead with the formal statements to make it legal." He turned to me. "When I give you the nod, you ask your questions."

I followed McKenna across the uneven ground to the wreck. We had to climb onto some rocks to see into the driver's side window. Ed had been flying when he lost control at the bend in the road. The left front of the Suburban had been crushed like an aluminum can against the boulders. Portable work lamps illuminated the wreck. Ed's lower body wasn't even visible beneath the twisted metal, but his upper body appeared unscathed. He turned his head easily as we approached, as if he were choosing to sit there and enjoy the rural night.

"My name is Karl McKenna. I'm a detective with the San Diego Police Department. Can you tell me your name?"

"Edward James Johnson." He sounded perfectly lucid.

"Mr. Johnson, I'm sorry to inform you that your injuries are without question fatal."

"I'm not dumb," he said testily. "I can see that."

"The doctor has informed us that when you're removed from the wreckage you will experience fatal blood loss."

He didn't say anything to that, so McKenna continued.

"Do you wish to speak with family members or a clergyman?"

"Hell, no."

"You do realize, sir, that you are about to die?"

He was playing it by the book, going through the statements required to allow Ed Johnson's dying declaration to be used in court.

Ed turned toward him. His face was white in the portable lights.

"What are you, deaf? I told you I know that. I seen more dead bodies in my lifetime than you ever will." He seemed proud to be such an authority on death.

"Do you have any hope of recovery?" McKenna's voice was flat and emotionless.

"Are you a retard or something? I said no already."

McKenna glanced at me.

"Very well, sir," he said. "Are you willing to answer some questions regarding the crime in which you were just involved?"

"Nope."

"Are you willing to make any true statement about the crime in which you were just involved?"

"That, I'll do."

"Go ahead, sir."

Ed pursed his lips, as if the words were bitter in his mouth.

"Fuck those goddamn Indians." He said it slowly, with finality.

McKenna looked at me and signaled with a nod to go ahead. I cleared my throat.

"Did Russell Cowan offer you money in exchange for murdering Dan Aquillo?"

Ed turned away from me and stared straight ahead.

"Did an agent of Mr. Cowan's, a man named Steve Hawking, offer you money in exchange for murdering Dan Aquillo?"

He turned his face to me and blinked, saying nothing.

"Did you murder Natalie Hurston to prevent her from identifying you as Dan Aquillo's killer?" The anger was leaking through in my voice. He tilted his head and watched me, as if amused by my feelings. The trace of a smile played on his lips. I sensed his spirit as a creature, dark and obstinate. I made one more attempt to reach his soul.

"Tell me, Ed, was it worth a lousy few thousand dollars?"

Edward James Johnson smirked and turned his face away. I stood staring, trying to comprehend his darkness, until McKenna took me by the arm and pulled me back. I climbed down the rocks and stepped away from the wreck, more shaken by this encounter than all the violence that had preceded it.

Moon and I stood back and watched as Johnson was pried from the wreckage. Fifteen minutes later he was pronounced dead and loaded into the helicopter.

EPILOGUE

I stood behind the railing of the widow's walk outside my upstairs parlor. Above me, the clear October sky glittered with
the ancient light of a thousand distant suns. I leaned my head
back and let the universe pour into my naked, wondering eyes.
Beyond the stars I could see, I could feel others stretching into
infinity. I steadied the tripod of my Celestron telescope and
pointed the lens southeast, toward Pisces.

The TV chattered through the open door behind me as I
adjusted the lens and brought Saturn into focus. Its rings,
hard and yellow as a frozen halo, looked close enough to
reach out and touch. I tried to comprehend that the planet was
nearly 800 million miles away, but my mind couldn't grasp
the figure.

"Okay," I called, "tear yourselves away from the God box
and come out and take a look at this."

"The God box?" Thomasina stepped through the open
door, elbows on hips. With her dark head wrapped in cobalt-
blue cotton above her long, gorgeous neck, she looked like a
Nefertiti for the new millennium.

"The TV is the primary altar of worship in this culture, far
as I can tell." I stepped aside and motioned her to the edge of
the widow's walk, pointing to the eyepiece on top of the telescope. "Look right through here."

She put her eyeball to the small glass square that opened to
the universe and took a sharp breath.

"You've probably seen the NASA photos on TV," I said,
"but they can't compare with the reality, if you ask me. Sequoia!" I called. "Come see this." I leaned in through the open
door.

Sequoia's feet were planted firmly in front of the TV.

"I think first you should see this," he said.

"See what?"

By the time I stepped inside, a savvy middle-aged actress

on the screen was suggesting for the hundredth time that I change my telephone-service provider. Sequoia muted the commercial.

"Not this," he said. "I just heard a teaser for the ten o'clock news. I think you'll want to see the lead story."

Thomasina poked her head inside.

"Hey, cuz, you should come out and take a look at Saturn."

Channel 8's Terry Baker came back on the screen, and Sequoia turned the sound back on. A photo of Russell Cowan and his mechanical smile appeared in the upper right corner as a somber Terry read from her teleprompter:

"California State Assemblyman Russell Cowan appeared before a grand jury today for questioning related to two murders on the Temecu Indian Reservation last month. The confirmed suspect in those killings, Edward Johnson, died in a car accident three weeks ago. Johnson had been an active member of Citizens Against Unregulated Gambling, a political group spearheaded by Assemblyman Cowan. Cowan appeared before the grand jury today to address allegations that Johnson may have been hired to kill casino manager and tribal leader, Dan Aquillo. Cowan has denied his involvement in the murder, stating that Johnson was an unstable personality, acting alone."

The set cut to Cowan's pudgy face.

"I am deeply saddened by the senseless loss of life in the tragic events of the past few weeks. No position taken to deadly extremism is ever justified. My heart goes out to the loved ones of the innocent victims." Cowan's face was convincingly pained.

The camera cut back to the news desk, and Sequoia muted the set.

"What I want to know is, was Cowan involved, or not?"

"The off-the-record answer is, not exactly," I answered.

Physical evidence had all but proved that the former Vietnam vet had murdered Dan Aquillo and Natalie Hurston. Aquillo's blood had been found on a hammer in Johnson's workshop. A .32-caliber Ruger recovered from Johnson's Suburban had matched the ballistics on the bullet that killed

Natalie Hurston, and her blood had been found in the Suburban's carpet fibers.

"Cowan's not denying that Hawking delivered money to the Pony Express," I continued, "but he's adamant it was for campaign expenses. As far as that phone conversation Chatfield and I tapped, Cowan says the campaign was planning to let Hawking go, and that's what Bello had meant when he speculated if somebody had tipped Hawking off. Cowan's explanation of the murders is that he made some off-hand comment to Johnson about 'nipping the pro-gaming movement in the bud,' and he thinks the guy just went off and took matters into his own hands."

Thomasina crossed her arms over her chest and smirked.

"Now we'll see if Cowan's cut out for politics," she said. "His career depends on how well he can spin this mess under control." Spoken like the PR mensch that she was.

Nero got up from the floor and put his face in my lap. I smoothed the top of his head. The fur felt like warm silk under my fingertips.

"Enough of this seamy stuff," I said. "Let's get back to our game."

The three of us returned to the dining room downstairs, where the nearly finished Scrabble game waited like so much unfulfilled potential. Thomasina was the clear leader.

Our conversation came in spurts, between long, concentrated silences.

"How's Wolf, Sequoia?" I asked.

In exchange for Wolf's confession to the scalping, the court had handed him a suspended sentence for mayhem and released him to an outpatient psychiatric program. I'd visited him once that first week, and he seemed to be doing well, but Sequoia would have the updated scoop.

"He's back in school," he said. "Also doing community service work at the library on weekends. I think he's gonna pull through okay. Lucy's sure happier than I've seen her in a long time."

It was Thomasina's turn at the board, and she was taking longer than usual.

"How's Hurston doing?" Sequoia asked.

"Great, so far," I said. "He's been hitting the Gamblers' Anonymous meetings pretty regularly, from what I hear. He's talking about this dream he has of opening up a low-cost medical clinic on the res. I hope he makes it come true. He should practice medicine." In my mind's eye I saw Hurston's tapering fingers. "He's got those healer's hands."

Sequoia nodded thoughtfully.

"Maybe some good will come out of this whole thing, anyway. Hey, I heard Rubio Valquez got out of the hospital last week."

Thomasina sighed heavily and got to her feet.

"Time out. I can't concentrate with you two jabbering. I'm going to make some cocoa. Anybody want some?"

We both put in orders, and Thomasina headed for the kitchen. I sat back in my chair, taking a break from the board. I'd been wanting to ask Sequoia a question all night. The time felt right.

"Who was the man in the window?" I watched his face for a reaction.

"What man?" The corner of his mouth curled up, contradicting his feigned ignorance.

"Before Ed Johnson opened fire, I saw a man through the window of the shop. If I hadn't stepped closer to look, Ed would've gunned me down as surely as he gunned down Valquez."

"No kidding. A man in the window, huh?" Sequoia's black eyes danced.

"Yes. In essence, he saved my life. What I can't figure out is, that window is up some stairs, ten feet off the ground. No way someone could be standing on the ground outside Norm's shop and be seen through the window. I wouldn't believe it myself unless I'd seen it myself." Sequoia wasn't reacting. "Maybe it was a figment of my imagination," I baited.

"Maybe so. Then again," he said slowly, "maybe it's not a matter of believing it when you see it, but more a matter of seeing it when you believe it."

"I believe the man in the window looked an awful lot like you."

"Me?" He smiled wide. Not a perfect smile, but beautiful in its warmth.

"Rationally, of course, it doesn't make sense. How could you know to look through that window right at that moment? Besides, your Jeep was nowhere in sight."

"Defies logic, you're right."

I dropped all pretenses, serious now.

"You're a shapeshifter, aren't you? One of those people who can travel outside the body and appear in another place. I've only read about it, wasn't even sure it was a real phenomenon. Is it?"

"What do you think?"

"I think you knew I was in trouble and you appeared, to get me out of harm's way."

His black eyes were steady now.

"You really believe that?" he asked.

"I don't know what to believe."

A tenderness in his face triggered another memory.

"That *was* you that night I got beat up coming back from Mystic Mesa. You comforted me by the side of the road." I felt a fluttering in my diaphragm. "You've been with me this whole time, haven't you? Before we even met. But how is that possible?"

An enigmatic smile crossed his lips, and he went back to studying his letter tray.

I struggled to understand. Sequoia was solid enough to flatten the mat on his chair, real enough to have a blemish on his chin and a few split ends at the bottom of his ponytail.

"How do you do that, Sequoia, travel and materialize that way? Do you think you can teach me?"

He slid the tiles across his tray, rearranging them.

"Maybe. My Aunt Christina taught me. Would you like to learn?"

Before I could answer, Thomasina broke in on us. In her hands she carried three steaming cups.

"What are you two jabbering about? The vibes are thick with conspiracy in here." She slid the cups onto the table. "Whose turn is it?"

"Yours," Sequoia said.

Thomasina sat down and sighed. A minute later she tsked and put down two measly letters.

"All right," she said. "Go for it, cuz."

We fell into silence as Sequoia studied his tiles. The only sound came from me, blowing across my cocoa to cool it down. I took a sip. The chocolatey liquid was smooth and sweet on my tongue. Moments later, Sequoia looked up.

"Don't get mad, okay? I'm going out on you guys."

Thomasina peered at his letter tray with an anguished face.

"You're gonna use up all six of those letters? Get out."

Sequoia winked at me and laid down his six remaining tiles, using a common *E* in the lower right corner of the board.

"Look at that," Thomasina moaned. "And such an ordinary word, too."

I stared at the board. A chill ran the length of my body, starting in my scalp and sending goosebumps down my arms and legs. Sequoia's last word spoke to me as surely as if it had been uttered out loud:

BELIEVE

The hot Santa Ana swept across the open desert, hissing through the bone-dry cheatgrass and shaking the stiff sagebrush. I did my best to ignore it. There was a red and white bull's-eye target tacked to a hay bale ten yards away. I was trying to keep my attention focused there.

Willpower, girl. Mind over matter. You can do it.

I locked an unblinking stare onto the target, drew back the bow string, and let the arrow fly. The slim, feathered spear shot forward but caught the breeze and veered left, missing the hay bale entirely. I sighed in exasperation.

"Great. What am I now, zero for six?"

The wind whipped a shank of hair across my eyes and I called it the F word. As if to mock me, the gust grew in strength, sending up a flurry of straws around the hay bale.

Sequoia stood motionless beside me, his long, black ponytail dancing in the wind. The Luiseno Indian's name suits him well. Sequoia is broad and tall, with skin the deep color of redwood. Like the ancient tree, something about him inspires reverence.

"This isn't about keeping score, Elizabeth. This is about using the power around you."

Spoken like the twenty-first-century medicine man that he is. A distant cousin of my best friend, Thomasina, Sequoia has lived most of his life on the Temecu Reservation east of San Diego. He claims to have learned his shamanic powers in Mexico from a mysterious woman he calls Aunt Christina. I believe he used those powers to save my life a few months ago. It's rare that I meet someone more versed in the unseen realm than I, which is why I'd signed on as his unofficial stu-

dent. I still wasn't clear what archery had to do with shaman-
ism, but had a feeling I was going to find out.

"What power would that be?" I asked.

"The wind. Don't fight it so much. Harness it." Sequoia
pulled another arrow from the leather pouch strapped to his
thigh and handed it to me.

I gave him a dubious look as I placed the notched end of
the arrow onto the string and drew back the bow. The wind
blew steadily, rustling the cheatgrass. I aimed at the target,
corrected for the breeze, and concentrated. *Harness the power
around you.*

The gust picked that moment to die and my arrow sailed
right past the hay bale, missing by an embarrassing distance.
Something inside of me snapped. I pulled my Glock out of my
waistband, set my sights on the target, and blew three hollow-
points into dead center. The gunshots reverberated in the open
air and left my ears ringing. I confess the release felt wonderful.

"There," I said. "How's that for using the power around me?"

Sequoia lifted his Wayfarers off the bridge of his nose and
squinted at the hay bale.

"Nice shooting, but you didn't harness the power of the
wind." He dropped his shades back into place. "You got frustrated and pulled your gun. That"—he nodded toward the bullet-riddled target—"was the power of your anger."

"So?"

"So your anger used you, instead of the other way around."

Sometimes he sounded more like a psychologist than a
shaman. Having once worked as a psychologist myself this
annoyed me, perhaps proving the point that doctors make the
worst patients.

"Who cares? I nailed the target, didn't I?"

The heat was getting to me. As if reading my mind, Sequoia pulled a flask from a large pocket in his cargo pants, un-
screwed the cap, and offered me a drink of water. Even
lukewarm, it tasted sweet and wonderful. I controlled my urge
to guzzle the whole thing and handed the flask back. Sequoia
took a sip and screwed the cap back on, a thoughtful look on
his face.

"When you act out of anger you might win the battle, but you're gonna lose the war. Anger makes you feel powerful, but it's the kind of power that doesn't last."

"But my anger got the job done," I argued. "I hit the damn target."

He walked toward the hay bale, collecting stray arrows along the way.

"What are you mad about?" he called over his shoulder. "Let's deal with that first."

I went with the easy answer.

"Tom's death."

It had been just a few months since my fiancé had been killed in an investigation gone bad. The emotional fallout lingered, and probably would for some time.

"Besides that," Sequoia said.

I tuned into myself. First thing I noticed was the aforementioned heat. On an October day when much of the country would be putting logs on the fire, southern California was baking. It was only nine in the morning and the temperature was climbing toward ninety. Plus, the wind was making me miserable. Blowing down from the high desert, the scorching Santa Ana had sucked all the moisture from the air. I ran my tongue over my lower lip, which had become a ridge of flaky skin. It felt like a wound.

"What's really bugging me is this weather," I called, raising my voice to be heard over the wind. "This Santa Ana makes me nervous, like something bad's going to happen."

Sequoia returned to my side, the fistful of feathered arrows a bouquet in his hand.

"Sounds like a premonition. Maybe you're afraid of what you know is going to happen, and your anger is covering up your fear."

A crow cawed in the distance. As I turned toward the sound, the Santa Ana blew another shank of hair across my face. The ends slapped my cheek so hard it stung.

"No," I said irritably, "it's just this damn wind. It's getting to me. Make it stop."

I brushed the flyaway strands out of my eyes and bent at

the waist, gathering my hair into a ponytail. I twisted it into a knot at the top of my head and stood upright. Sequoia had turned away from me and was facing east, into the wind. He'd once told me that if I ever had a problem I had no answer for, I could face east and the answer would come to me. I looked at his stoic profile and wondered if he was seeking an answer now.

At that moment the wind simply died. It had been blowing hard, but suddenly it was gone, as if someone had pulled the plug on a giant fan beyond the foothills. A hush came over the land and I found myself standing in complete stillness. After a morning of nonstop gusting, the change was as dramatic as a full eclipse. At first I figured it was a temporary ebb, but the calm stretched for over a minute.

"Sequoia?"

He stood silently, still facing east, where the sun had risen halfway into the sky. I tried to read his face, but couldn't see his expression behind his sunglasses. Watching him, I had a sense he was communing with someone—or some*thing*—I couldn't see. Without the cooling effect of the wind, the heat from the blazing sun intensified. Despite the broil, I felt goose bumps rising along my neck.

"Sequoia, did you make the wind stop?"

He didn't move. My question sat on the breezeless air, unanswered. Even the crows were quiet.

A high-pitched electronic beeping erupted from the pager clipped to my waistband, killing the moment. Sequoia turned to me and nodded toward the pager on my hip.

"Better answer that one."

I pushed the button and glanced at the display. I didn't recognize the phone number but did recognize the three digits tacked on the end—911. Whoever was paging considered it an emergency.

I reached for the backpack that served as my combination purse, briefcase, and tool chest. I searched and came up empty.

"Shit. I think I left my cell phone in the car."

"You can use mine." Sequoia dug into another pocket of

his cargo pants and handed over a phone. I dialed the number on my pager display and waited. After the first ring a somber male voice answered.

"Loebman."

"Hi. This is Elizabeth Chase, responding to your page."

"You the psychic PI?"

"That's correct."

A breeze had begun to riffle through the cheatgrass again. I got a funny feeling in my gut—whether it was from the wind or something else, I wasn't sure.

"Thanks for calling back. You know Detective McKenna?"

The name was fresh in my mind. McKenna worked SDPD homicide. We'd met on a case I'd worked recently and had stayed in casual touch.

"Yeah, I know Karl."

"He's the one who gave me your number. Said you were the real McCoy."

"And you are?"

"Oh—sorry. Bruce Loebman. I'm an area detective with the San Diego Sheriff, working the *Fielding* case." He emphasized the name, as if I should be impressed.

"Sorry, I'm not familiar with that one."

"The telecommunications mogul out in Rancho Santa Fe? His son's been missing for five days. It's all over TV. Crime Stoppers has been running public-service announcements on it every night. Surprised you haven't seen them."

Now I put it together. Frank Fielding was the CEO of a wireless communications firm headquartered in north San Diego County. In the past few years the company's stock had rocketed in value. Fielding became a multimillionaire and moved to Rancho Santa Fe, the community my parents had settled into long before the place became synonymous with obscene wealth. I remembered seeing the story about the kidnapping on the news and thinking that a family like the Fieldings was the perfect target.

There was no need to ask how Loebman's case was going. If he had any solid leads, he wouldn't be calling me. I heard a sigh on the end of the line.

"Anyway, Karl said it might be worth my time to talk to you so, uh, I'd like to do that." The hesitancy in his voice told me he wasn't sure about working with a psychic. I could have reassured him with my credentials—my double Ph.D. from Stanford, my state-certified PI license, my VIP commendations—but I hate self-promotion.

"Sure," I said. "Missing persons cases are my strong suit."

"Great." Hope was edging out his skepticism. "What do you pick up about the Fielding boy?"

I smiled to myself and forgave Loebman's naïveté.

"I don't know what McKenna told you, but this doesn't exactly work like a psychic hot line. I'll need to meet with you first and get briefed on the case. If I take it on, my standard retainer is five hundred dollars, plus expenses."

"Oh." Loebman took a minute to let that sink in. "Okay, that's doable. I'm at the Fielding place now. You got a pen? I'll give you directions."

"I'm not available right this minute. I'm way out in—" Sequoia's hand on my arm stopped me short. "Just a minute." I turned and looked into a face so solemn it took me aback.

"Go *now*," Sequoia said.

* * *

I slowed and put on my right-turn signal as I neared the Fielding estates, wondering why my abdomen was tightening. Perhaps it was a reaction to the intimidating design of the gate fronting the property. Constructed of sharply tapering iron bars, the gate spanned a wide asphalt driveway that snaked up into a forest of old eucalyptus. The loose limbs of the trees sailed like flags in the wind, showing just how much strength and velocity the Santa Ana had gained in the fifty minutes it had taken me to drive from the Temecu Reservation to Rancho Santa Fe.

I pulled up behind the unmarked silver Crown Victoria parked just outside the imposing gate. The passenger door opened and I hurried toward it, anxious to escape the wind. I dipped my head into the car.

"Detective Loebman?"

"Yeah, slide in."

A trim man in his mid-thirties gathered some papers from the passenger seat and held them over his lap as I got in the car. He wasn't dressed like any undercover cop I'd ever seen. His smooth face was freshly shaved, his crisp white shirt looked expensive and new, and the crease in his linen pants was as sharp as a paper fold. I eyeballed his outfit and smiled.

"Where we going—church?"

"Not if my rabbi has any say in the matter." He winked and cracked a lopsided grin. "Thanks for coming." In spite of his joke, Loebman impressed me as a solemn man. There was a sadness in his eyes that looked like it had been there for a long time.

It was hot in the car, hotter as soon as I shut the door. I could smell the citrus scent of Loebman's cologne in the close space. He studied me, a puzzled look on his face. I returned his look with an amused smile.

"Not what you were expecting, am I?" I was still clad in the jeans and tank top I'd worn to the reservation. A chalky dusting of desert sand covered my bare arms.

"Not really," he admitted.

"You gonna put that down?" I nodded toward the paper stack he was holding in his hands.

"Oh—I made an extra file for you. You want to see this stuff, or not? I'm not familiar with your, um . . . techniques."

Some psychics want absolutely no information from a case, fearing their imaginations will interfere with their extrasensory perception. I'm not the kind of psychic who can guarantee pulling information out of thin air, which is why I supplement my talent with a PI license. I reached for the papers.

"Yeah, let me see what you've got."

The top sheet told me that the Fieldings had filed a missing persons report late last Wednesday, the day their four-year-old son, Matthew, had disappeared. There's usually a forty-eight-hour waiting period before the cops will start the paperwork on an MP case, but underage kids are the exception. I skimmed the report but didn't go into it deeply, since there was a lot to cover. Documents from multiple agencies—Sheriff's Department, Search and Rescue Department, SDPD—

bloated the stack. I continued flipping through the papers and came across a missing persons bulletin. Above the text was a color photocopy of a little boy gazing, enchanted, at a cake ablaze with four candles. The candlelight played up his big eyes, silky blond hair, button nose, and dimpled chin. Innocence bestows an otherworldly beauty on every kid this age— there's no such thing as an ugly four-year-old. But the Fielding child had the kind of angelic face that tugged on the heartstrings.

"There's been no ransom note, no demand printed in the newspaper, nothin'." Loebman nodded toward the opulent grounds behind the iron gate. "But Fielding's one of the richest men in one of the richest towns in the country. Dollars to donuts, this is about money."

"You sure this isn't a custody dispute?"

He shook his head.

"There's no dispute here. I was ready to resent Fielding for being so damn rich, but when I interviewed the guy I felt bad for him, man. *He* is in church right now, by the way. Praying. His wife, Roxanne, is in there glued to the phone."

"Where'd the kid disappear from? Day care? Shopping mall?"

"Right off the property. Roxanne says one minute he was in the backyard, the next minute . . . gone."

I glanced at the photo and, in an intuitive flash, *knew* the child was alive. Almost immediately, my left brain—that logical doubting Thomas in my head—shot the insight down as wishful thinking. I've learned to go with my first impression. Dollars to donuts, the kid was all right.

"We've tapped every available resource." Loebman pointed to the bulletin in my hands. "That's gone out to every law enforcement agency we can think of. Plus the hospitals and shelters. Volunteer search-and-rescue teams have been combing the surrounding area since we got the call, handing out flyers. We called in the ASTREA helicopter, tracker K-9s, you name it."

"I can see that." I sorted through the agency reports. "What'd the dogs find?"

"They headed out to Camino del Norte here"—he pointed to the main road—"then lost the scent."

"So you think someone abducted the kid in a car?"

"That's what we're assuming at this point."

"Any leads from the Crime Stopper ads?" A twenty-four-hour hot line, Crime Stoppers offered cash rewards to citizens who called in tips that led to arrests in felony crimes.

"Nothing but the usual dead ends and nutcase calls."

I was staring at the photo again. *Where are you, Matthew?* I waited for images or any impression whatsoever. Nothing. Outside, a hot gust of wind blew so forcefully that the car shuddered. In the outside rearview mirror I saw a white van pull over to the side of the road about ten yards behind us.

"Who's that?" I asked.

Loebman checked the rearview and scowled.

"Channel Three news van. They've been camped here off and on, doing live telecasts from the scene of the crime. Let's get outta here. You ready?"

I nodded as I slipped the paperwork into my backpack.

He picked up the phone from a car caddy between us and dialed.

"Yeah, this is Detective Loebman, calling from the gate. The other investigator just arrived. We're ready to come in now."

Seconds later the massive iron gate began to roll open, moving with slow, electronically controlled precision. Loebman fired up the engine and the car's AC rattled to life, blasting air that was still hot and stuffy through the vents. When the opening at the gate was wide enough, Loebman guided the car through the entry and up the winding driveway. As we entered the forest of wind-blown eucalyptus, I turned back to see the heavy row of iron bars closing behind us.

* * *

The Fielding house crowned the pinnacle of one of the highest hills in Rancho Santa Fe. Covered by eucalyptus on its east side, the hill dropped off sharply on the west. Loebman and I walked along an adobe brick path to the front door, enjoying an unobstructed view to the ocean. Even at this elevation there was no relief from the hellish weather. We stood at the front entrance, where a jasmine-covered overhang blocked the penetrating rays of the sun. In spite of the shade, the alcove held the heat like an oven.

Loebman rang the doorbell and we waited in silence. The Santa Ana pushed a few dried eucalyptus leaves up the steps, delivering them right to the door. After a couple of minutes I shifted my weight from one foot to the other.

"Think anyone heard us?" I was having doubts.

"She knows we're here. Give it another minute."

Made of old California adobe and hardwood, the house was a beautifully maintained early ranch—I guessed circa 1928. I was examining the thick wooden door, looking for signs of age, when it swung open. A pale woman with dark circles under her eyes stood before us.

"Sorry to keep you waiting. I was—" The woman waved a limp hand toward the rear of the house, ending the sentence with a sigh. She searched Loebman's face. "I'm sorry, Detective, I've forgotten your name again."

I didn't need to be introduced to know that this was Roxanne Fielding. To Frank Fielding's credit, this was no trophy wife. Roxanne was approaching forty and wasn't going out of her way to fight it. Her blond hair was streaked with gray and she carried a sensible amount of weight on her frame. She was wearing a roomy cotton sundress and comfortable shoes. If she'd put on makeup today, she'd long since cried it off. I saw dignity in her face and liked her immediately.

"Bruce," Loebman said gently. "And this is the investigator I was telling you about, Elizabeth Chase."

She looked at me and smiled sadly.

"The psychic."

"That's me." I looked her straight in the eye.

She nodded, reluctantly accepting the fact of my presence, and stepped back to let us inside.

We followed her into a spacious, high-ceilinged living room where high-end, high-tech furnishings clashed with the home's historic architecture. A sleek black leather seating system dominated the center of the room. Cubist bookcases framed a stone fireplace on the far wall. The adjoining wall was almost entirely covered by a chrome-framed abstract painting that resembled nothing so much as a gigantic computer motherboard. The only concession to the past was the richly colored Persian rug beneath our feet.

Roxanne found a spot at the corner of the leather sectional sofa and sank into it with a sigh.

"Make yourselves comfortable," she said.

Loebman sat beside her and I settled onto the sofa section that jutted out at a right angle. Roxanne folded her hands together and lowered her eyes toward the rug, as if saying a prayer to the divinity she saw in its intricate pattern. There was an awkward silence before Loebman looked to me.

"I'm not really sure how you want to proceed here," he said.

I stared at Roxanne's downturned eyes, wondering if she really was praying. Most people, particularly the relatives in a missing persons case are at least a little curious about me and my work. But Roxanne had retreated from me completely. It almost looked as if she were dropping off to sleep.

Perhaps five consecutive days and nights of not knowing where her son was had beaten her into a shocked speechlessness. On the other hand, maybe she was hiding something. I stopped speculating and got to work.

"Give me minute." I closed my eyes, intent on quieting my thoughts, the necessary first step in opening up psychically. I relaxed my shoulders and took a deep breath through my nostrils.

I smelled smoke. Sharp and pungent, it hit the back of my throat, tickling the membrane. I coughed and opened my eyes. The nervousness I'd been feeling all morning turned to fear.

Loebman looked at me quizzically.

"You okay?"

"Something's burning," I warned.

A CONVENTIONAL CORPSE

A CLAIRE MALLOY MYSTERY

JOAN HESS

Farberville, Arkansas, is playing host to its first-ever mystery convention with five major mystery writers—each representing a different subgenre of the mystery world—making the trek to the local college for "Murder Comes to Campus." Bookseller Claire Malloy is looking forward to meeting some of her favorite writers. But when one of the conference attendees dies in a car accident, it's evident that in Farberville the murder mystery is more than a literary genre.

"Hess goes about things in a lively style. Her heroine, Claire Malloy, has a sharp eye and an irreverent way of describing what she sees."
—*The New York Times Book Review*

"Blends humor, eccentric characters, familiar emotions, and plot twists into an enjoyable lark." —*Nashville Banner*

AVAILABLE WHEREVER BOOKS ARE SOLD
FROM ST. MARTIN'S PAPERBACKS

Mystery's #1 Bestselling Author

The Witness for the Prosecution
AND OTHER STORIES

A MURDER TRIAL takes a diabolical turn when the wife of the accused takes the stand . . . A woman's sixth sense—and a loaded revolver—signal premonitions of doom . . . A stranded motorist seeks refuge in a remote mansion, and is greeted with a dire warning . . . Hercule Poirot faces one of his greatest challenges when his services are enlisted—by the *victim*—in a bizarre locked-room murder. From the stunning title story (which inspired the classic film thriller) to the rarest gems in detective fiction, these 11 tales of baffling crime and brilliant deduction showcase Agatha Christie at her dazzling best.

AVAILABLE WHEREVER BOOKS ARE SOLD
FROM ST. MARTIN'S PAPERBACKS

WFP 4/01